Praise for *The Dogs of Winter*, BOOK TWO in the
Russell and Leduc Mysteries:

"*The Dogs of Winter* is as much an exploration of a city and its
communities as a traditional crime novel. It's about power and
powerlessness in the dead of winter. And more than that, it's a
rollicking good read."

—ANN CLEEVES

"Like its predecessor, *The Dogs of Winter* does not shy away from
the darker side of Canada's history—nor its present—and makes
for compulsive reading. With Lambert's characteristic blend of
humour, pathos, and vivid prose, *The Dogs of Winter* should fly off
the shelves."

—ANNE LAGACÉ DOWSON,
Montreal commentator and activist

"Out of the ordinary? Almost everything skews that way in this
inventively plotted novel."

—*The Toronto Star*

"It's a red-hot potboiler that effectively pierces through any kind of
bone-chilling cold."

—*Montreal Times*

"Ann Lambert's excellent *The Dogs of Winter*, the sequel to the
similarly socially conscious (and terrific) thriller *The Birds That Stay*."

—*Winnipeg Free Press*

"…another simply riveting suspense thriller of a read and continues
to showcase the author's natural knack for the kind of narrative
storytelling that keeps the reader's riveted attention from beginning
to cliff-hanger-style ending."

—*Midwest Book Review*

Praise for *The Birds That Stay*, BOOK ONE in the
Russell and Leduc Mysteries:

Book Riot's list of "HIGHLY ANTICIPATED CRIME NOVELS"

"TEN THRILLERS THAT WILL KEEP YOU ON THE EDGE
OF YOUR SEAT UNTIL SUMMERTIME…The setting is the
Laurentians, north of Montreal. That leads one to inevitably think
of Louise Penny's *Three Pines*, but let the comparison stop there.
Yes, both are rural and very Quebec, but Lambert is telling a very
different story in a very different way."

—MARGARET CANNON, *The Globe and Mail*

"*The Birds That Stay* is populated with complex characters, not
one of whom has been untouched by some form of trauma, be it
divorce, addiction, abuse, abandonment, or betrayal. The skillful
way in which these characters are rendered is part of what makes
the book so engaging."

—*Montreal Review of Books*

"…a fascinating and gripping tale of suspense, and there's
even a hint of romance here."

—*New York Journal of Books*

"Lambert will scratch your murder-mystery itch, rest assured, but
she resists the common tendency to place the action in a sealed-
off world where murder is normalized. *The Birds That Stay* is fully
engaged with life."

—*The Montreal Gazette*

"Lambert's confidence in her characters, her intelligent plot, and
digressions that both instruct and delight make *The Birds That Stay*
is an engaging and un-put-down-able read."

—Jury comments for the Concordia
First Book Prize 2019 (Shortlisted)

WHALE FALL

A Russell and Leduc Mystery

WHALE FALL

Ann Lambert

Second Story Press

Library and Archives Canada Cataloguing in Publication

Title: Whale fall / Ann Lambert.
Names: Lambert, Ann, 1957- author.
Description: Series statement: A Russell and Leduc mystery

tk

Printed and bound in Canada

*Second Story Press gratefully acknowledges the support of the
Ontario Arts Council and the Canada Council for the Arts for our
publishing program. We acknowledge the financial support of the
Government of Canada through the Canada Book Fund.*

Published by
Second Story Press
20 Maud Street, Suite 401
Toronto, ON M5V 2M5
www.secondstorypress.ca

*This book is dedicated to all the people
who fight for our beautiful planet.*

*And of course, to David, Alice, and Isaac who rooted
for me through every chapter of this pandemic book....*

Dear God, be good to me. The sea is so
wide, and my boat is so small.
—Breton fisherman's prayer

"Man loots Nature, but Nature always ends
up taking revenge." Gao Xingjian

Chapter 1

THE WEDDING
SATURDAY NIGHT

Marie

"Do you, Marie, take this man, Roméo, to be your lawfully wedded husband, to love, cherish, respect, and protect no matter what comes your way?"

Marie smiled and held her gaze on Roméo's green eyes.

"I do."

There was a hushed quiet in the crowd, like they were all holding their breath until it was over. Anticipation. Or relief?

"And do you, Roméo, take this woman, Marie, to be your lawfully wedded wife, to love, cherish, respect, and protect no matter what comes your way?"

Roméo did not smile. He just tried to focus on the moment and Marie. Her dark brown curls, now flecked with bits of gray, framed her face and her deep, dark brown eyes. Her lips were painted a color he'd never seen before. He felt like he might cry, and swallowed hard, fighting to control himself.

"I do."

The officiant paused, and then added, "Are you *sure*? It's not too late."

A few gasps erupted from the guests. Heads turned and glanced at each other, wondering if they'd all just heard the same thing.

"Ruby!" Marie hissed.

Roméo took Marie's two capable hands in his own, and now, finally smiling, said, "*Je suis certain.* I am absolutely sure."

Just at that moment, Noah, Marie's grandson and the flower boy was startled by a spider on his arm and began to shriek. He hated bugs. Maya, his mother, calmly removed it from his arm and placed it gently on the grass under her chair. Then everyone returned their attention to the four people under the *chuppah*. Neither Marie nor Roméo was Jewish, but Marie's children were, and had decided to build their mother and Roméo a canopy made from the fallen trees around her house and garlanded with the wildflowers that grew everywhere and with such abandon in July in the Laurentian mountains. They had added a few cultivated roses, so the arrangements would survive until the next day without entirely wilting.

"Well, then." Ruby looked out at the guests with the confidence of an experienced college debater. "With the power vested in me by the Province of Quebec, I do hereby declare you wife and husband!"

Roméo leaned in to kiss Marie and managed instead to get her nose. They pulled back and tried again, giving each other a modest, awkward peck. The crowd chuckled and *awwwed*. Then Ben took the wine glass they had both sipped from and held it up for all to see.

"This glass symbolizes that every marriage experiences both joy and sorrow and is a reminder of Marie and Roméo's commitment to each other even during the most challenging times."

Then Ben carefully wrapped the glass in a white linen napkin and placed it at their feet.

Both Roméo and Marie stomped on it together as Ruby and Ben leaned into the microphone and exclaimed, "Congratulations! *Felicitations! Mazel Tov!*" This time Marie pulled Roméo to her and gave him a long, lingering kiss.

∞

Three hours, three single malts, and three glasses of champagne later, Marie sat in a chair by the dance floor massaging her sore feet. Although she'd switched to her flip-flops immediately after the ceremony, her feet were still complaining about being forced into high heels at all. Marie tipsily swallowed the dregs of her fluted glass, leaned back into her chair, and reflected happily on this extraordinary day. It had started with ominously leaden morning skies and a forecast of thunderstorms and violent winds. Marie was certain she and her guests would all be huddled under the big tent, getting drenched and hoping not to be electrocuted while pretending pouring rain didn't dampen the party. But somehow, Roméo's legendary good weather luck had held out and the storms thundered past to the south of Ste. Lucie. Instead, a luscious July day ensued with a blue sky uninterrupted by any cloud, and a delicious warm breeze that sounded like the ocean if she closed her eyes and just listened. As she had requested, Ben had walked her down the "aisle" in the tent they had put up in her backyard to the *chuppah* where she waited for Roméo, who was escorted by his daughter, Sophie. They said their brief but sincere vows to each other in French and English, each speaking the other's mother tongue. Being "given away" by their children and married by her daughter meant everything to Marie. Although they didn't need the paper to prove it, the ceremony was a public acknowledgment that they were all now, somehow, a family. Marie slowly twisted the brand-new gold band on her finger and wondered how this had happened. She had never planned to marry again. As if on cue, her ex-husband Daniel appeared beside her and loomed over her a bit drunkenly.

"I hope he knows how lucky he is."

Ruby and Ben had decided to invite Daniel who had traded her in for a newer model after almost twenty years of marriage. They felt sorry for him and thought his witnessing Marie's wedding would do him good. His second marriage had recently failed, and he had then tried half-heartedly and unsuccessfully to get back together with Marie. Before she had a chance to respond, Daniel was pulled to the dance floor by a woman he'd been flirting with all afternoon. Marie didn't recognize her at all. She must be one of Roméo's guests, probably someone's plus one. Not Daniel's. Typical. She was more than half his age for once, not pretty in that vapid way he liked, but attractive and chatty. Marie tried to wish him well, but even now she still had occasional dreams about his violent death.

After the hysteria of the traditional hora on a very crowded dance floor, and then a long run of Motown funk that no one could resist, the deejay gave everyone a break with a few sentimental and soppy slow dances. Marie thought about finding Roméo, but her feet were just too relieved to move.

Since she had already danced "their first dance" with Roméo and hugged and kissed everyone at the wedding at least once, she decided to just enjoy being a bit drunk for a bit longer. She emptied the last of a bottle into her glass and basked in the joy of being around this motley gang of people she had collected of over almost sixty-one years around the track. Marie felt an overwhelming rush of affection and tenderness for everyone. There was Roméo's daughter, Sophie, dance-clutching her new girlfriend, Pénélope, who seemed to make her happier than any of the men Sophie had dated. Marie had to admit that Sophie was a challenge; she could manipulate Roméo any way she wanted, and he was blind to her often narcissistic machinations. But Sophie had been through a lot, even if much of it was caused by her own behavior—and Marie had been softened by how excited Sophie was about this wedding. She had arranged for all the flowers, made all the table settings and little name cards, prepared thoughtful loot bags for all the guests. Marie was very touched by her attention.

She watched her oldest and dearest friend, Lucy Atwood, her arms wrapped around the neck of her perfect husband, Graham. Marie and Roméo had just asked their guests to dress "creatively" and typical of their generosity and enthusiasm about everything, they had. Lucy was wearing a saffron-colored, taffeta cocktail dress and a lime green fascinator with a dragonfly hovering over it. Graham wore an electric blue tuxedo with a saffron tie, to match his wife. Both were in bare feet. Suddenly, the deejay decided there'd been enough of a rest and the music abruptly shifted to Shania Twain. The couples disappeared from the floor and were replaced by most of the women and a few men they pulled along with them into a line dance.

Leading the gang was Manon Latendresse, in knee-high cowboy boots, a mini jean-skirt, and a bright pink peasant blouse. Manon was the local dog groomer, a highly sought-after landscaper, and had made Marie's wedding cake, which was a sublime chocolatey confection. She was very involved in local environmental issues and the rehabilitation of wild animals. She had also almost single-handedly rehabilitated Ti-Coune Cousineau, Roméo's old friend. Marie watched Ti-Coune watch the women execute their perfectly choreographed moves. Ti-Coune. He was wearing a black cowboy rodeo shirt with pink bucking broncos embroidered on it, and clean blue jeans. His long grey hair was gathered in a stringy ponytail, a few strands combed over to hide his encroaching baldness. He waved at Manon and smiled, revealing a black gap where one of his front teeth should have been. Who would've thought that Marie would be friends with Ti-Coune—former Hell's Angels wannabe and local low-life? But her relationship and now *marriage* to Roméo Leduc had taken Marie to *terra incognita* and beyond.

And then, there he was—the man himself, on the dance floor with his best junior detective, Nicole LaFramboise, who tried in vain to teach him the sequence of steps to *Man! I Feel Like a Woman!* She was laughing so hard at Roméo she could barely stand. Roméo was the happiest Marie had ever seen him, which was worrying. It could only go downhill from here. Marie felt like weeping with joy at the sight of Nicole's little boy, Léo, slow dancing sweetly with Noah, Marie's grandson, his pacifier glued to his mouth. Suddenly Léo grabbed the pacifier and threw it as far as he could. Marie waited for the pause, the realization, and then the explosion of Noah's howling. She was just on her way to comfort him when Ben swooped in and said, "I got this." Marie watched as her beautiful son, who it seemed had almost overnight become a man and father, fished out the pacifier from under the cake table, wiped it on his shirt, stuck it back in his son's mouth, and got him dancing again. Léo, sensing trouble, had run back to his mother and now was hanging off her leg as she tried to keep up with Shania.

Most of the guests were old friends and some newer ones of Marie's—Joel and Shelly, the old hippies and dear souls from down the road, her new neighbor Laura, who was a specialist in the devil. Literally. She toured the world lecturing on the role of the devil in medieval mystery plays. A few of Marie's colleagues and friends from Dawson College were also here, and her publisher from Toronto, a stern-looking septuagenarian whose face entirely transformed itself when she smiled, rare though it was.

Marie observed Robert Renard, Roméo's partner of many years, make his way back to the bar for another cocktail in his gray suit, black shoes, and pale blue tie. "Dressing creatively" for cops was too much of a challenge, apparently. Roméo trusted Robert with his life, but Marie had always felt wary around him. He was a man of many, effusive words until Marie joined the conversation. Then he would clam up. Did he think she wasn't worthy of Roméo? Or maybe was he jealous of her? Robert had divorced many years earlier and described his marriage as *l'enfer sur la terre*. Hell on Earth. Maybe she should introduce him to her devil specialist neighbor, who was single. Maybe Robert just didn't like women much, or their opinions. Marie knew plenty of men like that. She smiled at the sight of diminutive Steve Pouliot, who had worked with Roméo on his last big case, the LaFlèche murders in Montreal. He had stripped down to a skin-tight muscle shirt, his suit pants and bare feet. He was trying gamely to keep up with his plus one, a ripped young woman who was a foot taller. No Napoleon complex for him.

The music changed again to what Marie knew would be a run of classic wedding songs, starting with "We Are Family," and predictably, the dance floor filled up again. Marie looked for Ruby, who was the family's most committed and tireless dancer, although the most rhythmically challenged. Ruby had been tipsy and a bit gushy on the dance floor with her newish boyfriend, but they were not out there now. Then Marie remembered that they—well, Mohammed, as he drank very little—had kindly offered to drive Marie's mother, Claire, back to *Maison Soleil*, her long-term care residence in Ste. Lucie. Marie suspected they wanted a break from the nosiness of a few of her guests. Ruby, being Ruby, had gone to law school and fallen in love with the most complicated fellow student she could find, a soft-spoken refugee from Syria named Mohammed. Many of Marie's friends wanted to talk to him, get to know him, suss him out, and decide whether he was good enough for Ruby, whom they all adored. Marie was still getting to know him, but she loved that he was very solicitous of Claire.

Marie thought of her once-beautiful mother, whose dark brown eyes Marie had inherited, so lit up with intelligence and awareness. But Claire had lasted longer at the party than Marie expected. Lucy had decided that Claire, as the mother of the bride, needed to wear something very special and had crafted a fascinator for her as well. Claire had sipped at her glass of fizzy fruit juice with a hummingbird perpetually poised over a red flower on top of her head and smiled graciously at everyone who stopped to chat. She recognized almost no one, even her immediate family sometimes. Marie wasn't positive her mother knew it was her daughter's wedding day, but it didn't matter; Marie could see she was having a good time, and was so grateful that was the case, as it could quite easily go the other way when it came to Alzheimer's disease.

Missing from the party of course, were the many ghosts of the family. Roméo hadn't spoken to his estranged father, Claude, in over twenty years and only then at his mother's funeral. After years of abusing his wife and son, Claude had turned all that rage on himself through epic drinking binges and dedicated abuse of many prescription drugs. It was a miracle he was still alive—out of spite, if for no other reason. Marie's father had died in a car accident when she was twenty-two. Her sister Madeleine was also long dead—she took after their father and died after a brutal struggle with alcohol. Her other sister, Louise had initially agreed to come all the way from Calgary, and then changed her mind. She didn't want to leave her two beloved dogs, Humphrey and Bogart, behind. Humphrey had an ear infection, and Bogart was too anxious to fly. Marie had to admit she wasn't disappointed. She and her sister had always had a strained relationship, one in which Marie often felt that Louise celebrated Marie's losses and mourned her victories.

Suddenly, the music cut out and the deejay's voice abruptly announced, "All right, everybody! If you could all please take your seats, more or less at your assigned tables, we would like to hear a few words from a few choice folks." What? Marie and Roméo had specifically requested no speeches. They had already said their thank-yous and preferred to leave it at that.

She looked around for Roméo, but he had disappeared. Was he in on this? Marie watched in dismay as Robert Renard moved towards the microphone. But before he could reach it, Ti-Coune Cousineau did, and pulled out a tiny square piece of paper from his shirt pocket that he unfolded again and again. Then he put on his glasses, which slipped and perched on the end of his nose. He cleared his throat too close to the mic and startled everyone as they found their seats and politely prepared to pay attention.

"All my life I hated cops."

A few snippets of nervous laughter erupted from the guests.

"I guess there are a few cops here today. And a few of you probably remember the old Ti-Coune, when your...um...TV or sound system or firewood went missing."

Or worse, Marie thought.

"And I'm pretty sure a few cops hated me." A few approving chuckles now.

"They had their reasons, and I had mine." Ti-Coune paused to clear his throat again, but this time remembered to turn his mouth away from the mic. Marie realized he was trying to compose himself.

"But there was this one guy. You see, I met him in high school. And even then, he was different. He had a...bad time with his parents, too, like me. Well, me, I had no father, but my mother. She was mean enough for two."

There were a few uncomfortable chuckles now.

"But this guy, he was not like me. *He* was a hockey star. A good student. The kind of guy who everyone wanted to be. But him, he looked out for us little guys. *Il s'occupait de nous, les petits gars sur les bords.* The ones on the sides. The ones who didn't fit. The ones the others—the students, the teachers, the Child Protection gang—picked on. Bullied. The ones they knew were easy…prey." Ti-Coune paused again and swallowed hard.

"Roméo Leduc saved my life. More than once. He also saved the life of my dog, Pitoune."

There was a spontaneous smattering of applause.

"He's a good cop. He is a kind man. He deserves all the happiness in the world. So, I lift my glass—" Ti-Coune's glass had beer in it, so Manon hastily poured and handed him a fresh glass of champagne. "To Roméo and Marie!"

A chorus of "to Roméo and Marie!" followed. Then Ti-Coune leaned into the mic one last time. "May we all find what they have!"

Ti-Coune returned to his seat where Manon was waiting. She rewarded him with a beaming smile and a high five. Then, Lucy Atwood tripped up to the microphone. Marie laughed out loud. Lucy was a bit tipsy. More than a bit. Bright pink spots glowed on her cheeks. The dragonfly on her fascinator had begun to dip and stuck out at a right angle from her head. Graham applauded his wife as she unfolded her own paper and nodded at her approvingly. Adoringly.

"I have known Marie Russell since we were five years old. On good old Woodgrove Avenue in Beaurepaire. That was when a Montreal winter started in early November and lasted until mid-May. When summers lasted two months but felt like forever. When we started every day scrambling over the wire fence that separated our two houses—so we could play together every single day. I loved being at Marie's house. I loved her mom, Claire, who took care of me and loved me like one of her own daughters. I loved her dad, Edward, who called me *Lassie* and ran us down the driveway in a wheelbarrow if we asked him especially nicely. Marie always included me in everything she did, and in every part of her life. And she was in mine. Nothing felt like it had actually *happened* until I told Marie about it. Nothing felt complete without Marie knowing about it."

The guests listened attentively. Politely. Lucy was beginning to get a bit weepy.

"When I…when my family moved away—we continued to be best friends. Confidantes. Each other's number one cheerleader. I have known Marie since we were five years old. And, she is…she is the love of my life. So, I would like to lift my glass to my friend, Marie Russell! And her Roméo!"

As glasses were raised again and Lucy grinned tearfully at Marie and Roméo, she noticed a presence, a ripple of excitement just off the stage to her left. And so, it was Lucy Atwood who spotted the ghost first.

Chapter 2

A MEMORY

She had never felt so alive, so fully and completely a part of this planet, not on it, not of it, not beside it, but IN it. The morning had not begun with much promise. Although the sky was a clear, deep blue with no cloud threatening from any direction, there was a good breeze and a three-foot chop on the water. They had left that morning at six thirty, right after a hearty breakfast. She was the newbie here, on loan from the Monterey Aquarium where she had done her graduate fieldwork. She had loaded up on as many layers as she'd brought with her, because this was the North Atlantic, not the milder waters of Baja Mexico she was more accustomed to, even though she was a *Canadian* and used to brutal winters. It didn't matter. She was cold within minutes of leaving the dock, and now after five hours of bouncing up and down on the ocean in a sixteen-foot rubber boat she was frozen. She could barely move her lips to speak and was not sure she could open her hands enough to manipulate the camera slung around her neck. The head of the project ordered the intern to turn the boat one more time to the south. A lobster fisherman that morning had seen a pod of whales feeding there earlier. He announced over the whine of the outboard motor that they would try their luck there, and head back to the research station for lunch if no whales materialized. She glanced at this man from behind her fleecy jacket pulled up over her red nose. He had warmly welcomed her to the team and unlike almost every other man with whom she'd worked, did not immediately demonstrate his superior knowledge and experience to her. Instead, he was full of questions about *her* work, *her* discoveries, *her* team. He made her feel like she was the only person in that boat who mattered to him.

The evening before, during their first get together of this project, he'd opened a very good bottle of wine over supper (which, unlike every other man she'd worked with, he had helped prepare) drank more than half of it and fell asleep on the ratty sofa in the common room while everyone else argued over what DVD to watch that evening. She had listened while his team discussed him reverentially. It was clear that he was the sun they all revolved around, and each team member lit up whenever he shone his light on them. But he didn't seem to seek this or expect it. There was one other surprise as well. She had never felt much attraction to blond, blue-eyed men. It was of course irrational, but she always assumed that they were callow and entitled. She had always preferred hirsute, dark-haired men to men as pale and hairless as a piece of cheese. This man fell into the latter category, but it didn't matter. He was gob-smackingly beautiful, with a careless sexual energy that she assumed everyone felt, female and male alike.

Suddenly the boat lurched as the spotter shouted, "Blow!" The driver curved the zodiac in a wide arc as she sped towards the white puff on the horizon.

"I think it's Betty! I wonder if she has a calf!" The intern driver skillfully pulled up parallel to the whale and put the boat in neutral. No matter how many times she had seen one, a new calf was a thrill. Humpback whale mothers do not eat for the entire winter as they wait to give birth. But despite their hope, there was no calf with Betty, or whale #455. As they watched from a safe distance, the whale lifted her fifteen-foot white flipper out of the water, like a giant, featherless wing, and smacked it down. Then she rolled onto her back and looked over at the boat, which bobbed like a toy next to her. Marie tried to get her hands to thaw long enough to snap some ID shots of the whale's flukes, but they were stiff with the cold. Suddenly, she heard a huge exhale and a watery, fishy mist engulf her. Whale snot. A second whale came so close to the boat that she could practically see inside one of the blowholes that opened like giant nostrils and then closed again as the whale flipped her ten-foot tail up and smacked it on the water. Suddenly, several more whales appeared. They were in the middle of a pod of humpback whales feeding; they hadn't meant to get so close, but the whales had surrounded them. The water was churning with tons of whale—their flippers whitish green under the Atlantic blue, the fringy baleen plates of their mouths opening and swallowing the hundreds of herring that frantically tried to escape.

She was snapping ID photos of their flukes with the unwieldy zoom-lensed camera as fast as she could, while Magnus prepared the DNA dart gun with deft hands in the rollicking dinghy. He glanced at her for just a moment and winked. Marie knew that this was a man with whom she could fall dangerously in love.

Chapter 3

THE WEDDING

Roméo

Even though Roméo swore up and down that he knew nothing about the speeches, Marie didn't quite believe him. In spite of themselves, however, they sat together and listened to Ti-Coune and then Lucy's efforts with evident appreciation. Roméo was surprised and touched by Ti-Coune's words. Roméo was surprised and touched by everyone at the wedding, really. He never imagined he would be *feted* like this until his retirement, but that would be bittersweet at best. As the head of homicide for the St. Jerome district for the Sûreté du Québec, he had many people who liked and respected him in the SQ, but probably just as many who did not. Marie squeezed his hand.

"What are you thinking, about, my love?"

Roméo was thinking about how he would feel let down after the wedding. It was one of the reasons he had always resisted getting excited about the so-called Big Events all his life.

"*Post coitum omne animal tristum est.*"

Marie paused to translate based on her one year of Latin in high school. "After sex, all animals are…sad? Oh, Roméo—"

"Well, literally, yes. It is more the feeling you get after a moment you've waited so long for, but you feel like…there is something greater you missed just beyond your…fingers… your hands."

Marie was about to answer, "You mean out of reach?" when the microphone started screaming feedback. They paused to watch as the DJ fiddled with it.

"Roméo? If I don't go pee, I will explode."

Roméo touched his ear. "I can't hear you—"

"I'll be back in two minutes."

Roméo watched Marie hasten away. He relaxed back into his chair and took in the scene. There was Sophie, carefully carrying two fresh and spilling cocktails back to her girlfriend, who pulled Sophie to her for a quick kiss. It was strange for him at first—he had never thought of Sophie as a *lesbian*. She'd always had a steady boyfriend since grade eight and had never shown any romantic interest in girls. But there was no denying this girl was a vast improvement over the last boyfriend who spent all day playing video games and had been abusive. Roméo admired so many young people these days who didn't seem to care what gender their beloved was. He didn't really understand it, but he didn't need to; this was no longer his generation's world to make.

He smiled as Maya waddled away, Noah balanced on her hip with one leg straddling her big belly. Ben and Maya were expecting Marie's second grandchild—his now, too, of course. Roméo had grown to love little Noah and looked forward to the arrival of whoever this new human being would be. Roméo hoped it was a girl, as the *bris* debate last time had been difficult. Daniel, Marie's ex-husband, had acquired an obsession about his grandson's penis looking like his own and his son's, and had insisted they have him circumcised. They refused. Daniel's insistence was a control issue, Roméo thought. If he couldn't save his unravelling marriage, he could at least try to interfere with Ben and Maya's very personal decision by insisting on what some saw as an outdated tribal practice. Although he never got directly involved, Roméo could understand Daniel. Circumcision was the covenant, the defining ritual of their people. Daniel had finally split up with the wife who had replaced Marie and was now on the lookout for someone new. Roméo almost felt sorry for him. There was something about a person in his sixties still trying to find himself that he found sad, but in some ways admirable. Roméo realized how close he had been to ending up like Daniel. And then Marie came along.

For their honeymoon, Roméo had taken nine days off from his several active cases (well, five days and two weekends) and was very much looking forward to being with Marie in a tent in the middle of nowhere—including no cell phone— four hours by car north of Ste. Lucie. Between the demands of their jobs, kids, friends, and surprises life threw their way, undisturbed time alone together was rare. They had discussed other possibilities—hiking the Inca trail in Peru, scuba diving off the reef in Belize, a tour of the Icelandic volcanoes, but in the end neither one of them wanted to be far from home. But neither one of them could explain why, exactly. Roméo would be leaving Nicole LaFramboise in charge of his two active cases—an intimate partner homicide in Blainville and doing the preparation for the Jean Luc David trial for the sexual assault of Michaela Cruz.

Roméo now watched as Robert Renard made his way to the stage. Where was Marie? Was Robert going to making a bloody speech as well? Roméo found this particularly ironic, as Robert had spent a good part of Roméo's bachelor party trying to talk him out of marrying Marie.

"As your very good friend, Roméo," he had said, leaning drunkenly into Roméo's face, "I have to remind you that… you don't HAVE TO do this. She's…she's *ten years* older than you. You are a *man,* you could still have kids, *criss,* until you're eighty years old." Roméo had turned away from his fetid breath and tried to join the conversation next to him, but Robert persisted. "She can't, her. She's finished with that. A guy like you could get anyone you want. I've seen the way the women look at you. You could have had *Nicole.* Shit, she was hot for you…. *Tabarnac,* I'd give my right testicle for that."

Robert had clearly forgotten Roméo's romantic history, where he very much lived up to his tragic namesake. Roméo wanted Marie, and nobody else. How many women did he know who would save his life by clobbering his assailant with a log? Roméo considered the several policewomen at the wedding. Probably a few. But he wasn't in love with any of them. Robert's surprisingly respectful and mercifully short speech ended just as Marie slipped into the chair next to Roméo. As if on cue, all the guests were tinking their glasses, demanding a kiss. Roméo and Marie were not fond of performative intimacy. But Roméo leaned towards Marie and kissed her softly. As they separated, Marie turned back to their audience. Suddenly, her face turned quite pink. Was she blushing? Roméo found this quite touching but followed her gaze to the stage. A ridiculously handsome man was standing there, scanning the crowd like a rock star before a stadium of thousands. His roaming eyes finally settled on Marie, who was now blushing brighter red. Roméo recognized him immediately. Magnus Sorensen, the first love of Marie's life.

Chapter 4

THE MEETING

"Seven car dealerships. *Seven* car dealerships within a three-kilometer stretch of road. On a stretch of road that was once considered beautiful. This is Ste. Agathe's idea of sustainable economic development."

A few chuckles erupted from the eclectic group of people gathered around the room.

"And not a *one* of them is selling electric cars. That is their *limited, short-sighted* understanding of the future."

Now the group was silent, nodding, each thinking they had a real grasp of what the future needed. What it could, *would* bring.

The man who spoke these words gestured to the elaborate model in front of him. It looked like a modern version of a Breughel painting; at the center was a mountain, and all around it, miniature people were very, very busy. Skiing. Sledding. Skating. Swimming in a steaming outdoor pool. Eating in restaurants. Dancing in clubs. Getting massaged in spas. Shopping in the many stores that lined the streets of this imaginary mountain village. There was even a little church that people spilled out of. Unlike the good people of Breughel's world, however, not a one of them was making anything. Creating anything. The entire experience was devoted to the consumption of services.

"*Our* vision. Our vision of the future for this area we love so much that we have devoted much of our lives to, is to restore. Reinvent. And revive!"

Pierre Batmanian, charismatic restauranteur, entrepreneur, and real estate developer paused to catch his breath and lower the timbre of his voice. Now it was somber, ominous. "There are people...all around us here, who do not share this vision. Who do not want our project to go forward. Who have no sense of...our history. Our *patrimoine*. How our ancestors came here one hundred and seventy-five years ago and cleared rocks—*boulders*, the size of a house—in order to create this...little piece of the world for ourselves. How a ski industry was built from scratch. How Ste. Agathe was a place to dream—to dream of a better world. Of better health. Did you know it had one of the most famous sanitoriums for tuberculosis in North America? Even the Queen of England herself visited—"

He was interrupted by a few surprised *ohs* and a few boos and muttered protest. But he waved them down and continued, undaunted.

"The queen *herself* visited because this region was the crown jewel of Canada, then. Young people had hope then. There were good jobs. People had a sense of community. Of purpose."

Pierre turned to a squat, middle-aged woman with black-rooted blonde hair dressed in a navy pants suit and spiky high heels.

"Mayor Morin. Your grandfather built the little schoolhouse in Ste. Lucie. One of the saddest days of his life must have been when they had to close it down. Because there were *no children left* to fill it. Dare we dream of a bringing a school back to Ste. Lucie? Bringing young families back?" The mayor rose from her chair and turned to the crowd. "Yes. We do… um, can!"

The fifty or so people gathered before the speaker broke into vigorous applause.

"Now. Some say that the…collateral damage of our project will deprive us of the most noble part of our natural heritage. But we here? We say that the noblest part of our heritage is what *we* fashioned, what we carved out of the rock and hard earth here. What *we* built. And building a new world requires some…sacrifice. Of a few trees. And guess what? We have more than enough trees in Quebec."

To this, there was a scattering of applause and laughter.

"The Montreal Economic Institute says that we are not cutting enough to take advantage of our forests' regeneration capacity. They say that this adds to the economic suffering of the regions. And…the Quebec forest industry actually *removes* carbon dioxide from the atmosphere, so it helps to fight climate change."

Pierre paused to note that a man had entered the room from the double doors at the far end. No one else had seen him. He clicked them closed very quietly behind him and slipped into an empty chair.

"Some say that the clear-cutting of Mont Baleine to make way for Projet Leviathan will also drive away the animals. This is true. Some animals will be displaced. But *we* are also on the verge of extinction, if you will. Our little town. Our

Laurentian way of life. We need to bring jobs to young people again. We need to restore our way of life. Revive the heart of the Laurentians. Reinvent ourselves to face the future in this challenging and *changing* twenty-first century!"

Pierre finally seemed to have decided he'd had his say. But before he resumed his seat, he took one last look out at his audience, looking at each and every person directly as though daring anyone of them to challenge him. He had made this speech, or a variation on it, many times before. But every time he delivered it with the conviction and self-righteousness of an evangelical preacher

Then the mayor stood up and went to take his place, teetering on her heels and smoothing down her pants that had gotten stuck to her skin in the muggy heat of the evening. She pulled a pair of glasses on, as she had to read her speech.

"We are tired of being told by outsiders how to run our business. We are tired of outsiders, of people who are not from here, who have no connection to our little part of the world, telling us what we can or cannot do with it. We watched those people mount a campaign against us. Against this project. They obtained an injunction to stop it, but we have seen to it that that injunction will be lifted. Leviathan will not be stopped. A brand new, state of the art resort will be built. *Here*"—she pointed to the virtual map of Mont Baleine and the nature preserve outlined in green that surrounded it which appeared behind her on the smart screen—"and it will be built by us. The local people. And it will be managed by us. The local people. And the jobs, the profits, the many benefits will be shared by *us*!"

The room exploded with applause and shouts of approval. The mayor beamed at them, and then took her seat again, nodding briefly to the crowd. Pierre Batmanian stood up again.

"Tomorrow, as you know, a protest is planned against the so-called clear-cutting of the required area, due to begin in three days. Even though some of our local people, even some we know well, are part of this demonstration, we know the organizers are outsiders. *Agitators.* So, we ask that tomorrow, you prepare to greet these people. We have prepared handouts for you that includes facts and figures that counter the misinformation they have propagated and sold to the media."

He nodded to two young women who moved briskly around the room distributing the pamphlets.

"Thank you all for coming here tonight. You are about to become part of something much bigger than yourselves. Something your children, their children and *their* children's children will talk about with wonder and pride. You will *never* be forgotten!"

There was a brief hesitation, as though no one was quite sure the speech was over. Then, a final, enthusiastic clapping. Then a standing ovation. People began chatting excitedly as they checked their phones, shared bits of the latest gossip, looked over the handouts prepared for them. Some moved towards the maquette of Projet Leviathan to examine it, like kids at the window of a toy store. Others peered at the 3D version on the screen that constructed the project virtually from image to image. Pierre made his way to the back of the room and found the latecomer.

"Nice speech."

"Thanks." He glanced around the room. No one was paying them any attention. "How was the wedding?"

"Not bad."

He leaned in closer and muttered, "We can't have any more trouble about this. Right? You have it under control?"

The latecomer shook his head. If he'd had a cigarette, he would have pulled it from his mouth with his thumb and index finger and crushed it under his heel for effect.

"He's here."

Chapter 5

Magnus

Marie took a few moments to collect herself and then stood up a little shakily from her chair, her feet searching for her wayward flip-flops. She had to duck under the table to find one of them and pulled it on while hopping on the other foot.

"I…I have no idea what he is doing here."

"Why don't you go and ask him?"

Marie knew she was still blushing but hoped Roméo would think it was the champagne.

"Excuse me a minute, okay?"

"Do you want me to come with you?"

"Yes! I mean, not yet. Let me have a moment with him first? Is that okay?"

As if on cue, the DJ rebooted the dancing with Aretha's *Respect*, and Sophie, Roméo's daughter, tipsily grabbed his hand and pulled him away from Marie and onto the dance floor.

Magnus Sorensen appeared like a future version of

himself. His hair was now thinning on top but was still gloriously wavy with seams of palomino blond curling through the gray. He was tanned the color of expensive single malt, and was still lean, tall, with a prominent nose, long cheek lines, and a smile that left many people, especially women of all ages, shapes, and tastes, breathless. This was the man who had broken her heart so badly she could still, all these years later, sometimes feel the physical pain of it. After the split with Magnus, why hadn't she stayed out there on the ocean forever? Why had she come home, back to Montreal, hundreds of miles from the ocean and become a landlubber? Because Madeline, her oldest sister was really sick and needed her. Then, Magnus didn't wait for her and broke her heart. Then, she met Daniel. Then, she was pregnant with Ruby. Offered a stable teaching job with a pension and perks. If she went to the ocean, it was with her family on vacation to the touristy coast of southern Maine. In the early days of her marriage, Marie had tried to get herself onto whale research expeditions when she could, but it was a difficult life for a mother of two toddlers with a full-time job. Instead of being out in the natural world, she wrote books for kids about it. Her most recent one had even won a national award. But sometimes it paled in comparison to the life she might have had—the life she had studied for, prepared as her career, and had lived for a few exhilarating years. And all of a sudden, Magnus was *here*. He leaned in to kiss her on both cheeks, smelling faintly of Barrister and Mann's *ambergris*, a scent and brand Marie remembered even after all these years.

"I hope this is a good surprise, Marie." He said her name the same way he always had, with an accent on the e. Mari-é. Before she could answer, he pulled her close to him and whispered, "You look absolutely radiant. This man is good for you?" A question, not a statement.

"*How*...um, *why* are you here?"

Magnus took her hand with the new ring on it in both of his and squeezed.

"How? By plane and car. Why?" He smiled. "Well, that is the million-dollar question, to be sure. Your daughter Ruby invited me."

He still spoke with the inflection and slightly formal accent he acquired as a student in England, now diluted by the years he had spent in the United States.

"Ruby did? She didn't say anything to me. How did she even...? I don't understand—"

"Your daughter is a lawyer, no? Or almost one? She contacted our organization because she had heard I might be here for an action against this hotel project and told us who she was, more specifically whose daughter she was and mentioned you would be...getting married today. I then asked if I could...drop by. She responded yes, enthusiastically. I thought she would definitely have told you. I am sorry, Marie, if this is an unpleasant surprise. It wasn't intended to be."

He studied her face, as he had always done. She felt herself blushing again and turned away from him to seek out Roméo. It was then she first noticed that a not so small crowd of their guests had begun to gather, inching closer to Magnus. A few of her Dawson colleagues looked almost as excited as those crazed Beatle fans in the 1960's, who screamed and fainted at the sight of them. Amanda, her colleague from anthropology looked ready to take her underwear off and throw it at him. Even a few of the circling men were star struck.

"Are you pleased that I am here?"

Before Marie could answer, another face from her past appeared beside Magnus. The woman was almost as tall and tanned as he, but the sun had wreaked more damage to her finer complexion, like a patch of desiccated desert. Freckles that once were sprinkled on her nose now dotted every inch of her face. But her eyes were still a piercing, unavoidable blue, and her once strawberry blonde hair was now a beautiful silvery gray, still thick and held in a side braid that fell over one lean shoulder. She smiled at Marie, but the smile was pinched, hard. Her white teeth were still dazzling, though. She offered her hand to Marie, who was so startled she didn't respond. Then the woman leaned in to double-cheek kiss Marie with barely a touch of her lips.

"Marie. It's so *good* to see you."

Gretchen.

Chapter 6

Emily

He should have called by now. He had promised he would. At least to let her know what the plan was for the next day. At least to ask her how she was *feeling*. She checked her phone again, in case he had texted. Nothing. Just another message from her mother asking her again when she was arriving and where she was staying. She started to thumb an answer and then stopped. Her mother could wait a few more hours. Let *her* stew in her juices for a bit. She fell back into the king-size bed, sinking into the pile of extra pillows she had earlier requested. She should be finishing entering the data from the last few days of their research trip. She should be updating the website and uploading the latest blog to their social media accounts. She should be letting her few friends in Montreal know she was here. But all Emily Joly wanted to do was continue to lie in this enormous bed, stare up at the ceiling, and think about the myriad ways her life was about to change.

Three quick knocks at the door roused her from her

reverie, and for a brief moment she thought it was him, come to surprise her as he sometimes did. She gathered the thick, white hotel bathrobe with the embossed crest across her chest, tightened the cloth belt, and padded to the door, her feet pampered by the luxurious carpet that covered the entire suite.

Of course, they were the first thing the bellhop noticed. Like most men, he tried very hard not to look, but she knew it was a struggle. Even in an oversized bathrobe, her breasts were impressive. First in French and then in English, he asked her where she would like him to place the cart. She gestured to a corner of the room, and hastened to her knapsack on the bed, where she remembered she had a little Canadian cash hidden. As she bent over, she felt his eyes again on her body. When she straightened up, her bathrobe had relaxed, but he refused to let his gaze wander below her face. She tipped him a little extra.

Emily poured herself a glass of San Pellegrino and attacked the cheese and charcuterie plate. He wasn't here and she would eat whatever she wanted to. She was *starving*. Then she let the bathrobe drop to the floor and with a laden piece of baguette in each hand she went to examine herself in the full-length mirror in the sumptuous bathroom. No obvious signs yet. Her belly a bit swollen. Her breasts a bit tender. And growing bigger. Her nipples darkening. The rest of her firmer and more muscular than usual after the last few months toughing it out in the Pantanal jungle. Her phone pinged again, and she padded back to the bed to see if it was him. *Emmy, are you here?* She thumbed back *not yet call u soon.* Emily tossed her phone back onto the bed and thought about the news she was both dreading and thrilled to tell her mother. Her mother, who had certainly never stayed in a hotel like this in her entire life. Her mother, who had never even traveled beyond Canada and the US. Well, except to an all-inclusive resort in Varadero, once. Where she picked up *giardia* from infected ice cubes in her *Cuba Libre* and spent the next three weeks sicker than she'd been in her life.

Emily herself wasn't exactly used to this, either. Not like him. He grew up like this. He went to lycée in Switzerland. University at Oxford. Summers sailing off Sardinia and winters skiing in the Austrian alps. It made her love him all the more when she thought about how he gave it all up, turned his back on all that fucking *money*. Still, she knew he must still have access to some of it. How else could he do what he did? Not to mention afford a suite in a five-star hotel like this. She decided she really wanted to call him. Now. Interrupt him. Make him sneak off and answer his phone. He had promised he would get away as soon as possible. But he had to put in his time at the wedding of some old friend. Where *she* should be with him. But he wasn't ready for that yet. Emily smiled and rubbed her hand across her belly. She could wait a little bit longer. It was just a matter of time.

She perched on the edge of the gigantic bathtub and let the hot water run. The she selected one of the several proffered bath oils, jasmine, and let a few drops mingle in the water. Years of living on a boat in the middle of the ocean had taught her never to take a hot bath for granted. She picked up a tiny remote control perched on the edge of one of the two sinks and pressed ON, wondering what it controlled. A TV suddenly came to life in the bathroom mirror. And then, as if on cue, he appeared on the screen, running his hand through his wavy hair the way he often did when thinking of the right way to say something. *La phrase juste.*

It was an old interview from the IPCC summit in Geneva, and there was Greta Thunberg next to him, alongside his old, estranged partner in the eco-wars, Tor Hanyes. She went to unmute the sound and then changed her mind. She'd heard this one many times. Analyzed it. Parsed it for sound bites and inundated their social media platforms with it. He had been particularly persuasive and compelling that day. He could explain how eco-Armageddon was coming if we didn't address global warming against a backdrop of the world on fire and still make you feel hopeful. Like there was something still to be done. This was his gift. *One* of his gifts. She watched him turn to Greta and listen to her in that way that makes his interlocutor feel they are the center of the universe. *My God, he is beautiful.* Emily returned to the bedroom to fetch her phone. No message yet. She held the phone out to get as much of her body as possible, snapped the photo and sent it. *waiting for you, my love. hurry.*

She swirled the bathwater twice and was just lowering herself into the tub when she heard a knock at the door. Shit. She hadn't ordered anything else. No one knew she was here. Except Magnus. Maybe he'd sent flowers? Chocolate? Chocolate and flowers? She clambered out of the bath, threw on the robe and hastened to the door. But when she opened it, no one was there. Just an empty hallway and a chambermaid vacuuming the extravagant carpet by the elevator. She peered down the hallway again and closed her door. This time, Emily made sure to drop the locking door chain into place.

Chapter 7

Louis

Despite its name, *Maison Soleil* was not a particularly sunny place. A former elementary school converted into a long-term care residence, it still had an institutional atmosphere. As soon as anyone walked in the front door, they could easily imagine a bunch of kids lining up dutifully, according to gender, before a stern nun in a full black habit. In an effort to brighten it up, the concrete walls were painted bright, mustard yellow, and the doors to each room a loud pumpkin orange. The carpets, which lined every hallway and each of the activity rooms were the color of dirty sand. The effect was meant to be cheerful but was mostly off-putting at best and nauseating at worst.

It was as usual, completely quiet by ten o'clock at night, the only sound the hum of the fluorescent lights over the collection of vinyl armchairs and tired magazines on a coffee table in what passed for the lobby. One bulb kept flickering and had needed to be changed for weeks. Karine, the night attendant, was tipped back in her chair at the welcome desk and busy swiping for love on Tinder. Two residents were slumped in overstuffed chairs in the games room in front of the TV, sound asleep.

But one resident wasn't asleep, or staring at the walls, or playing a game on a phone, or dreaming their pain away, or staying alive with memories or trying to forget trauma. Tucked away in his tiny room in the warren of other tiny rooms, Louis Lachance was on his knees foraging for something under his bed. It wasn't easy. His bad hip was worse, and just lowering himself involved several painful steps. Finally, he was in what looked like the downward dog position, his arthritic, bony hands scrabbling for the cache he had been squirreling away for several weeks. He slid it out from under his bed, took a few seconds to get his breath back, and then slowly, slowly got onto his knees, leaned onto his bed and hoisted himself back up. In the little *Hello Kitty* knapsack his granddaughter had given him was a bottle of red wine he had saved since the Christmas before, two plastic wine glasses, a little polka-dotted tablecloth, two matching napkins, a heel of cheddar cheese he had pilfered from the kitchen, two bread rolls from tonight's supper, and la *pièce de résistance*—a *Rosette de Lyon saucisse* his daughter had brought him on her last visit. Then he dropped his ancient Swiss army knife into the pocket, zipped it up, and tucked the knapsack under his blanket. He was ready.

Louis sat on the edge of his narrow bed and wondered if he would be able to fall asleep. Thirteen hours to go. He picked up and rearranged the several framed photos of his *petit-enfants* on his bedside table. Even now, all these years later, he still could barely look at the one of his grandson,

36

Charles-Etienne, but he had to have him there, his handsome face framed and smiling, forever nineteen years old. Louis wiped the dust off the photo of Michelle, his wife who had died in her sleep last January 26. It was not a good one. She was squinting up at the photographer directly into the sun, so she looked annoyed and cranky. Which she often was. But she could also be silly and at times, almost joyful. And she had loved him in her fashion and looked out for Louis for almost sixty-seven years. When Michelle died, the ground had fallen away from him, even worse than when Charles-Etienne took his own life. Louis had had a series of small strokes, and his children decided he was too feeble to take care of himself. Then they convinced him to sell the home he had shared with Michelle for almost sixty years and almost all of his tools, acquired proudly and stubbornly over a lifetime of being the most reliable and affordable *homme à tout faire* in the region. His grief over Michelle left him in such a state of lethargy that he submitted to the wishes of his daughter, Dominique and his son, Francois. He had allowed them to take charge of his life. *His* life. And allowed himself to be locked up here. It was as though he had slept through the entire ordeal, and then woke up from the nightmare too late. Louis was still furious with himself, and for weeks and months had wept like a child every time he thought of his house. Michelle's modest wardrobe packed up and taken to the *friperie*. Francois loading his car with the remainder of Louis's tools, the ones that hadn't already been cannibalized by garage-salers and his son's free-loading friends. His remaining four grandchildren still visited him dutifully once a month or so. But he could sense they were counting the minutes until they could get away. From the smell of old people. From their grandpapa who used to take them fishing at all his secret places. Who treated them to hot dog *stimés* every other Sunday at their favorite *Casse Croute*. Their *grandpapa* who was sure as hell no fun anymore.

The people who ran this place—no, not them—the people who did the actual *work* here were kind for the most part. Except the night-time *preposé*, who could be a real shit—cruel and condescending. But Louis's day was divided into slices of inane activities. That was fine for the ones living on the third floor, but for him? *Insupportable.* Bingo. Scrapbooking. Découpage. Playing cards. *Coloring books.* Or worse, some stupid board game missing half its pieces. Once you passed through the doors to *Maison Soleil* you become an old, old person. With the mentality of a child in pre-school. *All ye who enter here abandon everything you once were.* He had asked to be allowed to do some handyman work. He had asked to get some of his tools back so he could maintain at least the strength in his hands, but for both insurance reasons and union restrictions he was not allowed to work at the residence. Yes, his tiny strokes had left him a bit paralyzed on one side once and slurred his speech a little. But Louis was all there. Was all *here*.

And then there was Kutya. Madame Newman's dog that Louis had taken in when she died. Of all his recent losses, Kutya was perhaps the worst. They were allowed pets at *Maison Soleil*, as long as they were small enough to fit into a lap. But Louis had lobbied for the Labrador mix that was Kutya, and for several weeks they had shared Louis's tiny room. Louis had tried to walk him on a leash without being dragged across the small yard around the residence. But Louis realized *Maison Soleil* was no place for a big dog who had never been leashed, who was used to following wherever his nose took him through the forest, flushing out rabbits and turkeys and sometimes, thrillingly, a deer. Louis had finally asked Manon Latendresse, the local kennel owner and stray animal savior to take him. And she did. She was also kind enough to visit with Kutya once every few weeks. Louis kept a stash of dog treats for him as well, but he was obviously now Manon's dog. Growing old, Louis thought, was being forced to accept one loss after another. You'd think he'd be used to it by now, but for several months after Louis had been incarcerated in *Maison Soleil*, he had wanted to die. And then, one day, everything changed. Claire moved in. Claire Lapierre Russell.

There was a sudden knock at his door, and before Louis could answer, she had opened it and looked in. It was the night nurse with the very large bum who walked like a duck. He hated how they knocked and then just opened the door. That was another criminal offense of old age. No privacy.

"Are you looking forward to the picnic tomorrow?"

Louis slid the knapsack a little further under the covers.

"*Bien sur, Mademoiselle.*" Which one was she? Carole? Karine? Maybe Karine.

She smiled again, wrinkled up her nose and in a babyish voice that made him cringe asked, "*Vous avez pris votre douche ce soir, Monsieur Lachance?* Did you take your shower tonight? Will you need some help?"

Louis wanted to scream *I don't need any bloody help*. Instead, he smiled sweetly and admitted he had yet to take his shower, and no, he would be fine.

Carole/Karine briefly considered pursuing this line of inquiry, then decided to move on. She wished him a *Bon dodo!* like she was talking to a five-year old and continued on her way. Louis checked the time on the clock radio by his bed. Twelve hours to go.

Chapter 8

Here's to the beginning of a brand-new diary! I haven't kept one since grade 9 or 10. How can that already be seven years ago? I am so OLD! But this one seems special. This time I'm not calling it a diary. I'm going to call it a JOURNAL which sounds much more…important. Or maybe a logbook. More maritime? Or maybe a chronicle. So. To all ye who open these pages:

This book shall hereby contain all the Important Observations and Significant Experiences of the brand-new INTERN on the SS Star of the Sea. (Our little rubber zodiac boat doesn't really have a name, so I have christened her with what my name, Molly, actually means in Irish.

I have told no one this, of course.

So, what shall I name thee, diary/journal/logbook/chronicle?

After some thought, I have settled on a name from a book that I know I should have read. A classic. And IMPORTANT. But I could never get past the first few chapters and had to resort to the Classics for Kids version of it. All

I remember from that monster of a book is "Call me Ishmael" and "Whenever it is a damp, drizzly November in my soul... it is high time to get to sea as soon as I can."

So, dear...whatever you are...I shall call thee Ishmael. I remember from Bible study that Ishmael means "God hears." And these words in this whatever it is? Are for God's ears only!

Chapter 9

Gretchen

You would think by now, after almost thirty years together, that there was nothing new he could do to surprise her. But this? Informing her he wanted to attend *Marie Russell's* wedding? She did not see this coming. But as soon as he announced that he would support this protest against some hotel project in Ste. Lucie, wherever that was, she should have known something was up.

She watched as he worked the room, leaning in intimately to a person he'd just met, gently touching the bony arm of an older woman to make a point, running his long fingers through that mane of gray-blond hair as he chatted with a young man, the silverback reminding the other of the hierarchy. They were literally lining up to shake his hand, kiss his cheek, get an autograph, lift a glass to his and clink, each one of them rendered a bit giddy by being in his presence. Sometimes she imagined him raising bejeweled hands and blessing each one of them, like the pope. Oh, he could work a room, that man. He could persuade a televangelist to build an abortion clinic if he put his mind to it. There was a very brief pause in the bustle around him, and Magnus caught her eye observing him. He shrugged his shoulders and grinned a bit sheepishly. Gretchen smiled back. This little scene from the five-act play of their life together had been performed a thousand times. Or more.

She continued to watch from her perch at the edge of the dance floor as an older couple, dressed like the aging hippies they probably were, buttonholed Magnus and talked at him enthusiastically. Was that the couple that had contacted him about the project in the first place? The woman threw her head back and laughed, her big, slightly buck teeth exposed. Gretchen couldn't hear what she had found so funny, but she was hanging on to Magnus's arm, her rather ample cleavage pressed against it. Suddenly, Marie appeared beside Magnus, probably introducing him to the couple, or elaborating on what they'd already told him. Marie looked entirely self-possessed. Confident. Happy. Not a woman who looked for herself in the eyes of others. It was very attractive. Still, she could see why Magnus left her. Marie had *settled*. For a life with hubby, home, and kids. A teaching job at a junior college—what do they call them in this crazy province? *Cegeps*. The requisite divorce twenty years in. Ticking off those milestone boxes on the long stumble towards the end. The Marie that Gretchen had known all those many years ago was fierce. Irreverent. Fearlessly dedicated to the cause. Someone who never backed down. Also, a lousy cook who sang cheesy pop songs badly and off-key in the kitchen. Magnus was crazy about her. Until he wasn't.

Gretchen watched a smaller, auburn-haired version of

Marie tap her mother on the shoulder and turn to present herself to Magnus. Marie wagged a finger at her daughter—who seemed like a bit of a smart ass—a lawyer, she was told. And that must be her boyfriend trailing after her, like a puppy. Middle Eastern, Gretchen guessed. Interesting. Now the son was clearly introducing himself, a toddler in tow. Now *he* was gorgeous. He must look like the father who Magnus said is here somewhere. He was young to have one kid already and another one on the way.

"You must be Gretchen?"

Gretchen looked up into the bemused eyes of the groom.

"Yes, I am. And you are of course, Roméo. May I offer you my congratulations?"

Roméo thanked her and received a double-cheeked kiss. An awkward silence ensued. As if on cue, both of them turned to watch Magnus and Marie, who were now chatting with another couple, a man with a greasy ponytail and a missing tooth, and his rodeo queen girlfriend.

"Is it…strange for you to see Marie after all these years?"

Gretchen considered this for a moment. "Yes, a bit. But lovely as well. She was the one who got away, you know. Broke his heart."

Roméo frowned. "Oh? I heard it was the other way around."

"Sometimes I think he still pines for her. But I guess I'm not supposed to tell you that on your wedding day."

Roméo leaned closer to Gretchen and whispered, "I certainly don't blame him." He looked at her empty champagne flute and asked, "Can I get you another?"

Gretchen smiled and replied quickly, "No, thank you. I've had more than enough for today."

Roméo didn't have time to excuse himself properly before a quite masculine-looking young woman who had to be a cop grabbed him breathlessly and pushed him toward the dance floor. Magnus had actually proposed once. He had even bought the diamond ring and got down on one knee. Gretchen had said no, shocked by his concession to a conformity they had always rejected. Gretchen had never understood why anyone got married. In pre-Hellenic times, the concept of marriage—the very idea of being mated to one person for life—was absurd. Women could enjoy sex with whoever *they* selected, and the men were forced to submit to the authority of the women. Then those matriarchal cultures were forced to accept the idea of male superiority and male control. The world was never the same. Of course, the proposal was many, many years ago. Most of her married friends eventually divorced. Most of the unmarried couples she knew had stayed together, more or less successfully. Should she have said yes to Magnus? Would that have changed anything?

Gretchen could not stop herself thinking of an incident a few weeks earlier. Magnus had called home to tell Gretchen he would be late, as he was meeting his oldest friend and partner, Paul, to talk over some personal issues Paul was going through. Gretchen had called Paul to see how he was, but of course he didn't answer his phone. Magnus then called her to say he was going to spend the night out on the Cape with Paul who was drinking too much and feeling really depressed. But Gretchen recognized the tell-tale tone in Magnus's voice. She decided to make the hour-long drive out onto the Cape, to the offices of *See Change*. And there, of course, he was. Conveniently standing outside the front door in the foggy evening, illuminated by the yellow porch light. She watched the two of them kiss, Magnus leaning down to the much smaller girl. Woman. The new—was she still new?—social media and brand strategist. She wanted to jump out of her car and confront them. She wanted to aim the car at them and hit the gas full throttle. Instead, she took out her phone and called Magnus. Astonishingly, he answered, squinting at the caller ID and then turning away from the girl.

"Hi! Hello?"

"How is Paul?"

The girl stood there and waited, her arms wrapped around herself against the invading fog, watching.

"Oh. He's much more depressed than I thought. I don't know what is happening to him, but I think I must stay the night with him. He needs me. I hope that's all right with you?"

Magnus was leaning against the railing on the landing, staring absently out to the sea which the fog had obliterated.

"Are you with him now?"

Magnus hesitated. "Of course. He's just in the other room. We're planning on finishing the bottle of vodka we started, and then we'll both fall asleep in front of a movie, no doubt."

Gretchen watched as the girl came up behind Magnus and wrapped her arms around his waist. With his free hand he clutched one of hers.

"Please say hi to Paul from me?"

"I will, of course. I'll be home tomorrow evening. I'm in meetings all day. Okay?"

"Okay."

"I'll see you tomorrow." He turned away from the sea and seemed to be staring right at her. "I love you."

Gretchen hung up. She could still aim her car at the landing and take them both down. But she had been through this scene before and survived. Besides, there was something in that office that Gretchen wanted, that she needed. She had waited as the two of them descended the stairs and disappeared into the fog. Then she turned off the engine of her car, slipped on a pair of gloves, and stepped into the darkness.

ℬ

Magnus placed his hand on her shoulder and squeezed gently. "Everything okay? Are you all right?"

She knew she should touch his hand. A small gesture. But she couldn't.

"I am. Perfect."

He leaned down and gave her a peck on the mouth. It took every drop of what self-control she had left not to pull him to her by that mane of hair and scream at him to stop. Just…stop. Gretchen handed him her glass. "Could you go fill this up for me, please?"

Gretchen watched as Magnus dutifully headed towards the lineup at the bar. Then she scraped her chair away from the table and found a quiet, hidden spot in the garden, just outside the tent. She pulled out her phone. It rang five times and then went to voicemail.

"Did you do it?"

Chapter 10

Paul

He tried not to, but he couldn't help but check himself out in the massive mirror behind the hotel bar, all gilded edges and smoky surfaces. He had tried to clean up a bit, but he still looked like some kid's idea of an old salt who'd wandered off a boat smelling of fish and whiskey, bumping his peg leg along the streets of the big city until he'd stumbled into this joint. He'd put on a shirt with long sleeves and his best trousers, which he realized too late had a largish hole near the crotch. He had also brushed his mop of hair, now entirely gray and even more unruly than ever. He looked back into the mirror and tried to tame a few wayward strands that stuck out at right angles from his ears. A haircut was long overdue. A good massage. A decent meal cooked for him by a good woman. A good meal cooked for him by a decent woman. Or not.

He watched the bartender expertly pour him a shot of bourbon, an exact ounce and a half, not a drop misplaced. He tried to imagine her without the crisp white shirt, black bowtie, and black vest hugging her small frame. Her black hair released from the severe ponytail. She might indulge him if she knew who he was, or rather, who he worked for. Who his best friend was. But the bartender tucked the bill for his drink discreetly by his napkin, gave him a cursory smile and turned away to another customer, clearly a regular who was rewarded with a warm *Bonjour!* and a double-cheeked kiss.

Paul glanced around the swanky room. Of course, Magnus had put her up in a hotel like this. The rest of them were used to the Motel 8's and crappy quarters the world over. Paul leaned back on his stool to let the familiarity and comfort of the bourbon work its warmth into his gut and down into his legs and recalled with startling clarity when he first met Magnus. It was the summer of 1987, and Paul had already run a few campaigns for PlanetGreen UK, first coordinating from the cramped London office in Camden and then out in the field. It was a heady, hopeful, and thrilling chapter in his life. He and his comrades still believed they were changing the world. That what they did *mattered*, could still change the *course of history*. They used to hang out in a local pub called The Lion and The Lamb that was dark and dingy no matter what the weather was outside. It smelled of beer, vomit, and fried fish, and of course they adored the place. Paul had first laid eyes on him when Magnus joined them at the pub to meet a girl from PlanetGreen that Paul had been desperately trying to date. Magnus had just finished up his graduate degree at Oxford. He was almost everything Paul loathed. Stupidly, blindly, fecklessly rich, and with the indecency to be handsome and smart as well. Of course, once the girl met Magnus it was game, set, and match. For a month or two. Then Magnus extricated himself from her as he always did, in such a way that the girl practically felt like *she* had ended the affair. Paul had learned that Magnus was a poor little rich boy, the son of a Norwegian oil baron who assumed that his son would gratefully rule his kingdom when the time came. In two words: entitled asshole. And the *enemy*. And yet. When Paul told Magnus what he did for a "living," Magnus listened raptly. It was Oedipal of course—the son of filthy rich, morally bankrupt man gets back at his father by sabotaging his life's work. But when Magnus told Paul in that damp and dreary pub that he could fly a plane *and* a helicopter, that he had in fact often flown his father to one of his several estates around Europe, Paul had suggested that maybe he put those skills to better use.

He couldn't quite remember exactly how it happened now, but somehow Magnus did not end up flying a helicopter. Instead, with no background or training in the environmental movement, he ended up in the zodiac boat that was bringing supplies to the activists who had occupied, an oil platform off the coast of Norway that was scheduled to be scuttled to save money, dumping one hundred tons of oil and toxic waste into the North Sea. Of course, the picture that made headlines around the world was not of all those like Paul who'd put in years of work fighting eco-criminals, but of newly minted Magnus, young, gorgeous and determined, heroically flying through the waves, dodging the water cannons from the biggest oil company in the world. David versus Goliath. A star was born. But that image. That image was so powerful, it caused a boycott of service stations across Europe and forced the giant to its knees. The oil platform was not scuttled, and the laws allowing the dumping of toxic waste into the sea were changed forever. One battle won. But what did it all add up to? Did they move the dial? Yes. They'd won a few battles, but now they were at war, and it was probably too late. All they could do was try to mitigate the most devastating effects of climate change and hope for the best. Maybe the geniuses who dreamed up a way to block the sun, or a pump that cools coral reefs, or plastic-eating enzymes could still save the world. But Paul knew it was over. Hope? Time? These were the two commodities they couldn't sell anymore. Mother Nature always bats last.

Paul hesitated for just a moment before he gestured to the bartender to pour him another shot. She was starting to warm up to him a bit and rewarded his request with a smile. He checked his phone. Three text messages from her. And just now, a voice mail. Paul swallowed the shot in one go. He was going to have to deal with her, too.

છ

After Paul had paid a shocking amount for his two bourbons, he made his way to the elevators and pressed the button for the ninth floor. An impeccably coiffed and dressed elderly woman gave him a barely perceptible nod and a keen once over as he stepped beside her and tried not to inhale the perfume she had spilled all over herself. He made his way along the silent, carpeted hallway, rehearsing his impending conversation. Even though Paul had done it for over thirty years, he still resented cleaning up after Magnus. There are people who use you up and throw you out, he thought. And there are others who use you over and over, again and again. And somehow you keep coming back.

He knocked on the hotel room with three quick raps and waited. He knocked again, twice. He was pretty sure she was in the room—he could see a light under the door and hear what sounded like running water. Shit. He did not want to have to come back. Just as the thought of downing a few more bourbons and looking to see what other souls might be frequenting the Four Seasons lobby bar sounded like a plan, the door opened to the end of its chain.

"What are you doing here?" she asked, peering at him through the space between the door and its frame.

"I'm ah...I'm sorry to interrupt whatever it is you're doing, but I need to talk with you. It's urgent."

Emily Joly hesitated. Then she slid the chain from its metal slot and opened the door a few more inches. She gathered the two lapels of a rather plush bathrobe tightly under her chin.

"I'm kinda busy. You can talk to me right here."

He looked up and down the hallway. A chambermaid had appeared and was busy refolding towels onto her cart. She was within earshot.

"No, I can't. It's. It's something about Magnus. You need to know. Now."

Emily sighed and crossed her arms. "I think I know a little more about Magnus than you do, Paul." She frowned at him. "Wait...did you knock on my door a little while ago?"

"No. Why?"

"Never mind. I thought maybe it was you."

"Look, can I come in?" Paul did not want to have this conversation in the hall. He tried to step into the room.

"For fuck's sake, Paul. Let me get some clothes on—"

"Well, that would be a first."

Emily Joly went to close the door on him, but he was faster, blocking it with his knee and shoulder. In one movement, Paul Pellerin was in her room, and had clicked the heavy door shut behind him.

Chapter 11

THE PARTY'S OVER

Two hundred cocktails had been shaken and swallowed, and a dozen drunken, impromptu toasts had been made. Ruby had pulled everyone into a wild hora finale, Roméo had danced sweetly with Noah balanced on his shoes (before he carried him to his big boy bed that he'd only just grown in to) and someone had puked in the bathroom. Nicole's Léo had got into the remains of the wedding cake and had had a nuclear sugar meltdown that had ended with both of them in tears—but now, at last, the wedding was almost, finally over. The last few diehard partiers had abandoned the dance floor, said their good nights, and wandered back to their cars, *oohing* and *awing* at the starry night. The DJ and bartender had packed up most of their stuff, but in the wake of the party there was still an epic clean up. Ben, Maya, and Lucy had half-heartedly started picking up glasses and packing them into the caterer's boxes, but the wine had eventually caught up with Lucy who was snoring loudly on Marie's sofa. Graham had long since passed out in the guestroom. Marie had ordered Ben and Maya to bed, and they did not protest.

Gretchen had left hours earlier for the house she and Magnus had rented, claiming she was exhausted from the travel and had to get some sleep before the big protest the next day. But Magnus had stayed late in deep conversation with Ruby while Mohammed listened, watching him with a kind of wonder. Marie was too tired to move or join them. Was she getting *old*? She watched as Roméo towered over the kitchen sink, tipsily working his way through the mountain of dishes while he whistled what she now recognized as a Beethoven violin concerto. How many men were there in the world like Roméo? His bride's ex-husband and ex-boyfriend show up at their wedding, and he takes it all in stride. There was nothing sexier than confidence. The knowledge that what you were was enough. A man happily doing dishes was pretty sexy, too, she thought.

There were two more guests who seemed to be in no hurry to leave. After Nicole finally got the chocolate icing washed off Léo's face, hands, hair, shirt, and pants, he had passed out like a drunk, and Roméo had offered to let him sleep it off in Noah's old crib. She gratefully accepted and went into the spare bathroom to wash the sticky mess off herself. When she came back out, Steve Pouliot, who had offered to stay and help clean up, was busy carrying boxes of glasses out to the front porch.

Nicole sat on the ottoman at Marie's feet. They both watched Steve in his tight undershirt, which he filled perfectly, his arm muscles straining against the weight of the boxes.

"What happened to his date?" Nicole whispered to Marie.

Marie turned to Nicole. "I'm not sure, but I think she left with my ex-husband."

Marie recalled a moment earlier that night when she saw Steve's Amazon woman strolling arm and arm with Daniel along Marie's little lakefront path. Then, she realized both seemed to have left the party. So that's who he was after.

"He's very cute. And nice, I think. He's very short, though."

Marie took in Nicole. "You're not exactly tall yourself."

"I don't like to be taller than the guy I'm dating."

"Who said you're dating?"

Nicole blushed.

"And what's with your sexist bullshit? Men have to be taller than us?"

As if on cue, Steve glanced over at them and smiled, then stacked up another couple of boxes and grunted his way to the door.

"Marie, I am never, *ever* dating a cop again. Normand is now down to one day a month with Léo. And even that seems like a real obligation for him. It makes me so sad. For Léo. Myself, I don't care. Dead weight. Good riddance." Neither one of them of course mentioned the intense one night Nicole and Roméo had spent together, a night that still sometimes haunted them.

Steve Pouliot suddenly appeared beside Marie with his shirt and jacket back on, his tie hanging around his neck.

"*Merci*, Marie. It was a fantastic party. Thank you for inviting me and...for inviting me."

"Thank you for working so hard, Steve. I don't know how you have the energy. But then, you're young."

He nodded and jangled his car keys in his hand. Then he turned to Nicole.

"Do you have a lift home?"

"I'm calling a taxi."

Marie raised an eyebrow. "At this hour? Maude—she's the local taxi—she usually knocks off by nine pm."

Steve shrugged his shoulders. "I could take you home."

"And my giant comatose toddler as well? Do you have room in your car?"

Steve shrugged again. "Sure."

He stood awkwardly before Nicole and Marie. "I'll just go and say good night to Roméo then."

Nicole got up off the ottoman with a groan and headed towards the bedroom where Léo had passed out. And now, Marie noted, Roméo was ceremoniously handing over the dish towel to Mohammed while Ruby plunged her hands in the sink to continue the washing. When Ruby first brought Mohammed home, he would sit and wait to be served, while the rest of them ran around getting the meal to the table. He wouldn't lift a finger, like he had no idea or experience of men getting up to do dishes or help clean up. Marie was very gratified to witness this moment. She had taught Ruby well.

Steve emerged from the bedroom with Léo passed out in his arms, his head nestled into Steve's shoulder, his limp legs bumping against Steve's knees. The toddler looked half as big as the man. Nicole followed, a diaper bag slung over her shoulder and the car seat in her spare hand. She leaned in to kiss Marie good night. "What the fuck am I doing?"

Roméo moved behind Marie and gently massaged her neck as they waved Nicole and Steve off. "Well, *that* was unexpected."

Marie felt a touch on her arm. Magnus had left Ruby and Mohammed to the dishes and looked like he was ready to go, too, she hoped.

"Look. um…Gretchen took the car back to our rental and it's a bit far to walk—"

Roméo and Marie both looked at the abandoned sofa, but neither said anything.

"If it's not too much bother, I would love to just head down by your lake, throw a blanket down, and sleep under the stars."

Marie and Roméo both protested. "No, that's…no. Roméo will give you a lift—"

"Just give me an old blanket. It's so warm tonight. Just something to cushion these bones a little. I haven't done this in years—it'll do me good."

Before they could protest any further, he added, "I'll be gone in the morning—you won't even see me."

Roméo shook his head. "You have to join us for breakfast. You and I? We haven't had a chance to talk."

Marie went and grabbed the two crumpled blankets off the sofa. "Here you go."

Magnus stepped out into the muggy night air, and the moonless starry night. Roméo had already turned back into the house, but Marie watched as Magnus glanced around a bit furtively, then took out his phone and made a call. His body language told a clear story; Magnus was calling a lover, and Marie was pretty sure it wasn't Gretchen. What neither Marie nor Magnus knew, though, was that someone else was watching Magnus too.

Chapter 12

The mountain was the verdant centerpiece of 5,000 hectares of public land and a network of eco-corridors that connected precious natural areas in a region infiltrated by more and more urban sprawl. It was a wonder of biodiversity, with a vast water network and swaths of forest over ninety years old covering 90 percent of its territory. Some two hundred animal species lived here, including twenty protected species. It was frequented by wolves on its eastern flank, and on its northern slope was the one of the biggest lynx habitats left in southern Quebec. Although not seen in these forests for decades, many locals hoped the cougar would one day return. Some said it already had. The mountain was known as Mont Baleine, even though there wasn't a whale to be found for at least 500 kilometers, not until Tadoussac, where the Saguenay River emptied into the St. Lawrence. The local Mohawks, whose hunting and fishing territory included its southern flank, more aptly called it *Oh'kwa:ri*, or Bear Mountain, as its rounded peak looked more like a black bear's rump than a whale. By whatever name it was known, the mountain seemed impervious to the hive of human activity below it trying to prevent one tiny speck of the damage its species had done for centuries.

Even though the sun had only just risen, there were already dozens of people busily getting ready for the big day. On the little gravel beach of Lac Noir at the foot of the mountain, the organizers were setting up the tables that would soon be covered in leaflets of information about the Mont Baleine nature preserve and what would happen to the entire eco-system should Projet Leviathan come to pass. Others were putting the finishing touches on an enormous, colorful banner, and still others were preparing drinks and snacks for the hundreds of people expected to come and support their cause. Many were wearing matching T-shirts with their protest logo STOP LEVIATHAN! emblazoned on the front. Manon Latendresse, one of the chief organizers of the protest, sported a different T-shirt—one with a single leafy tree on it. It read: *I Photosynthesize. What's Your Superpower?* She pulled her phone from her back pocket and texted him again. *you're late. where are u?* When Manon looked up, she spotted Ruby and her boyfriend, Mohammed heading towards her. She gave them both a forceful hug and smacking kiss on the cheek, grabbed Ruby's hand, and pulled her up onto one of the picnic tables.

"*Bonjour tout le monde! Hey! Écoutez! Écoutez, tout le monde!*" She gestured at everyone to come together. "*Je vous présente Ruby Russell.* This is Ruby Russell. A few of you know her, the daughter of Marie Russell, our local author. It's because of Ruby that he's coming today—Magnus Sorensen is coming today. So, just give her your attention for a minute before the big gang gets here and things get much louder and crazier!" Ruby was hungover and had not prepared anything to say.

Her tongue felt fuzzy, and she was desperately thirsty. She grabbed Mohammed's water bottle and took a long swallow.

"*Bonjour*! So, I…we are here today to help with any legal questions you have, and we brought a hard copy of the petition—" Ruby held a fluttering piece of paper above her head and waved it at the crowd—"that already has over four thousand signatures and will get more today! Please encourage everyone you know, have met, and ever will meet to sign it at our office in the village, or on-line. Also, please share it on all your social media." Ruby began to step down from the table, but Manon stopped her and nodded for her to continue. "I…I…have read Magnus Sorensen's book about how he fought to save this one pack of wolves in Norway—like, just forty wolves. Many people wanted them dead. They just didn't see the use of wolves. They didn't see the *point* of wolves." Ruby turned to take in the view behind her. "If they destroy this mountain, if they *kill* this mountain for this…big hotel, for Leviathan…." Raucous booing erupted from the small crowd. "We'll hear the chainsaw, not the howl of a wolf. We'll hear the sound of cars, not the call of loons." Ruby searched for another image, but her foggy brain stopped right there. Manon smiled and started to thank Ruby for her wise words. But Ruby continued. "One thing I took away from Sorensen's book is, is to tell a good story. Whatever small battle or major war you're fighting, make it a good story. So today, we're going to tell a story that everyone understands, that everyone can feel, deep inside here." Ruby touched her stomach and then her heart. "He also wrote about his campaign against Big Oil that it's all about putting on a good show. Well, today, with the help of Magnus Sorensen, I think we'll do just that!"

Ruby did finally step down off the picnic table and Manon

took her place. "Just one more thing. The media will be here soon. And there will be the people from *their* side here—and they will be here to provoke us. This fight is not just to keep our mountain *pretty*. This is an environmental *emergency*. We don't want people screaming at each other here today. Don't shame people. Don't preach at people. *Persuade* them. Explain in language they can understand what this project *means*." Manon paused for dramatic effect. "Remember that people on both sides of this all want what's best for our kids and for our collective future. We just don't agree on how to get there."

Manon gestured to an older woman wearing an intricately beaded jacket.

"I would like to ask Tracy Jacobs of the Mohawk Council to speak to you now."

The woman chose not to get up on the table. She began to speak in a measured, quiet voice that shut the chattering crowd up immediately.

"The Mohawk Council has never been consulted about the Leviathan Project, which borders our reserve, our hunting and fishing territory of one hundred square kilometers over which we hold ancestral rights. It is a violation of the constitutional obligation to consult us when there is an impact on ancestral rights, but also a violation of the obligations imposed by the Quebec law on sustainable forest management. They had a duty to consult us, but they have never done so." There was a smattering of boos again.

"We must preserve what we have NOW. For our grandkids, our great-grandkids and our great-great grandkids. We must protect what we have. We can't just look at the trees and the land as something to USE. Something to exploit. As just another way to make more and more money. Because one day, money will be worthless." Manon squeezed her into a big hug, and applauded her back to the crowd, which was starting to disperse and return to their preparations. Then she heard it. The unmistakable sound of Ti-Coune's ancient pickup truck with the muffler held in fragile place by a bent hanger. She checked her phone. Late, of course. He slammed on the brakes too close to another car being emptied of its boxes, threw it into park, and stepped out.

"*Câlice de tabarnac.*"

"You're late—"

"They trashed my house! Those bastards were at my house last night, okay? When we were at the wedding. I drove by on my way home from your place this morning—thank fucking God Pitoune was at your place because who knows what they would have done to her!"

A few people heard the commotion and wandered over to hear what Ti-Coune and Manon were arguing about.

"They knocked over my fucking fridge and now it don't work anymore. They threw all my food on the floor. And they tore down the curtains that you made for me, Manon—I never had no real curtains in my whole life before. *Cristie.*"

For years, Ti-Coune's little bungalow was derelict, with piles of rotten wood, rusty lawn chairs, and various broken appliances and car parts dotting the yard. Under Manon's firm supervision and guidance, the whole place, and Ti-Coune's life as well, had been transformed.

"Who did this, Jean-Michel?" an elderly protester asked, shaking her head in disbelief.

"The same people who vandalized our place." Joel, Marie's friend and neighbor announced. Shelly, his wife, put a comforting hand on Ti-Coune's shoulder. "They killed three of our hens and spray-painted a swastika on the side of our house. It's a hate crime." Without realizing it, Ti-Coune pulled the sleeve of his shirt down to cover the old, faded swastika tattooed on his forearm, a shameful remnant of his old life.

"I am so sorry, Ti...um, Jean-Michel. We'll give you a hand cleaning up. Joel can take a look at your fridge. He can save almost anything."

"They pissed all over my bed. I mean, that's not the first time it happened. Why do people keep breaking into my house and pissing on my bed?"

A few people chuckled grimly at the attempt at humor.

"Did you call the police?" Joel asked. "We did. They came quickly enough. But they wrote up their report—and after three weeks? They 'have no clue who did it.'" Joel said, the last part in air quotes.

"It was probably them who did it," Tracy Jacobs offered. "We all know most of them are big fans of Leviathan. Don't go to the cops. They won't help. When we have vandals on the reserve? We find out who they are and take care of them ourselves."

Ti-Coune lit a cigarette and exhaled a stream of thick, white smoke through his nose. "I'm gonna get those bastards."

"What are you going to do, Ti-Coune? You gonna go piss on their sofa? And who are *they*? I can tell you. They love to race their gas-spewing motorboats around our lake. When they're done with that, they hop onto their ATV's and drive into the forest where they've left a mountain of carrots to lure the deer to them—so they don't have to walk very far carrying their *heavy* gun, and then shoot them. It's very sporting. But then, they never fight fair. So, I don't know what you *think* you're gonna *do* to those bastards. And I wonder if all the...

protests and…petitions in the world will stop this, this… Leviathan from happening!"

Everyone was shocked into silence. Those were the most words that had ever been spoken in one breath by Lucien Picard, the famously taciturn local mailman. The only time he could ever be described as loquacious was when he was sharing his expertise on wild mushrooms during the harvest season.

"*Criss, mon vieux*, you been keeping that in for a while!" Ti-Coune said, breaking the silence.

Bob Babineau, the councilor for the nearby little town of Saint Esprit clapped his hands to get everyone's attention.

"*Okay, mes amies!* We've got three hours left to get ready. You all know what you're doing, right? Let's focus on the task at hand, and we'll circle back to unpack this later." Bob loved words like "unpack." His other favorite was "stakeholder."

They were just all returning to their various stations, still marveling at Lucien's eruption when Manon held up a hand, still reading a text on her phone.

"Someone just set the mayor's car on fire. Mayor Morin." Manon held up her phone. "It's completely destroyed."

"Was she in it?" Ti-Coune asked.

Shelly gave him a withering look. "That's not funny. I mean, is this who we are now? We're burning the cars of people who support Leviathan? Who don't *agree* with us? This is not us. Well, it's not me."

"This doesn't look good for our cause. Just gives them some leverage," Bob Babineau opined. "I *really* hope nobody here did this."

No one said anything. Everyone was checking their phone for images of the burning car.

Out of the crowd, a voice shouted, "Maybe it's time we do act more like them. Maybe we need to burn a few more cars. Send a message ourselves."

Joel glanced at the faces around him, trying to find the source of that opinion.

"That is the stupidest idea I've heard in a long time. If I find out any of us is responsible for this, this…idiocy, I am out of this whole thing."

Ruby suddenly waved to get everyone's attention. "I just got a message from Magnus Sorensen. His ETA is at one-fifteen pm. Exactly. We have a lot to do. Let's go give them a good show!"

Chapter 13

Claire

"I thought you might like to wear this little sundress today, Madame Russell. They're announcing very warm weather. And you'll be so pretty in this."

Claire Lapierre Russell looked at the woman with bright brown eyes that often looked startled now. "Pretty?"

"Yes! You are so pretty! Especially for someone your age."

The caregiver, Carole, marveled at Claire's skin and at her eighty-six-year-old face, marked by very few wrinkles. She perched Claire on the edge of her single bed, and without being asked, Claire obediently raised both skinny arms above her head and allowed the dress to be lowered over her and pulled into place. Carole carefully stood her up and helped her slip on a pair of snug shorts over her diaper. Carole winked at her.

"Just to make sure no one sees something they shouldn't."

She slipped Claire's feet get into her sandals and tightened the Velcro straps.

"You can put your arms down now, Madame Russell."

Claire dutifully lowered her arms and waited. She was feeling excited but could not quite remember why.

"How was your daughter's wedding yesterday? Was it beautiful?"

Claire smiled at her.

"What is your name again?"

"I'm Carole. You know my name!"

Claire repeated it like she'd never heard it before. "Carole." Then she added, "Carole. Did you know that I almost got married to Tony?"

"Oh. No! Who was Tony?" She leaned in to Claire and whispered. "Were you engaged to someone else before your husband, Madame Claire?"

"My brother, André? He and I, we used to go out on Saturday afternoons after we worked all week. You know, to…walk along and look at people. Flirt a little bit. We used to walk along *boulevard Mont Royal*—all the way from our apartment on Boyer Street to the foot of the mountain. We were never supposed to go that far, because that meant crossing *boulevard Saint Laurent*, where all the immigrants and the Jews lived. My daughter married a Jewish man. She loved him."

Claire looked confused. "Not yesterday. Yesterday it was Mr. Roméo."

Carole glanced at her watch. "Madame Russell, I have to hurry now. I have two others to dress."

"On one of those walks I met Tony, my first love. A singer. Oh, he was so handsome. And so nice. Then I met. Ed…Ed."

"Edward? Your husband?"

"Yes! Edward. So, I was dating both boys. I couldn't

choose. I was sitting at home one Saturday morning with Papa. And he said, 'Claire, you are twenty-three years old, and you must choose who to marry.' So, I decided I would choose the first one who came to my door that day."

Claire looked at Carole. "Can you guess who it was?"

"Edward, I think?"

"No! It was Tony. Handsome, dark Tony who loved to sing. And he was Catholic, so Papa was happy. But I decided that Tony would never make enough money. And Edward was so blond, and tall. And English. Oh, Papa was not happy at all. A *Protestant*. But I chose Edward. He was an alcoholic. He died. A long time ago."

Carole gave Claire's hand a squeeze.

"We'll bring your cardigan in case the weather turns a bit cool, okay? I'll be back to get you soon."

"I have a new boyfriend now."

"You do?"

"Oh, yes. Do you know him?"

"Does he live here?"

"He had his own house. His wife is dead."

"Madame Russell? I love listening to your stories. But I have to go."

"We're going on a picnic together!"

"Yes, we are!"

Carole quickly grabbed the little hairbrush on Claire's tiny dresser and ran it through her thin, white hair.

"There. You look *beautiful*."

Chapter 14

Marie

Marie opened her eyes to the morning just after sunrise, the clean blue sky streaked with salmon pink clouds—the kind of morning that made it impossible to question being alive. She leaned over to breathe in Roméo who was still asleep, his mouth slightly open. He smelled of scotch, sleep, and a bit of sweat from the warm night and the quick, quiet sex they'd had the night before because the house was full, the walls were thin, and there were only two bathrooms for ten people. She thought about staying in bed with Roméo for the rest of her life but decided to get up because the birdsong symphony though her open window was so extraordinary, she had to get outside and hear it in stereo. She kissed Roméo's cheek, then decided the best way to shake out of her booze fog was a swim. She slipped into her bathing suit, grabbed a towel from the bathroom, and stepped down the stairs silently. Marie loved the being the first one up—loved feeling that the house was entirely hers before the others woke up and started their days with their own habits. Of course, someone else was awake. Dog sat by his bowl and awaited his breakfast with a slowly wagging tail. Marie dropped a cup of kibble into his bowl which he inhaled. Barney, Marie's fifteen-year-old Puggle, was curled up nose to tail on the sofa, sound asleep, too deaf now to hear the sound of food, which in his prime would have had him torpedo off the sofa and to his bowl in the blink of an eye. Marie toed her feet into her flip-flops and went out the door, Dog hard on her heels. A slight breeze lifted the branches of the aspens and balsams lining the forest path to her little lake and set them in gentle motion. The sky was now almost cloudless, an intense blue that promised no change for the next few hours at least. Marie stopped to listen to sort out who was singing that morning. The ovenbirds were *teacher-teacher-teacher-ing* insistently. She could just make out the ethereal, fluty notes of the wood thrush echoing deeper in the woods. Then the ecstatic trill of the winter wren, a bird that could sing harmonies with itself. She heard the squeak of nuthatches, a squawking baby blue jay, and high overhead, the iconic shrill whistle of a broad-winged hawk that would send the songbirds fleeing for cover. There were too many warblers joining in for her to identify, but she could hear the black-throated green warbler, singing the five opening notes of *Into the Woods* that Marie was pretty sure Sondheim had heard as well and borrowed. What a sensory orgy July is in Quebec, Marie thought. Everything was so *erotic*. The juicy grasses, the coy wildflowers, the waving ferns beckoning her down the trail and closer to the lake. The raspberry bushes were heavy with ripeness. The blueberries were still two weeks away yet, but so full of the tiny green berries that she expected a spectacular harvest this year. If she got to them before the bears did. And Dog.

As she approached her dock, she realized Magnus had to be awake—the birds were so loud he couldn't possibly sleep though their morning chorus. But as she glanced at the clearing by the boathouse, she could see the hump of his body still swaddled in the blankets off the sofa, and no movement at all. She dropped her towel on the dock, kicked off her flip-flops and without hesitation, dove in. Dog jumped in next to her one second later.

Nothing on this beautiful, miraculous planet was more delicious to Marie than a swim around the lake on a July morning. The sun was still rising, and the water sparkled and danced in its light. Marie knew every little detail of its shoreline the way she knew her own body: the alder tree the kingfisher liked to fly out from, dive-bomb her and then fly back to and chide her for being there. The cove where the loons hid their nest in a tangle of long grass. The pile of rocks where the merganser mother and her dozen ducklings camouflaged themselves from predators. The inlet where the snapping turtle lurked, and the stock-still heron waited patiently for a fish. Suddenly, a horse fly buzzed her head. They were aggressively territorial, and Marie had invaded his space. She swam underwater to lose him, and when she came back up, Dog had decided he'd had enough of a swim and was heading back to shore. He would frantically follow Marie and make sure she was still alive from there. As she came back up for air, two loons appeared just ahead of her. At this point in the summer, they were so used to swimmers and boats they were practically tame. The male *hooed* softly to the female, reminding her that Marie was nearby and reassuring her. Marie was always anxious about the return of the loons every May—she felt if they didn't return some terrible thing could happen. For years she and Daniel saw themselves as the loon pair—crazy and mated for life. The second half of that statement proved itself wrong, and Marie had recently learned that loons were more like her and her ex-husband than she had thought. If a chick was not produced, they often split up and looked for a more fruitful partner—and if an invading male came into the wrong territory he could be stabbed through the heart by a rival's sharp beak. This pair had had no chicks again this year. But as Marie began a leisurely breaststroke through the dappled water, the two loons were now peacefully preening. Marie looked back towards the shore where Dog had stopped to watch her. He was very close to the ruins of a little cabin, which was well over a hundred years old. When they were little, her kids dared each other to play in it, convinced that a witch lived there who was out to get them. She and Daniel had played along, maybe not entirely certain themselves the place wasn't haunted. Marie liked to imagine being alive at a time when people believed in witches and otherworldly spirits. Or a time when people believed the world was so full of gods that one could be encountered at any time. He or she might be an animal or a passing stranger. Of course, Joel the local historian, told her that the cabin had actually been a speakeasy, a place where the settlers who cleared these forests to farm (and who had failed so spectacularly—you cannot plow Laurentian Shield rock) had a place to get away from their wives and many, many kids. The Catholic church—so dominant in Quebec until the Quiet Revolution of the 1960s began to challenge and ultimately quash almost all its power and control—did not allow any contraception. So, what was a man to do while his wife washed diapers, fed their brood, and maybe didn't want to have sex every night even though the local priest told her it was her sacred duty? Marie slowed her stroke to watch the water striders skate ahead of her on the calm surface. The locals called them Jesus bugs. Two patrolling dragonflies zipped by her on perpetual hunt. She lazily treaded water and let her breathing relax a bit, as a smile broke on her face. She was now married for the second time. Her second *husband*. To a cop. To a vegan. A classical music lover. A *cat* lover. Someone who was gentle, funny, kind, responsible, and fully grown up. How many people, let alone men, could you say that about?

Marie signaled to Dog that she was turning back for home. He jumped to attention and started racing to their dock. Marie switched back to the more efficient crawl and swam as quickly as she could to get her heart rate up again. When she slowed to catch her breath, she was already almost back at the dock, just in time to catch a glimpse of the beaver who slapped his tail on the surface of the water to warn her off. He then vee-lined away from her back to the shore. The beaver reminded her of the new book she was researching and outlining for her publisher. It was about animal revenge, inspired by the behavior of a colony of beavers at her neighbor's house. Although beaver dams create wetlands, which are among the most productive ecosystems in the world, her neighbor didn't appreciate them and had destroyed their dam on the pond next to his house. A few weeks later, he had to go to the city on business for a few days. When he returned, he discovered that the beavers had chewed down almost every single tree around his house. There were many other stories Marie had found: the orcas in Spain, for example, who had been attacking and sinking boats all this past summer. It was believed one had lost her mate to a boat strike. Was she a vengeful whale widow? And just the other morning someone told Marie that an otter had attacked a woman in a nearby lake. An *otter*? This was unprecedented. Marie hadn't believed it until she saw an article in the paper with pictures of the traumatized woman recovering in hospital. In spite of herself, she quickly glanced around to see if any killer otter was following her. Dog waited for her at the end of the dock as she pulled her dripping self up the metal ladder. As she toweled the water off, she closed her eyes and just breathed in the morning air that was already turning muggy as the sun rose higher and the humidity of an impending thunderstorm was starting to gather. Suddenly, she was shocked out of her reverie by a scream. Not a playful one. A terrified scream. And then another. Marie sprinted along the path towards the sound with Dog right behind her.

Chapter 15

Dear Ishmael,

Today was one of the best days of my life. Maybe the best. Well, okay—maybe second best to the day Anton asked me to marry him. Maybe this is my last big hurrah before I get married and become a married lady—haha! Anton is so wonderful. He encouraged me to do this internship. He wants the best for me. Caroline, of course, says he's too nice. Too doting. Too…what's the word she says? Besotted. How can you be too kind to the person you love? Maybe I should date one of her guys—rich party boys who get her drunk and then dump her at parties with a bunch of sketch people?

Wow. Totally sidetracked there as usual by my sister. Same old same old. Back to my best day? I've only been on this job, (well, internship and unpaid, but still) for three DAYS and THIS HAPPENS!!!!! We were following these two humpbacks who were avoiding us. We try not to stress them by getting too close, and they clearly didn't want us near. They're often supposed to be very curious and friendly, but these two were skittish. ANYWAY. Magnus (the boss) said let's try something. So, he cut the engine of the zodiac, and we just sat there quietly bobbing in the waves. Then he said, "they like it sometimes when you sing to them." We took a minute or two trying to choose a song, and we finally all started singing some song I didn't know—My Bunny Lies Over the Ocean? That didn't work. The whales kept moving away. Then we tried some old folk song I also didn't know, and it still didn't work. Finally, I just started singing O Canada. Really loud and proud. I'm the only Canadian here, so no one else knew the words, but I do. In English and French. And I couldn't BELIEVE IT. Those two whales turned right toward us and came up alongside the boat—one so close I could look right into her eyes. I've never felt anything like that in my life. It was like looking at the stars or God—she made me feel so small, but also like we were all a part of this. Together. Human and whale. One is no more important than the other. Both part of a world where one could not survive without the other. Or would survival be worth it without the other? Maybe for the whales. Listen to me! I'm a philosopher.

Anyway, the whales moved off and we started heading back to the research center (it's really an old shacky-looking house on this little island) and a pod of dolphins followed the boat. They were like friendly little torpedoes of muscle. Then when we got back, the sky was so blue and the sun still so hot (rare) that most of the crew stripped off their clothes and jumped into the sea. Should have taken a picture of that for the folks back home. And Anton. I did it too. Stripped right down to my birthday suit and plunged right in—for about ten seconds. That water is like 54 degrees. Paul (the guy who kinda runs the place) opened a case of beer and we all got just a little bit drunk. What a DAY! If died right now at least I could say I had really lived something special. But OMG I want to live so MANY MORE DAYS LIKE THIS!

Chapter 16

THE MORNING AFTER

Marie came to a stop and doubled over, her chest heaving and her hands on her knees as she tried to get her breath back. Just at the end of the lake path in front of her house stood a few of their overnight guests. Not Magnus. Had she run past him while he was still sleeping? They were gathered together looking down at something, shaking their heads and murmuring to each other. Marie straightened herself up and jogged closer. Roméo saw her first and broke away from the group to go to her.

"What is it? Who was screaming?"

Roméo put an arm around her shoulder.

"It was Pénélope. She came outside to take a little stroll with her coffee and—Marie!"

Marie pushed past Roméo. Pénélope and Sophie had stepped away from the group and were now sitting on the steps to Marie's house. Penny looked shaken. Marie peered between Ben and Graham, almost afraid to see what they were all looking at.

"What is it?"

Ben stepped back and turned to his mother.

"He's still warm."

What Marie saw was a raccoon. Or rather, what was left of a raccoon. Its gray head with the black-masked eyes was intact, still connected to its shoulders. The rest of the animal was gone, except for a bloody tangle of bone and muscle.

"Poor thing."

"Pénélope just about stepped on it—you know, enjoying the beautiful morning in the country...." Ben continued in a whisper. "And we know how much she *loves* the country."

Pénélope, Sophie's new girlfriend, hated the country. She hated the quiet. She hated the bugs. She hated the birds who woke her up too early. But she seemed to love Sophie, so she tolerated these occasional visits. This was not going to help.

"I'll go get a shovel."

Roméo, Graham, and Marie continued to examine the animal.

"What the hell did that?" Graham asked.

Marie shook her head. "I'm not sure. Maybe a coyote? A wolf? Could even be a big owl. I have *never* seen this before."

Ben returned with a shovel and started to scrape the animal into it. Its head tilted at an odd angle. It had almost been decapitated. Marie turned to Roméo.

"We'll need to keep an eye on Barney. Even Dog. There's a predator on the loose. And it's close to home."

Just at that moment, Magnus sauntered up the path, his hair wet from a swim, the folded blanket in hand.

"Sounded like quite a commotion here. Is everyone all right?"

ಐ

Pénélope's screams had woken all the guests—at least two hours earlier than most of them had wanted to. Although everyone was feeling a bit unsettled after the "event" and in various stages of being hung over, the conversation around the mound of bacon, eggs, and toast that Ben had prepared, and the oatmeal and bowl of fresh berries that Roméo had served was lively and generous. Magnus had tried to leave, but Roméo insisted he stay for breakfast, and he said yes without much persuading. The shyness the others had felt the day before at the wedding around Magnus had dissipated. Now they were all eagerly asking him questions about his many years in the limelight of activism. Lucy wanted to know if Michelle Obama was as wonderful and authentic as she appeared to be. Pénélope wanted to know if the movie star Matteo DiAngelo was really a nice guy or an asshole. Magnus answered all the questions with humor and just enough indiscretion. Then he glanced around the table and seemed to notice two people missing.

"Where are Ruby and Mohammed? Still sleeping?"

"They had to get the protest early," Ben mumbled through a large piece of toast.

"Of course," Magnus nodded. "They're very involved in this."

"We're all going over this afternoon. We have our signs ready, right, Noah?"

Noah looked up at his father from his bowl of oatmeal. Ben was trying to get some of it in his mouth, but he kept turning away from the spoon. Most of it was on his face. Noah lived on air, bananas, and cheese sticks. He ate nothing else.

Magnus turned to Roméo.

"Are you going to protest? Or is that a bit complicated for a senior police officer?"

"We would have," Marie interjected. "But we've had this campsite booked for almost a year. It's a tough reservation to get. We only have five nights and we don't want to miss one."

The truth was Marie wasn't exactly a keen camper. Roméo was the one who thrilled to sleeping in a tent. To gathering wood and cooking over a fire. To trying to get comfortable on a leaky air mattress that was flat and hard by morning. To packing up enough gear to survive a lifetime on, and then schlepping it all into a canoe. She didn't really get it.

The other truth was, despite the fact that Marie was dead set against Projet Leviathan and had been to more protests in her life than she could count, she didn't really want to go to this one. She had—if not friends, then neighbors and people she liked on the other side, and she wanted to be able to continue to like them. It was like agreeing not to discuss politics at a family dinner when doing so could mean years of resentment.

"I'm a homicide cop. It's not my beat. But I understand the *Sûreté du Québec* will be there, keeping a low profile." Roméo said. Then he added with a wink, "I hear a famous person will also be there and is planning some kind of a stunt."

"I have no idea what you are talking about, Detective."

"Come on! Won't you give us a clue?" Lucy asked.

"No. One of the keys to the success of an action is only the people who need to know, know," Magnus said as he popped a big strawberry in his mouth.

"Is Gretchen picking you up here?" Marie asked him.

Magnus avoided Marie's eyes.

ANN LAMBERT

"She's not coming to this one. She's flying back to Boston this morning and then heading home. I'm staying on here another two days."

Marie wondered if his extended visit had something to do with the phone call she saw him make. Had Magnus taken up with someone new?

Magnus turned to Roméo.

"I hear you are a vegan."

"Yes, I am."

"Isn't that unusual for a policeman? But then, I think you are an unusual man."

Before Roméo could answer, Sophie piped up.

"Cops mostly eat donuts and coffee, but my father isn't one of them."

"Isn't that a stereotype?"

Roméo laughed. "One that's mostly true, I'm afraid."

"And you seem to live amidst a group of carnivores."

"That is also true."

Marie crunched into a piece of bacon. "Let's keep this conversation clean, please."

"I'm a vegetarian. So is Noah. Converting this crowd is impossible," Maya said, throwing her hands up.

"I know I shouldn't eat meat. But I am trying to eat less of it. I eat more chicken." Ben looked at her with a sheepish smile. "Chicken is a vegetable, isn't it? OW!" Maya had punched his arm.

Magnus helped himself to a spoonful of scrambled eggs. "Eating meat is a bad choice for the planet. Driving a car is bad. Catastrophic climate change is happening. It's been happening for years. We all know this. We know what we do causes this, so we feel extreme stress because there is a

83

conflict between our beliefs and our behavior."

Magnus smiled and wagged a finger at Ben. "Between 'meat-eating is bad' and 'I like eating meat.'" But our brains want to resolve this conflict by either changing our beliefs or our behavior—so most people who know that meat-eating is bad, make excuses for their behavior rather than giving up meat."

"Cognitive dissonance!" Sophie exclaimed. "I was just studying that."

Magnus nodded. "Exactly. And...we'd have to give something up—sacrifice something—but who wants to? That's the challenge—"

Sophie interrupted him. "You put your body where your mouth is—you *have* sacrificed yourself for the cause. Many times!"

Magnus smiled and shook his head. "In the old days, yes. Not so much anymore. Listen. I own a car. I fly a plane. I fly all over the world. I live an absurdly entitled life. A double life... like almost everyone else."

Magnus picked up the glass of soymilk Maya was drinking.

"It's never black and white, is it? Like this glass of soy milk. Soy is 'good', right? It harms nothing. Cow milk is 'bad.' The cows suffer, forest and wetlands are cleared for land to feed them, and then they create insane amounts of methane which causes global warming. Okay. But consider this. We just spent the last three months in the Pantanal in Brazil. Trying to prevent major expansion into the Amazon jungle by multinational soy traders. Did you know that large-scale soy farming in the production of animal feed has overtaken ranching and illegal logging as the main cause of deforestation there? It's true that soybean producers tried to clean up their act in two thousand and six when they signed a pact to stop buying the soy grown in deforested areas of the Amazon. But they're back at it. Deforestation in the region is at a twelve-year high under President Bolsonaro—"

"Ruby told me you were shot at down there," Ben interrupted.

Magnus grinned. "We did seem to upset a few people. We got enough death threats to hire a driver and a bullet-proof car. But if the Amazon dies? We all die. Makes you look at that glass of soy milk a little differently, no?"

"I guess there'll always be that tension between…our need to exploit and consume everything to keep our economy going, and the protection of the planet? We need a tectonic shift in thinking." Marie said. Then she put back the extra piece of bacon she'd on her plate.

"Or one day, the planet may take its final revenge."

"The new book I'm writing is about revenge. Of the animal kind."

Magnus nodded at Marie. "I look forward to reading it. In the old days I would be resistant to that kind of anthropomorphism. Revenge? It's a human construct. But now? I'm not sure. The exploitation of wild places where animals live— puts us at risk of catching new zoonotic diseases."

"What the hell is that?" Pénélope asked.

"An infectious disease that's transmitted between species—from animals to humans. The destruction of natural habitats increases their risk because of increased contact between humans and wild animals. Remember SARS? MEERS? Ebola? Well, that last one mostly killed Africans, so nobody cared. There's revenge for you. The next one might be coming for us," Magnus offered quite cheerfully. The conversation paused briefly, and then was interrupted by the insistent buzzing of Magnus's phone. When he checked the caller's number, he excused himself and disappeared into the kitchen. Marie couldn't make out the words, but could hear his voice, intimate and tender. Two minutes later Magnus returned to the table and announced he had to leave. Everyone scrambled up from their chairs like they'd been summoned by a teacher. Magnus hugged each of them in turn. Then he shook Roméo's hand.

"I will see you all this afternoon! Well, most of you. And...remember to look *up*! It has been a pleasure to meet you. Thank you." He turned to the door. "Marie? Can you walk me out?" Marie followed him out the front door. Magnus took both her hands in his.

"We didn't get much of a chance to talk."

"I am happy you came to my wedding, Magnus. I *am* happy to see you. But I don't want to talk about the past. I don't want to talk about us. That's all water under the bridge. Oceans under the bridge, actually. Six of them to be exact."

"Marie...I—"

"I wish you well, Magnus. Take care of yourself. You're working at such a crazy pace. You've got yourself spread pretty thin."

He took a deep breath. "That's going to stop soon, though."

Marie raised an eyebrow. "Oh?"

"Yes. I'm making some changes. Big changes. I'll be going back to Norway for a while. To live."

"Norway?"

"Yes."

Marie was surprised. Magnus never much liked living in Norway. He loved the staggering beauty of his country but often found the people to be small-minded and hypocritical.

"Well, whatever is taking you back to Norway—I hope it's what you are looking for."

There was an awkward pause. Thirty years of silence hovered between them.

Just at that moment, Roméo emerged from the house.

"Do you need a lift, Magnus? As I recall, you don't have a car."

Magnus let out a belly laugh. "Yes! Of course. I totally forgot Gretchen had taken the car. Thank you!"

Roméo walked past Marie and Magnus jangling the car keys.

Magnus turned to Marie and said goodbye in the way they used to, so many years earlier before long separations: "See you in a minute."

Then he trotted down the driveway after Roméo. Marie watched as two of the three most important men in her life got into the car and pulled away. Her past and her future.

&

They drove in silence for a few minutes, until Roméo began to make the turn towards the highway. "It's near Val David, right?"

"Oh, I'm not going back to the rental house."

Roméo stopped at the intersection.

"Where am I taking you then?"

"Do you know the Rasmussen place on Lac St. Simon? Can you drop me off there? I know it's a bit out of the way, but—"

Roméo smiled. "The place with the plane *and* helicopter?"

"That's the one." Magnus raised his hands sheepishly. "He's an old friend."

"Will you be making use of either of those vehicles today? Marie tells me you're an experienced pilot."

"I may."

Roméo glanced at the man in the seat next to him. "I am a bit sorry to miss it."

Magnus put a hand briefly on Roméo's shoulder.

"Don't be. You are going to be off with Marie on your honeymoon. As we say in Norway, *Å være midt i smørøyet.*"

"What does it mean?"

"To be in the middle of the butter's eye."

"I have no idea what that means. Maybe because I speak French I don't—"

"No. It is one of those idiomatic expressions that doesn't translate literally, of course. It really means that you are right in the best possible spot."

Roméo followed the back road toward Sainte Josephine, a tiny little hamlet that didn't even have a dépanneur. Every town in Quebec had a dépanneur. Then he continued past it and into the rolling mountains to the northeast. As the car swung down yet another roller coaster hill, they spotted the sprawling main house and outbuildings of the estate below.

"It looks a lot like southern Norway around here. No ocean, though," Magnus noted.

Roméo pulled up to an enormous iron gate flanked by two stags in stone. Magnus opened his car door. "I can jump out here. I have the code for the gate."

"Let me drive you up—"

"No, it's not far to walk. You've done more than enough."

Roméo turned to get out of the car to shake Magnus's hand and say a proper goodbye. Magnus seemed to have second thoughts and clicked his door shut.

"Roméo. Listen. I don't know if I should show you this. But…." Magnus reached into his back pocket and pulled out some crumpled pieces of paper. Then he placed each one in turn on his lap and flattened out the wrinkles.

"Since I've been here in Quebec? I have received these notes, I guess you would call them. I got this one first two days ago at the rental house. It was left in the mailbox."

Roméo took it from Magnus. On a small piece of paper was written *The last big hurrah*.

"Then, at your wedding, I found this one. Under my glass of champagne that I had left unattended. The same font. You see?" Magnus read it aloud. "*I had lived enough.*"

Roméo took that paper as well. Then Magnus showed him the last one.

"This I found this morning in the pocket of my shirt. I think it could only have been placed there when I was asleep. By the lake. It was not there before." Magnus looked at Roméo searchingly. The note read *Today is the day*.

"Do these words mean anything to you?" Roméo asked, examining each one.

"Not at all. Except that they are…expressions or sayings of some kind. Maybe it's silly to mention them, but I did find them odd."

"Do these seem like some kind of threat to you? Why would someone leave these for you?" Roméo was speculating, not really asking.

Magnus shook his head. "I have no idea. I mean. I receive threats—death threats—all the time. On social media.

Sometimes by email. It is all a part of this life I live." Magnus looked at his phone. "Oh! I'm very late—I must go." He opened the door of Roméo's car and extricated his long legs from the front seat.

"Can you leave these with me? It would be good to hang on to them in case...you know. We need to find out who sent them. In the meantime, if you have any ideas about them at all, just text me." Roméo fished out his card from the glove compartment for Magnus and handed it to him. "I will be out of contact for a few days, so I will alert my detective Nicole LaFramboise, about this."

Magnus reached out to shake Roméo's hand, then to Roméo's surprise, pulled him into a stiff hug.

"Thank you. And thank you for being Marie's new man. I think you are the only one who ever deserved her."

Magnus turned away from Roméo, and without looking back went directly to the gate and punched in a code. Roméo was already in his car and turning back towards the main road when Magnus stepped between the two silent deer and the gates swung closed behind him.

Chapter 17

Paul and Gretchen

Paul Pellerin was driving just a bit too fast for the gravel road he was on, winding his way through the thick boreal forest of the Laurentians north of Montreal on his way to her. He checked the GPS again. Where the hell was it taking him? Was he on the right road? And who the hell was Saint *Elge*? She had told him the place was in the middle of nowhere and she wasn't kidding. He hadn't seen another house for at least fifteen minutes and had passed the last gas station and convenience store about half an hour earlier. Saint Elge. He had never been anywhere else in the world—even Portugal and Spain—where virtually every little town and village was named after a saint as they were in Quebec. He'd never even heard of Saint Elge—was that French for Elgin? Helga? Algae? Was it a man or a woman? He was pretty sure they made up a lot of saints—how many could there possibly have been? He remembered getting little cards at his Catholic primary school for being a good boy, doing well on a test or demonstrating high moral character. They were like baseball cards except on each one a haloed saint was depicted in some state of ecstasy or suffering—kind of the same thing for saints, he figured. It was usually the nuns who handed them out and Paul was always thrilled. One day the cool, young priest attached to the school offered Paul a coveted card of Saint Francis of Assisi if he would come into the back room with him. Paul cheerfully followed him, but at the last minute got a creepy feeling and said no. Dodged a bullet there, he thought. He never went near that priest again.

He looked at the GPS again and realized he must be very close. But he was dreading this conversation. He'd had a job to do, and he had failed. And everything, *everything* was at risk now. Suddenly the sign appeared on his right—*Paradis Perdu*. Paradise Lost. What a weird name for a rental cottage. Where he was from, they had names like *Bide-A-Wee* and *Cozy Nook*. He turned the car down a long driveway towards a large, boxy house with huge windows from floor to ceiling. There wasn't much to see out of them though, except trees, trees and more trees. Whoever built this place really wanted to get away from it all.

The front door opened before he had even knocked. She searched his face with those shockingly blue eyes before she turned on her heel and gestured for him to follow her. She was wearing a blue silk kimono with a purple dragon clinging to the back. Her hair was loose and long, and she gathered it into a top knot as she sat on the sofa in the middle of a sunken living room. She was still heartbreakingly lovely.

"You didn't really have to come all this way. We could've talked on the phone."

Paul shook his head. "I had to drive up here anyway. I'm

meeting Magnus at the protest today."

"Really?"

"Yes. He wants me there on the ground just in case."

Gretchen nodded. "I made coffee. In the kitchen, which is *that* way. There's cream in the fridge. Help yourself."

Paul went and poured himself a cup. The kitchen was spotlessly clean. Lots of stainless steel and granite with nothing extraneous on the counters. Like a staged house for rent or sale. As though no one had ever lived there. He returned to a not very comfortable looking armchair across from Gretchen, who had tucked her long slim feet up under her and awaited him patiently. She looked like a beautiful, self-possessed cat.

"And so? What news do you have for me? You never answered my call. I left three messages."

"Well, first things first. Did you get a chance to talk to Magnus?"

"Tell me about the girl first."

"No. I need to know if he's still in."

Paul Pellerin had invested everything he had in *More Than Meat*, a company that made fake meat from soya beans. Magnus was a major investor, but more importantly had promised to endorse the product. But Magnus had recently confided to Gretchen that he was pulling out, as the product had serious problems that compromise Magnus's brand.

Soya was no longer a 'clean' or green product, and, besides, one of the biggest meat producers in the world, was getting in on the fake meat game, Carney Meats—who also happened to be Paul's major investor. Magnus was all set to endorse *More Than Meat* before he visited the Pantanal in South America and witnessed how Carney operated down there. He was now refusing to invest. Paul needed both

Magnus and Carney Meats' money to make it happen, so Magnus's withdrawal would completely tank the company. And his friend. The quid pro quo they had arranged was this: if Paul could get rid of the girl, Gretchen would make sure Magnus stayed on track with *More Than Meat*.

"He can't renege on this deal now. It is *way* too late. I'll be ruined!"

Gretchen regarded him coolly. "I've done my best, Paul. He *hates* Carney, you know that. They're one of the worst agro-polluters in the world, and they're playing for both sides now. He won't do business with them."

Magnus had often told the story of Carney Meats in Brazil. They destroyed swaths of old growth rainforest to raise cattle. For dog food. For the US market. Meanwhile, the local farmers, mostly Indigenous, ate rice and beans if they were lucky. The image of cows grazing on that land for American dog food never left him. Magnus would not be associated with that.

"But he did business with *Nestlé*! I mean, these people convinced women to use their baby formula instead of breast milk and their babies starved—"

"Nestle signed the soy moratorium in the Amazon."

"But they are *evil*—"

"Paul, if you get in the mud with the pigs, you'll get dirty. But just remember. The pigs enjoy it."

"What the *hell* does that mean?"

Paul leapt out of his chair and started pacing the room.

"Gretchen, you got to make him understand what this means to me. He doesn't make a move without you."

Gretchen sipped her coffee, her long fingers wrapped elegantly around the mug.

"I'll see what I can do. I promise. Now tell me about the girl."

He stared out the window at the many trees.

"She's nobody's fool. I can tell you that."

Gretchen said nothing. Paul turned to look at her.

"I don't know what to tell you. She's not going anywhere."

Gretchen placed her mug carefully on the coffee table before her. "They all go *somewhere* sooner or later. All of them. They never last."

"I'm not sure about this one."

"Why? What makes her so special?"

Paul inhaled deeply, steeling himself for what was to come.

"She's pregnant."

Gretchen heard nothing more. Her ears were ringing. Paul's mouth was still moving so she assumed more words were coming out of it. But she couldn't hear them. She squeezed her eyes shut. The ringing slowly began to diminish. Gretchen opened her eyes.

"How do you know? She told you?"

"She didn't have to. Her robe opened and…I saw it. I'd say she's about four months along."

"That's not possible."

"I think it is. I think it's very possible. He…he's been talking about Norway, going back to—"

"He always does. It's his little fantasy."

"I'm so sorry, Gretchen. You must be—"

Her voice had not changed in tone. It held that same smoldering rage of knowing what Paul said was true.

"You did explain to her what this means? We will no longer protect him from the truth of all those years ago? We will give him up."

Paul shook his head and stared down at his hands.

"She laughed at me. She just said *you won't do that*. He's worth much more to you as he is than disgraced and discredited. I know how he has helped you. I know what you owe him."

"We owe him nothing."

"She *is* a branding expert. That's what we hired her for. She knows that Magnus *is* the brand. She's not like the others, Gretchen. This is a new breed of women who know what they want and will not be pushed around."

Paul hesitated. Then he asked, "Did you and Magnus— did you ever think of having…?"

"No."

Gretchen remembered the abortion she'd had so many years ago. Magnus making it seem like it was her choice. *Her* decision. But she knew he didn't want it. And she didn't want it if he didn't. Their lives were too crazy then. They were just building *See Change* and seeing the world as infinitely possible. The agreement was their lives were too busy and too peripatetic to have kids. The 'understanding' was they might consider it later, and then when they did, it was too late. For Gretchen. By the time *he* seemed ready.

"Fucking men. You guys can have kids until you drop fucking dead, can't you?"

Paul moved closer and tried to take her hand in his. He remembered her beautiful legs, wrapped around him, pulling him inside her. The consolation prize.

"Don't touch me!"

"I am so sorry. I think they are planning on having this baby—"

"I never thought he'd do this to me."

The truth was, Gretchen had known something was wrong. Very wrong.

"I don't think I can help you anymore, Paul. With *More Than Meat*. I think he'll pull out and you'll be fucked."

"He can't. He cannot do that to me."

Gretchen smiled grimly.

"He went to see his lawyer. Alone. I saw the appointment in his private book, the one he doesn't think I know about."

"So?"

"Well, Paul. If Magnus is thinking of…," Gretchen paused to compose herself. "Of having a *baby*. Then he may want to change his will. To have something for that baby. And her."

"He wouldn't cut you out. Or leave less for me. He wouldn't do that."

Gretchen said nothing.

'Listen. I have to go—I said I'd get there early to set up. I'm late already. We will talk about this later."

She looked up at Paul but still said nothing.

"What are you going to do? Gretchen?"

"I am going to pack up and get out of this fucking hellhole. I am going home."

Paul checked his phone. "Christ, they've sent me a dozen messages. I'm really late."

"So, go. Go and do as you're told, Paul."

He grabbed his car keys and took a last sip of the coffee, which was now cold.

"We could always contact *him*. Let him know we are willing to tell the truth. It would pressure Magnus. He'd never want to see that opened up again."

Gretchen regarded him evenly. "But the girl is right.

Damaging Magnus's brand damages us. He *is* See Change. We are just the people who built it. And him."

"I got to go. I'll call you when the thing is done. This is not over, Gretchen. Not by a long shot."

Chapter 18

Robert

Robert Renard exited the little dépanneur in Ste. Lucie with a big bottle of soda in one hand and a jumbo bag of potato chips in the other. The Chinese owner of the store stocked a very poor assortment of snacks, but he did carry Robert's favorite—Barbecue Ripples. Robert slipped into his car and immediately drank a third of the bottle in one swig. He never understood why Coke didn't market itself as the most effective cure for a hangover known to—well, him anyway. His head at least had stopped pounding. Why had he done those last few shots at the wedding with the gang from the Ste. Lucie precinct? He was too old for that shit now. He ripped open the bag of chips and left it on the passenger seat for easy access. Then he swung his car northeast onto the road towards Mont Baleine. He gestured perfunctorily at the few people strolling through town or chatting on the sidewalk. A few kids carrying towels and beach toys waved at him. They must be heading to the little beach on the shore of Lac Canard, the tiny lake at the center of town. It was appropriately named, as it was inhabited by too many ducks whose poop was the cause of many a swimmer scratching himself all the way home after a dip.

Almost everyone in these parts still knew him from his thirty years as a *Sûreté du Québec* officer, the last eleven years in this district. Robert loved being a cop. Even when he worked in Montreal in vice, he loved serving. The sense of purpose. But after years of a daily diet of the destitute, the desperate, the drug addicted, dealing with people at the lowest point in their lives eventually got to him, and he asked for a transfer to *les régions*, the country. One of the first things he noticed in his new life as a rural cop was when he waved to a kid he got a wave in return, not a fuck you middle finger. In these little towns that dotted the Laurentian mountains, he felt like he was at the center of things. Yes, the job could be boring, but just when he thought he couldn't take the routine of it all, there was always a surprise. Sometimes hilarious. Sometimes horrific. He still couldn't get the image of one house he was called to a few years earlier, on a domestic abuse call. The three kids hadn't been washed or fed in days. There was no running water. No food in the fridge. It was freezing. The mother had both eyes beaten shut. He'd called Child Protection and tried to get her to press charges, but she refused. How did this happen in a little town where people look out for each other? The truth was people were garbage everywhere—and sometimes it was easier to hide it in plain sight.

After he became a detective, Robert was thrilled to join major crimes, and especially once he'd teamed up with Roméo Leduc in homicide. When he and Roméo finally cracked that maple syrup heist case where the fuckers had killed a security guard and they very nearly lost one of their team, it was like conquering Everest, or winning the Stanley Cup. That feeling of working so hard for something and it paying off. It was rare enough in his world. Robert had hoped that Roméo would retire, too. He'd hoped they'd retire together and make plans to do things together. Hunt? No. Roméo, although he was the squad's crack shot, did not hunt. He was a *vegan* for fuck's sake. Roméo and Robert did one thing together: being cops. And now that was over. And that *casse couilles*, that ball-breaker of a wife of his—who'd invited her ex-husband *and* ex-fucking boyfriend to their wedding—and her snotty lawyer kid were putting Roméo on the wrong side of this situation. It wasn't like Roméo not to be reasonable. He was the most rational and even-handed guy he knew. Leviathan was solid. Visionary. And environmentally friendly whenever and wherever it could be. It was as fucking *green as green could be without being ridiculous*. But it wasn't enough. It was never enough for some people. Over the years he had worked in these communities, Renard had mostly encountered the wealthier people through the activities of the Thibodeau twins, who made a living stealing their various expensive toys. These people were almost all a specific type. They hated hunting, snowmobiling, fishing, ATVing, motor-biking, and for that matter, any boat with a motor on it. They were "pro-nature"—they'd never cut down a tree except to clear the forest to build their mansions. Protect the wildlife? As long as that wildlife could be enjoyed by them on their own private land for their own private consumption. Robert couldn't wait to go toe to toe with the tree huggers.

He drove past the entrance to Tio:weroton, the summer hunting territory of the Kahnawake Mohawks in Montreal and glanced at their gated entrance. Now *they* were tough fuckers. He had a lot of respect for them. They had gotten the entire country to apologize for its past shitty behavior. After years of putting up with government bullshit they were fighting back. He admired that. Most of them were against Projet Leviathan, and that was a problem because people were actually listening to them now. But Robert also knew that some of them supported Leviathan. They understood the need to develop the area and wanted a piece of the action before they were shut out. As they'd been for the last two-hundred years.

He turned onto the access road to Mont Baleine, the only one in and out of the area. It was a very pretty stretch of gravel road that ran up and down the hills that finally culminated in Mont Baleine. Still, Robert always had a funny, almost creepy sensation on this road. Like he was being watched by something. Or someone. He couldn't explain it, but once he had mentioned this experience to one of his buddies, and he had reported the exact same sensation.

As he crossed a bridge over a stream made lazy by the recent lack of rain, he spotted his people up ahead. There were four of them, in full SQ uniform, manning a kind of barricade. He recognized two of them. A few dozen others in the pro-Leviathan camp were milling about, getting ready to head to the protest themselves. He would have a word with their leaders: there was to be no violence. At least none anyone could *witness*. That business with Ti-Coune Cousineau's house was stupid, but that had more to do with his past than his present. Lots of people still didn't like him. Lots of people would be more than happy to do a lot worse than trash his house. And the old hippies' place? Killing chickens? Painting a swastika? What was *that*? Stupid people could so easily sink the whole project. But then who set the Mayor Morin's car on fire? Was it one of his people looking to discredit the other side? Or had one of them decided to play a little dirty? That made Robert quite happy. It was a pleasure to see these pricks take a fall from their moral high ground.

Robert nodded to one of the cops who was speaking into his shoulder mic. Robert knew this guy loved all the police toys, imagined himself like the cops on TV. He nodded to him, and then shook hands with his buddy Yvan, who he took aside to speak to privately.

"*Écoute. Le business avec les gens du coin, la. C'est fini.* I don't want no one killing a chicken or breaking into someone's house, *Christi!*"

"That wasn't us!"

Almost on cue, they both looked over at a couple of guys in camouflage pants, vests, and backwards MAGA baseball caps. One was wearing a jokey T-shirt that read on the front: PETA=People Enjoying Tasty Animals! And on the back: VEGAN: Very Enthusiastically Grilling ANimals! These guys thought they were living in the United States, apparently. But Robert knew they were the outliers. Most of the people who supported Leviathan wanted to offer their families a better life. They really needed the jobs this development would bring. A few others were preparing effigies of Magnus Sorensen and other leaders of the protest. Robert lit a cigarette and blew the smoke out his nostrils in a thick stream.

"So? What's going on? Everything under control?"

"The media went through already—the TV and newspapers. A few from Montreal. That should have the old hippies pissing themselves with excitement, *anh*? And that Swedish guy coming? The big ace up their sleeve?" Yvan laughed.

Robert crushed the cigarette under his heel.

"He's Norwegian. But they're in for a bit of a surprise there."

"*Oui, Monsieur*! He won't get through. There's only one road in and one road out and…we're here."

"Good. His ETA is around one pm. He'll probably be with his entourage, so just delay him as long as you can. I mean, *stop* him if you can."

"Yes, Boss. We'll do our best."

Another thing Robert loved about being a cop was the brotherhood, the sense that a certain group of men understood you. *Got* you. Yvan? Roméo? These guys would die for him—he knew it.

"We should get that injunction reinstated any day now, and we can finally put this to bed."

But Robert knew that if this project didn't get final approval, he would lose everything. Including the shirt off his back. So would quite a few people he'd convinced to go in on this with him. He couldn't even begin to imagine the fallout.

"Listen, Yvan, I can't be seen around here. I'm going back to town."

Yves saluted him with a big grin on his face.

"Understood."

Robert was about to go back to his car when he got a text.

"*Tabarnac!*"

Yvan glanced at his phone.

"What?"

"He's flying in. He's fucking flying in. That guy never takes a car if he can waste more gas and make a spectacle of himself."

Robert texted back frantically. *Where's the plane?*

It took a few seconds before his phone pinged the answer. Then he ran to his car, jumped in, and sped down the road. Right back where he'd come from.

Chapter 19

Magnus

When Gretchen told Magnus she wasn't coming to the protest and instead would be flying back early to their house in Cape Cod, he was concerned, but secretly delighted. Concerned because it was quite out of character for Gretchen to abandon him to an action, they had both chosen to take part in, but delighted because, well, he felt it was an auspicious sign. He had called Emily as soon as Gretchen informed him of her new plans and asked Emily to join him on the Leviathan protest. Magnus didn't care anymore what people thought of them. Of her. He had always been careful to protect Gretchen because he loved and respected her. He would always do right by Gretchen. But this woman, this fucking amazing woman was going to have *his child*. And he wanted her next to him until the day he died. Magnus practically danced his elation along the floats as he did his pre-flight walk around the plane, careful not to take a misstep and land in the water. He had flown this beauty many times, but it had been a while. Given the extra precious cargo he'd be flying in that day he would be meticulous in his check out. He inspected the water rudder cables and struts, checked the float compartments for excess water. He double-checked the propeller and took a look at the engine. His friend had filled the gas tanks and promised him that the plane had been regularly serviced. Magnus looked at the lake he'd be taking off from. It was small, but private, so no worries about dodging boats or swimmers. He noted with relief that there was a bit of wind, which was good. That meant there'd be some chop on the water, which was much safer than flying into flat, glassy water, which could be deadly. Once Magnus had come in for a landing on a glassy lake and misjudged his height above the water—on flat water it was hard to see the surface even when you're on it—and his plane flipped right over. Luckily, he was alone, and knew how to extricate himself from the cockpit. No, the conditions today were perfect. He couldn't wait to get up there. He had wanted to parachute from a plane and land on the beach with Matteo DiAngelo, the Hollywood A-lister. Matt had cleared it with his agent and was keen to do it, but Paul had vetoed that. Too expensive, too show-boaty. One of the new interns had suggested creating papier maché lynxes—like the 1600 pandas action the World Wildlife Fund did in Paris, but there hadn't been enough time to prepare. When his old friend offered Magnus his float plane, they had decided that his landing on this beautiful lake, despite the wrong message about fossil fuel, was dramatic and effective. Emily said his brand and name were so recognizable that just *being here* to lend support against Leviathan ought to be enough to sink the project. Investors do not like negative publicity. They do not like lawsuits and injunctions. Magnus had learned over his many years hustling money that they were cowards, most of them.

Paul was still pouting about the use of the plane today. But then, Paul was negative about almost everything these days. They'd had a huge argument about the power of protest just recently. Paul felt they didn't work anymore—he told Magnus that he always felt like he was on the outside looking in, at the ones who really had the power to make changes. He argued that even their iconic North Sea action which most people believed had helped turn the oil company toward greater environmental responsibility hadn't really worked. They were still drilling for oil in the Arctic. He said someone had called this "the thin yes"—a yes without meaning or belief. Magnus had to agree that he too was moving towards a type of activism that asks for a complete shift of attitudes. Like wearing a seat belt. Like quitting plastic bags. But still, he was shocked by what seemed like Paul's rejection of years of work. It was like Lenin becoming a capitalist. Or Greta Thunberg driving a Hummer. Magnus felt like Paul was giving up. But maybe it was more his stress about that company Paul would give up his first-born child to if he still could. Paul's first and only born was now a diffident man in his late twenties who worked like so many of them in an IT start up. Sitting all day in front of a screen. Probably most of the night, too. Magnus did know how to compromise. Tor Hanyes had never understood that, pure old soul that he was. Well, Tor was dead now and Magnus was alive. But the Chinese had invested in Paul's *More Than Meat*. So had Carney fucking Meats, which were like the polestar of climate change evil. Magnus could not get involved with them. He hated to disappoint his oldest friend, but he had to draw a line. He could not give up. He couldn't. He had a child coming. What greater act of hope was there in this life but to bring a child into the world?

Magnus squeezed into the cockpit and saw that the key was in the ignition as promised. A yellow sticky note hung from it: *Sorry I missed you. Just put her back where you found her. Call you next week.* He smiled and checked the instrument panel. He looked out the windshield at the beauty in front of him. They were calling for thunderstorms later that evening, but you'd never know. The sky was an uninterrupted blue, the wind ruffling the lake's surface like feathers. He couldn't wait to show his child this magnificent world. His thoughts drifted to his father, Fredrik. Had he been as excited as Magnus when he learned he was going to be a father? Of course, he'd been half Magnus's age. Magnus really should be a grandfather by now. Did he dream of the world he'd build? Did he already know the kind of crap he'd be doing to build his empire? Magnus barely knew him the first few years of his life; and Fredrik had no interest in children until they could have a proper conversation, and only on a subject that interested him. He had slowly driven Magnus's mother crazy—literally. One of his two sisters worked for the family business. Magnus was convinced she was a psychopath, like his father. Like 20 percent of all CEO's of huge companies. His other sister, her twin, was the one who wasn't quite as pretty or charismatic or ruthless. She dropped out of university her first term and tried working with their father for a while, but her twin always overshadowed her. She ended up doing a lot of dope in high end hotels and the homes of callow men around the world.

Magnus hoped she wouldn't die of an overdose. What do you do when there's nothing you *have* to do? When everything is handed to you as your birthright? How do you find meaning? What do you strive for? Why *not* party until you drop dead? He would always be thankful to Paul for rescuing him all those years ago in that cruddy pub. He would now be working for his father's company, no doubt. Or worse yet, he could *be* his father who had died four years ago of a brain aneurism. Of course, many suspected that he'd been murdered by a rival he had fucked over. Magnus thought the rumors might be true.

He stepped out of the plane and did once last check of the floats. One seemed to be lying pretty low in the water. But he had just checked the water levels. Odd. Then his phone started to vibrate, but when he answered he heard nothing. He had no service here. Mikael had warned him about that— it was spotty at best. He checked the number. Emily. And Paul had called as well. He jumped back onto the floating dock and held up his phone, like some kind of ancient ritual of worship. There was no signal. He walked past the plane to the end of the dock. Nothing. He remembered he'd had service a way back down the road, so he turned to go back towards the house, his phone still held high over his head, practically bumping into a figure who had appeared out of nowhere.

Chapter 20

The morning was already warm, anticipating the very hot and humid day the weather channel had gleefully forecast. Léo had woken up at his usual five am, but she had dragged herself out of bed and mercifully gotten him back to sleep with a bottle and a quick cuddle. Then she fell back asleep herself, into a series of weird dreams. In the last one that she remembered she had suddenly acquired a pet iguana that had the run of her house. He sat at the kitchen table and ate breakfast with her, he watched TV with her and followed her everywhere. In her dream, she kept trying to shoo him from her bed, and in revenge he shit all over it—leaving huge goose-turds all over her sheets. What the hell was *that* about? Was this an image of her ex-boyfriend she'd dredged up from her psyche? As her eyes started to focus and she saw how bright and sunny it was outside she checked her phone. *10:07 AM?* That wasn't possible. Nicole bolted from her bed without stopping to pee and ran to Léo's bedroom. He wasn't there. She raced into the kitchen, screaming his name. And there he was. Sitting at the kitchen table eating a piece of apple and string cheese. Next to him sat Steve Pouliot. Every man (all two of them) that Nicole had dated since she split with Léo's father had treated Léo like something to be tolerated at best, or a kind of animal to be tamed at worst. One had tried to discipline him on their second date. One had played so rambunctiously with him that it had taken her hours to get him calm. Normand, his father, claimed he had wanted this baby more than anything in his life and had lasted exactly eight months and three days before he fucked someone else and settled for a visit with Léo every other weekend. Now he saw him maybe once a month. But he never, not once *fed* him without being asked to. Now, Normand wasn't exactly the brightest. *Il n'est pas le pogo le plus décongelé de la boîte*, not the most thawed Pogo in the box, as one Quebec politician had recently said about an opponent. Like some men, Normand had loved the *idea* of a child. Just not the exhausting, relentless, unstoppable, real live human being. It was an impossible kind of fatigue to explain to people who didn't have kids. One of her cop girlfriends had a new puppy that she often complained was like having a toddler. Nicole explained that when she had carried that dog inside her for nine months and pushed it out her vagina then she could make that claim.

ॐ

Steve Pouliot was reading a *book* to her son, who was peeling strings of his cheese and dropping them into his wide-open mouth, his tongue trying to catch a wayward strand. Léo had many good qualities, but a long attention span was not one of them. She could never get him through an entire book—even Dr. Seuss and the shortest of picture books. He'd usually be halfway up a bookcase that he'd turned into a personal climbing gym while she was still reading to him.

Steve looked up. "Good morning!"

They hadn't slept together. She'd made up the couch for him. Why was he so cheerful? Nicole found the whole situation a bit creepy.

"Good morning. Um, how long have you been up with him?"

Steve checked his watch which looked huge on his small arm.

"Just under three hours. Why?"

Nicole was at a loss for words. Steve filled the silence in. "I thought you might appreciate a sleep in. So, we watched a bit of TV—cartoons only—and then we had a little breakfast. He told me what he likes to eat. Then we went for a walk. Léo showed me the hole where the squirrels live. The huge poop the neighbor's dog made that no one picked up. Oh, and the big tree where you let him climb up to the first branch. Then we came back here and now we're eating second breakfast. Or first lunch."

Nicole went to Léo and kissed him on the top of his head. He squirmed away. Then she sat down at the table opposite Steve. He got up and poured her a cup of coffee from the pot he'd apparently made.

"You already know your way around my kitchen."

Steve smiled. "I didn't think you'd mind. But if you do, I apologize."

She took a sip of the coffee. It was delicious, of course. Better than any coffee she'd ever made in the same machine.

"Did you sleep well?"

Nicole nodded and smiled. "Oh my God. Yes. I had lots

of very strange dreams though—don't worry! I won't start telling them to you—"

"I'd love to hear your dreams."

"No, you wouldn't. If you did, you'd never agree to see me again…I mean—"

"I'd like to see you again."

Nicole nodded. He was a cop. And short. Way too fucking short. And a cop. Steve scraped his chair back from the table. He was even shorter than she thought. He was still wearing his wedding suit though and looked very dapper and handsome. He scribbled his number on a stray piece of paper he found on Nicole's kitchen counter.

"Here's my number. I could drive up on the weekend. Take Léo to the beach? Take you both to lunch?"

"I'll definitely think about it."

"Well, that's all I can ask."

He flung his jacket over one shoulder and removed his car keys. He moved like a much bigger man. Then he leaned over Léo and tousled his long hair.

"Ouch! Stop that!"

Nicole laughed. "He hates having his head touched."

"See you next time, Léo."

Nicole stood up and walked Steve to the door. "I'd ask you to stay a bit, but I have to head over to the Leviathan protest. Roméo asked me to keep an eye on things."

"Okay."

Nicole waited. She thought he might lean in to kiss her cheek. Kiss her on the mouth. Do something. Instead, he turned on his heel and started through the door.

"Steve!"

He turned around, jangling his car keys.

"Yes?"

"Thank you. I mean it. For everything."

"Anytime."

And with that, he was gone. Nicole watched him get into his car and pull away. He was too short. And he lived in Montreal. He was a *Montreal* cop. Impossible.

She turned back to the kitchen just in time to catch Léo standing on the kitchen counter trying to retrieve a box of Fruit Loops on the top shelf he couldn't reach. She saved his life again, for probably the thousandth time since he was born. Then she took Steve Pouliot's phone number and tucked it into her shirt pocket.

Chapter 21

Magnus and Emily

She was almost there. At least according to her GPS, which was pronouncing each of the French directional names that she drove past with such a hilarious English accent that she couldn't stop giggling. She had managed to make it all the way from downtown Montreal to within minutes of St. Donat without stopping to eat, but then she felt such overwhelming hunger she pulled into a gas station dépanneur for a snack. Ever since she got pregnant, she hadn't stopped eating. At this rate, by the time she gave birth she'd weigh about 300 pounds. She thought about the humpback whale mothers she had observed in the Dominican Republic. They go there to give birth, and then do not eat for six months while they nurse their babies. *Six months.* Those tropical waters have little food, so they just live off their body fat until they return to temperate water in the spring. Emily remembered observing baby humpbacks nursing. The milk is sort of injected into their mouths, as they have no lips to suckle with. The mother humpback can feed them 400 liters of milk *a day*.

She reached into her shirt and touched her right breast, which was quite tender, and tried to imagine what it was going to feel like to nurse a human being. She had already consumed half a dozen books about breastfeeding, what to expect when pregnant, what foods to eat. She glanced over at the bag of cheesies on the seat next to her—that wasn't one of them. The dépanneur had no fresh food, except for one tired-looking banana that Emily had already devoured in three bites. She would be sure to eat a healthy supper and get to a proper grocery store by tomorrow and stock up.

Emily turned onto a gravel road from the paved main road towards St. Donat and slowed down. Magnus had said there was a tricky turn and she had to pay attention. Her heart was starting to pound at the thought of seeing him again. When he had called and asked her to join him on this action she hadn't hesitated to say yes, although she wasn't really sure about flying in—or the whole stunt for that matter. It seemed pretty old school. One of those mind-bombs they used to talk about from the good old days when he and his old whale head buddies had a few beers and started reminiscing. They were like the first wave of the climate justice movement, old fashioned Extinction Rebellion—and Emily loved them for it. Ever since she was a little girl, she had felt pain and injustice deeply, especially when it came to animals. She had wanted to be a vet but realized early on she couldn't stomach seeing sick and abused animals all day long. She wanted to save wild animals—she was devastated by what she had read about mass extinction, especially of large mammals, and so she volunteered first for PlanetGreen, then the One World Foundation, and then *See Change*.

She smiled at the memory of the first time she ever laid eyes on Magnus in the flesh. She and her then boyfriend went to hear him speak at a fundraiser at their alma mater. Magnus had called for a complete, tectonic shift in our way of inhabiting this world. He'd said that we must see the whole project of existence as sacred and understand all living creatures to be as sacred as humans. His talk had changed her life. She volunteered for *See Change*, then got a job there, and then finally she worked her way to the inner sanctum. And that was where Magnus Sorensen first really *saw* her.

For a long time, Gretchen didn't seem to notice her at all. Emily wasn't important enough to be on her radar. But she was now. The fact that she was accompanying Magnus to this action felt like her—what else could she call it—*replacement* of Gretchen had taken another huge step forward. She knew Magnus would always love Gretchen—he had made that clear. But her time with him was over. He was Emily's now. A few of her girlfriends had wondered about their sex life. They all agreed he was pretty hot for an old dude, but what it was like making love with an old man? Was it gross? Did he take forever to get it up? Did he pop a Viagra? Emily never gave any details, but just smiled and said, "Better."

She turned off the AC which she never usually used because it was such a pollutant and rolled down her window to breath in the fresh country air, which hit the car like a steam bath—hot and humid—a real Laurentian July scorcher. Emily leaned her elbow on the open window and scanned the road ahead for the turn-off. Would Magnus marry her? He had mentioned it, but she didn't want to appear too keen. He had never married and was known to be opposed to the idea of it. He felt strongly that marriage was good for men and bad for women—studies had proved it again and again—and he didn't see the fairness in it. But she was excited to move to Norway—Magnus had shown her on Google earth where his maternal grandfather's old wooden house still stood on a beautiful piece of land on the coast near Bergen and they had discussed the possibility of living there. He had always said his was one of the most beautiful countries in the world, blessed with such an abundance of natural gifts. He also said Norwegians were similar to Canadians in that they felt a bit morally superior to the rest of the world, even though they did little to earn that reputation.

"Norwegians are petroholics," Magnus always said. "We depend so much on the income from our oil. We want to stop, but we don't know how." Emily had read that it was called the Norway paradox: they export almost all the fossil fuels they produce and keep their emissions "clean" at home—like laundering their carbon. Magnus called it classic Norwegian hypocrisy, and he hated it. Still, they'd discussed having their baby there, or whether or not they should have her in a country where neither of them had citizenship like the US or in another European country, but in the end, they decided that Canada was best. Her mother lived here. One or two of her childhood friends were here. They would spend the first few months probably in Montreal, then make the move to Norway. She'd had a moment of panic that Magnus would dump her there and leave her to manage alone. He traveled a lot. But he assured her that those days were over.

Suddenly a car appeared, hurtling over the rise in the road above her. Emily had to swerve quickly to avoid it. She felt her tires slip on the dry gravel and the car fishtail until she righted it. Fucking idiot! She looked in her rear-view mirror to see who the hell it was, but the car was hidden in a cloud of dust, and she couldn't quite see it. She often wished at moments like this she could drive like some action hero— turn her car around, chase him down, force his car off the road and teach him a good lesson. Or her. Terrible drivers were usually men, but every now and then women could be assholes as well. Emily watched as the dust poured out from behind her car like she was crop-dusting the road. They really needed rain. Then out of the corner of her eye she noticed the two stags at the gate Magnus had mentioned. She immediately pulled over, backed up and turned around. Although Magnus had given her the code for the gate, it was open. She was relieved she wouldn't have to get out of the car and deal with it. The heat was staggering, and she could feel her back was soaking wet against the car seat.

℘

Emily drove slowly up the tree-lined driveway until she arrived at an enormous house. A manor house, really. A castle. There must be twenty rooms at least, she thought. There was a garage that would hold about a dozen cars, what looked like riding stables behind the house, and an absurdly green and luscious lawn that rose and fell like a carpet towards the lake. There didn't seem to be anyone here. Emily stepped out of her car and groaned while she stretched out her back. He had said just to come and find him at the dock, so she grabbed her water bottle and headed towards the lake. She felt dizzy with the anticipation of seeing him, of touching him. Of him taking her in his arms and reminding her again that this was all really happening. She hastened down to the end of a landing dock where she could see the red and white wings of the floatplane. It bobbed gently in the chop of the lake.

"Magnus?"

There was no answer. Only the sound of the water slapping against the dock and a far-off lawn mower.

"Magnus?"

Where was he? Had he gone back up to the house? She saw no sign of him being here at all. She didn't feel like walking in the heat. She felt like jumping in the lake instead. But she dutifully started the rather steep climb until she remembered to pull out her phone and call him. There was no service. Not one bar. How was that possible? Emily dropped her phone back in her pocket and started up towards the house again. Wait. She hadn't checked the boathouse. Maybe he was in there tinkering on something and couldn't hear her. She stepped back down onto the long, wooden dock and pushed open the door. It was completely dark except for the spill of sunlight through the crack in the door. As her eyes adjusted, she could see no Magnus. She checked her phone again, although she knew it was pointless, and emerged from the cool of the boathouse into the heat of the sun, even though a breeze off the lake made it more bearable. Just as she went to turn back up to the house, she glimpsed what looked like a pile of mud or rock sticking up out of the water next to one of the floats of the plane. And then she saw an arm undulating with the waves. Emily raced towards it. When she got close enough to recognize the T-shirt and then his face, she began to scream his name. But no one could hear her.

Chapter 22

The protest was effectively over. The drummers were quiet. The chanters were yelled out. Tired kids who started the day with brightly painted faces and their cheerful parents were cranky and tearful. A few were in the middle of a full melt-down. The television crews who'd come from Montreal were busy packing up their tangles of cables, their cameras and equipment. The demonstrators were thrilled that CNN had come to cover the protest, but their van had already left in a cloud of dust, their reporter furious that the promised celebrity hadn't shown up. One last interview was being conducted by the CBC. A red-faced, overheated reporter was getting a final word from a pro-development father of four. A few protesters and a few supporters of the project were still gamely waving their signs behind the interviewer: *Stop Leviathan! Save The Whale! Forestry Feeds My Family! Respect Existence or Expect Resistance!*

Even though there had been a great turnout, Ruby, Manon, and the other organizers were disappointed. Joel and Shelley were dejectedly emptying the dregs from the huge urn of coffee they'd brought. Tracy Jacobs and her crew were rolling up their banners with the Mohawk insignia and packing up the leftover bannock they had brought to share. Bob Babineau and his team were busy picking up stray fliers to use again. Everyone was trying to put on a positive face, but the truth was they were all feeling a bit disillusioned. *Décue* as they would say in French. *Deceived.*

Paul Pellerin, whom they had all figured out was Magnus's point man, had been at the event earlier but was now nowhere to be found. Ti-Coune Cousineau stopped loading signs into the back of his mini pickup truck to go talk to Ruby and Mohammed.

"Hey. So, what happened to your mother's friend?"

Ruby shook her head. "I have no idea. It's so weird. I've been texting him and calling. Nothing. No answer."

"I guess it was too small potatoes for him in the end—"

"I don't think so. He takes these small grass-roots actions very seriously; they're the bread and butter of *See Change*—"

"Maybe in the end, he was too much a bigshot, you know? A *vedette*? Too big a star to shine here in Ste. Lucie?"

Ruby could practically taste his disappointment. She said nothing, just shrugged her shoulders. Mohammed, who was gathering the petition and other legal papers into a large file folder, said quietly, "Well, it's not her fault he's not here."

Ruby looked up at Ti-Coune and Manon, who had spotted them after the interview she'd just finished and crossed the sandy parking area to them.

"Manon? I can't believe he was a no-show. He was coming. I know it."

Manon smiled warmly and touched Ruby's arm gently. "It was a success today!"

Ti-Coune spat into the sand at his feet, just missing his own boot.

"Maybe people like him they commit and don't mean it. *Plein de merde* all of them. And where is that prick—Paul something or other—who works for him?"

As if on cue, Paul Pellerin had returned. He seemed to have snagged one last interview with the CBC reporter who was clearly on her way out. Ti-Coune started towards him, but Manon held his arm.

"Voyons. Laisse faire. Calme-toi! Calm down!"

Ti-Coune pulled a filthy bandana from his butt pocket and wiped his sweaty face. "*Tabarnac, il fait chaud.*"

Manon patted Mohammed's back and turned to help the others load the last of the tables, crossing paths with two of the pro-Leviathan people. One was an off-duty, pro-development cop who'd had a few run-ins with Ti-Coune in the past. He sidled up to him and said quietly while he indicated his appreciation of Manon walking away,

"*Ey?* Ti-Coune? I hear your girlfriend used to be *la guidoune du village*, the town pump. She liked to pull on a few hoses. But don't worry. We'll take care of her. Maybe feed those dogs and cats she likes so much to a few wolves on Mont Baleine—"

But Ti-Coune didn't hear the rest. He shoved the man away from him and then fell on him in a frenzy. The guy was much bigger and threw Ti-Coune off him like a small child. Ti-Coune bounced to his feet and went at him again, but the man dodged him, tripped him, and then he kicked him a few times in the gut, hard, as he fell. Ti-Coune lay in the dirt gasping for air, as the man wiped a smear of blood from his nose.

"You just attacked a police officer, little man. Idiot."

Suddenly, a few of the pro-development people were gathered around them, like kids cheering on a schoolyard scrap. They would have yelled, "Fight, fight, *fight!*" if it hadn't been over so quickly. Robert Renard watched from the sidelines. He could not get involved in this one, but he would see to it that that low life fuckhead would come up on charges. Just enough to make his life very difficult.

Manon, Ruby, and the other protesters watched as Ti-Coune was handcuffed and led away by Robert Renard who at last had stepped in. They insisted that he let Ti-Coune go, that the cop had started it. Renard leaned into Ti-Coune's ear and whispered, "Roméo Leduc is not here to protect you either, my friend. Neither is his little lackey, Detective LaFramboise. Tant pis pour toi."

Paul Pellerin thanked the reporter as he finished the interview and watched as Ti-Coune was led away. The guy looked pretty rough. Not at all your typical hippie tree-hugger stereotype that still persisted. Just as he was making his way over to the stunned crowd of Ti-Coune's friends, his phone buzzed. Paul could barely make out what the woman was saying. It sounded like Emily. And she was screaming.

Chapter 23

Claire Lapierre Russell was a survivor. She had survived the death of her mother at three years old, and then being sent away by her father and stepmother to be raised in a convent where looking at herself in a mirror was a sin. She had lived through the Depression, World War II, *Le Noirceur* of the Duplessis era, The Cold War, 9/11, and now the climate crisis. She had given birth to three daughters, survived a marriage to an alcoholic who had lost everything they'd worked for, and then the loss of both her husband and one daughter to the same disease. Finally, she had survived losing some of her cognitive faculties and being moved to an expensive long-term care residence where they drugged her so heavily, she had been almost catatonic. She had survived the move to *Maison Soleil*, which was not as expensive as her last home, but where she felt much safer and happier. Claire Russell was not done yet. Not by a long shot.

She sat on the edge of her bed, feeling excited and nervous. She looked out her window at the enormous old maple tree that was catching the sun so gracefully in its leaves. It reminded her of a tree in another summer—was it thirty years ago? Forty? Maybe seventy years ago? Her stepmother didn't like her underfoot when she was home from the convent, so she arranged for Claire to spend three weeks on a second cousin's farm near...near...the waterfalls. Waterfall. *La... chute? Lachute.* That was it. Oh, the freedom of that summer! There was no supervision at all. They could do whatever they wanted as long as the farm chores were done. She remembered a big, ancient tractor that the oldest boy used to drive as they circled the fields cutting the hay. The smell of it so sweet it seemed edible. Claire understood why the horses loved it so much. And she loved the horses, who seemed to understand everything she confessed to them. She rode with the farm kids on a big old plow horse—barefoot and bareback— down to the nearby river, three kids at a time. She learned that according to the boys, horse manure makes a great ball for poopball—take a swing at it and see who gets hit by the exploding turd. She learned that cows like to be milked and chickens aren't dumb. What eggs still warm with freshness taste like, what an egg should taste like. She drank the cream on the bucket of milk before it was skimmed off. She turned it in a wooden butter churn by hand. She felt her city-girl soft arm muscles harden. She shyly showed them to the oldest boy, who had a bit of fuzz above his lip that he tended to with dedication and a forelock of streaky blonde hair that Claire found very attractive. She loved to watch him run his hand though it and try to tame it to the side. He touched her new muscles, and then he grabbed her and kissed her, forcing her lips open with his tongue. She was thrilled and appalled. She ran all the way back to the house and made certain she was never alone with him again.

Claire remembered one night she heard strange, painful sounds coming from the parents' bedroom. She crept out of her bed and went to their door to see if one of them was hurt. When she peeked through the slightly ajar door, she watched the father on top of the mother, her legs wrapped around his hips. He was speaking very vulgar words to her. Very vulgar. Claire discovered that they did this every Saturday night. And then the very next morning they piously went off to mass like it had never happened. She resolved never, ever to have intercourse. It was for pigs and goats and dogs. Not humans. Claire remembered all this with a smile. In the first few years of their marriage, she had liked sex with Edward, her husband. Not like a lot of women she knew. But that summer, she remembered like it was yesterday. As the August days grew shorter and cooler, that meant Claire would be going back to the city. To the convent. She remembered the actual, physical pain that caused her. She had wanted to stay so badly.

And now Claire was going to see a place that Louis had promised was more beautiful than anywhere she'd ever been. She knew she was supposed to wait for him and had done exactly what he told her. She had changed out of her pretty sundress and put on a pair of long pants and a long-sleeved blouse even though it was still stiflingly hot. She carefully placed her pillows and extra blanket to look like a person sleeping and threw her duvet over it all. Her radio was left on very quietly, because they knew she liked to fall asleep that way. Claire took another deep breath and sat up straighter on the edge of the bed. When would he be here? She couldn't wait any longer. She felt like a little kid running away from home.

They'd never even notice they were gone. He was sure of

it. By this time every night most of the residents on Claire's floor had already been given a pill and were either fast asleep or might as well be. Claire lived on the third floor, where they put the people with some cognitive impairment. On the fourth were the ones so far gone that they didn't know whether they were up or down. It was like the higher they put you, the closer to heaven you were. Or wherever you were headed. Louis was on the second floor—for people with more autonomy who just had a little trouble doing everything for themselves. Of course, that was not him. He didn't belong here at all.

With his knapsack filled with the precious treats he stepped out into his hallway and closed the door to his room very quietly behind him. No one was about, as usual. Good. Being seen with the bag might attract some unwanted questions. As he made his way to her room, he could feel his heart pounding. He was eighty-eight years old, for God's sake, and he was feeling like a boy again. A boy in love. Louis knocked very softly on her door and opened it. She was there. Ready. He grabbed a cardigan from her closet and stuffed it in the knapsack. Just in case. He had also tucked the cellphone his grandkids had given him for Christmas last year into the side pocket. Unfortunately, his server didn't work very well in this area—Ste. Lucie was a bit of a dead zone—so reception was spotty at best, non-existent at worst. Still, he thought it would be a good idea. Louis took Claire's hand, bent and twisted with arthritis, and kissed it.

Louis placed the key card that he had borrowed from one of the orderlies back in his pocket and held the heavy emergency exit door until it clicked quietly shut behind them.

He could smell that some weather was coming—the air

WHALE FALL

was fragrant with the anticipation of long-awaited rain—but
not until tomorrow morning. He had checked the weather
channel obsessively. Thunderstorms were expected. But only
tomorrow afternoon. Hand in hand they walked carefully
across the back lawn, past the copse of white pine trees that
framed the property of *Maison Soleil*, past the rocking love
seats, past the splintery picnic tables, past the little garden that
no one tended to properly. Louis thought briefly of Madame
Newman, his client of many years. His *friend* who had been
killed. She would have taken that sad little pile of dirt and
turned it into Eden.

The sun was a glorious, buttery yellow, just starting to
settle in the tops of the trees around them. Louis figured they
had two hours. Two hours to get there, drink a little wine and
enjoy the cheese and *saucisse*, and watch the sun set. That
would be plenty of time. He glanced back at the residence to
double check that they hadn't been spotted. Then he squeezed
Claire's hand and held it close to him. Their adventure was
underway.

Chapter 24

Everyone, no matter where they live, thinks their little piece of the world is beautiful. Some places looked like they were designed by a benevolent cosmic force to represent a human's idea of paradise, and maybe her little piece of the planet did not rank as one of them. But to Marie, there were few places more beautiful than Ste. Lucie in the height of summer. So, she wasn't entirely sure why they had driven north for four hours to The Middle of Nowhere that looked a lot like where they lived, only with perhaps even more trees and rocks. By the time they had bumped down someone's idea of a road for the final two hours, unloaded the endless piles of stuff they'd brought and then crammed it into the canoe they'd rented from the local outfitter, Marie was tired, hot, and cranky. But she had to admit that when she and Roméo had stepped gingerly into their canoe and began to head down the Salmon River to their campsite, the human world began to fall away. And as it did, Marie began to feel the delicious intimacy between them in the quiet rhythm of their paddling. Of being both completely separate and completely together. Two hours later, Roméo spotted the painted yellow X on a pine tree by the shore that marked their campsite, and they pulled their canoe up onto a little rocky beach. It was absolutely perfect. Their tent faced the western sky, there was a little stone fire pit with a few logs around it to sit on, and a flat mossy area to pitch their tent. Marie and Roméo set to unpacking again, and within an hour they were done. Roméo hoisted their food supplies up a tree and inside a metal canister, as this was bear country and they were notoriously fearless around campers. They saw no sign of bears, but Roméo did disturb a red squirrel who indignantly started chastising them. Marie took out her cell phone.

"I told you there was no service here. That was the point."

Marie shrugged her shoulders. "I thought I'd give it a shot, anyway."

He pulled a satellite phone from his smaller dry bag. "That's why I brought this. In case."

Suddenly, Marie put her index finger to her lips and shushed Roméo. About ten meters away, a skinny orange fox had popped his head out of a thicket of berry bushes and stopped to watch them. Marie and Roméo froze so as not to spook him. Because of Dog, Marie almost never got to see a fox up close—they were way too skittish. There was a fox that sometimes stopped in her front yard to scratch himself, then rolled on his back to get at another itch. Dog, usually the most phlegmatic, un-predatory dog when it came to most things—other dogs, cats, birds, people—went into full hysterical hunter when he saw a fox, rabbit, or groundhog. He would hurl himself at the screens of her porch while making a high-pitched howl like he was being tortured by some Bond villain. Well, in a way he was. That genetic need to hunt was being thwarted, and it was agony. After ten minutes of pacing, crying, and imploring Marie to release him to chase the fox, Dog would finally settle down, and flop on his bed with his head in his paws, emitting the occasional muted sigh. Roméo raised his arm to swat at a mosquito, and the fox vanished without a sound.

Marie went to drop her useless phone in the tent and stopped to take a deep breath.

"Oh my God! Can you smell that?"

Roméo looked up from the fire pit where he was preparing the logs for a fire. "Makes Ste. Lucie smell like the city."

Marie closed he eyes and inhaled again. "It's the smell of petrichor, the oil plants make that gets absorbed by the rocks and soil and released into the air? It's that smell after a rain, especially when it's been dry. Isn't it divine? I think it means the liquid of the gods on stone. Or something. It must have rained here earlier today." Marie smiled at Roméo. "It's kind of the smell of trees talking to each other."

Roméo threw a few more branches into the fire pit and asked, "Trees talk to each other?"

"Yeah. There's this researcher—a woman who's proven that trees 'talk' to each other through an underground network like the internet through these fungi that they have a symbiotic relationship with—you feed me, I feed you. Remember that idea that trees competed for sunlight and space? They actually cooperate. Large, healthy trees share resources with trees that aren't doing so well. They even help seedlings grow and get this, especially when they recognize them as their own family. There's even cooperation across the species barrier. Isn't that unbelievable? It's a whole new way of looking at a tree. Maybe there's still hope for us humans."

Roméo put an arm around Marie and pulled her over to the fire pit. He sat her down on one of the logs, but first rolled up his jacket to make her a pillow. "I am sorry to say I have to burn one of these chatterboxes, but at least they're not alive anymore. I'm making us a fire, and I want you to sit here, get comfortable, and in a few minutes, I will be serving the *hors d'oeuvres.*"

Marie perched herself on the log. "I wonder how the protest went. Ruby was really nervous. And don't you love that Mohammed has become so invested in this? What a lovely guy. Anyway, I hope it was a great success."

Roméo struggled to get the match lit. "I have no doubt it came off very well. Your old boyfriend may have saved the day. He's a hero."

"I wonder what his stunt was. God, it was so top-secret. He didn't even tell me."

Marie watched as Roméo looked for another pack of matches that weren't damp.

"That Leviathan project is just so…stupid and short-sighted. And will probably be a disaster. How could we have let these people run the world for so many years? For what? Another hotel that will bankrupt the little towns?"

Roméo finally got a match to light the dry spruce branches that ignited instantly.

"Marie," Roméo interrupted. He was a bit tired of the endless circular conversations about Projet Leviathan. "Do you want to start with a cheese plate, or shall I open the champagne?"

"You brought champagne?"

"Yes. Of course. What is a honeymoon night without champagne?"

"Thank you!"

Roméo leaned down to kiss Marie gently on the lips.

"I wouldn't get too close. All that paddling? I am sweaty and I smell like an old sock."

"You smell lovely to me, if a bit gamey. Like a moose. In rut."

Marie swatted Roméo. "Maybe I'll go for a swim first."

Marie pulled off her T-shirt and slipped out of her shorts. She walked gingerly over the little pebbles to the edge of the water and started wading in.

"How's the water?"

"Come on in and find out."

"I'm not a big swimmer, as you know. I prefer the surface."

Marie dropped into the river to her shoulders and flipped over to float on her back. The sky was deepening to cobalt blue. A thunder cloud was just starting to gather on the horizon. It would be a spectacular sunset. Marie swam back to shore and grabbed a towel from her pack.

"I guess I worry about what I will tell Noah and New Baby about what I did to save this world for them. Nothing."

"You teach and inspire people to do good. You write books explaining these…miracles all around us—"

"And you catch the bad guys. That's tangible. There's an objective and a result."

"I don't get most of them."

"I just feel this paralysis, not knowing what to do, how to fight it. Like I fought and protested my whole life for things I believed in. I was trying to explain this feeling to my class last spring just before the end of term—I can't even remember the context—I think I was telling the story of when I gave Ronald Reagan the finger at a protest against US policy in El

Salvador—"

"Do I know that story?"

"Yes, I've told it many times. *Anyway*. This little jerk in the back of the class says under his breath, 'Okay, Boomer.'"

Roméo looked up from the cooler he was digging around in. "What does that mean?"

"It's a shitty, ageist way to confront an old person. But maybe he was right? These kids must feel such environmental anxiety. And they see baby boomers leaving them to clean up our mess."

"Making an enemy of us won't help. And you, my love, are a good person who has at least tried to do the right thing. None of us succeeds all the time." And with that, Roméo popped the cork on the champagne. The sun was starting to drop lower on the horizon. As Marie expected, it was stunning. She sipped at her champagne while Roméo placed a few cheese slices, grapes, and baguette on a plastic plate. Then he ducked back into the tent to grab her a fleece. Even though it was still quite warm and humid, she'd gotten a bit of a chill from the river. As he foraged through her bag, he noticed the satellite phone in his bag was beeping red. There were already three urgent messages from Nicole LaFramboise. When Roméo finished reading them, he felt like someone had kicked him in the gut. Marie called over to him from the fire, her face softly illuminated in its glow.

"Thank you for today, my love. It was absolutely perfect. Hey, what are you up to in there? Got another surprise for me?"

Roméo dropped the phone back into his dry bag. He hesitated.

"No, that's all for today." Roméo returned to the fire,

wrapped his arms around Marie. and kissed the top of her head. "I love you very, very much."

Marie looked up at Roméo quizzically. He wasn't someone who said *I love you* very often. He showed his love with action. Not words.

"Me, too." The she added. "I love me very, very much. Kidding. I love you, Roméo."

And with that Marie dug into the cheese plate and emptied the rest of her glass in one swallow. She leaned into Roméo by the flickering fire as the sun continued its descent and stained the clouds an otherworldly pinky orange. It didn't get much better than this.

Chapter 25

Dear Ishmael,

Well, I have now been an intern for six weeks, and in some ways, I feel like a total newbie, and in other ways I feel like I've been here forever. I have learned so much these past weeks it makes me wonder what the hell I was doing with my brain all these years? When I could have been challenging myself every day? First of all, I'm learning so much about whales—about how to identify them from their tails (humpbacks) or their chevrons (the marking on their side, finbacks). I'm also becoming a very good whale spotter.... This morning I had the 6:00 to 8:00 shift up in the tower. I made a good hot thermos of coffee, got in my fleece and hat, and climbed the spiral staircase to the top where the scope is set up, but I usually just use my binoculars. Then I scan that endless ocean for a whale's blow—it's like a white poof of smoke on the horizon. Easy to see when the water is calm, way harder with chop and when the seas are gray. Then I radio to the team in the zodiac that I've spotted a whale and send them in the right direction,

I'm learning to measure distance by eye. It's a real skill. Like I said, we identify humpbacks by the markings on their tails, what we call flukes. Each one is as different as a fingerprint. I study the photographs and compare them to the identified whales in our catalogue—and I recognized the fluke scars on a whale that they identified and named in the late 1970's!!! in Stellwagen Banks in Cape Cod.!!!!Her name is Notch (because there's a notch missing in her tail, from a boat strike probably). It was thrilling. I mean, six weeks ago I was selling seal and whale stuffed toys at the aquarium shop!!! How did I get so lucky? I have to thank Anton for encouraging me— no, convincing me I had to do this. The people here are so AMAZING. So ACCOMPLISHED. I feel like a nobody. What have I done with my life? I've done everything I was told to do since I was a little girl. There were expectations put on me, especially since my sister felt none of them. She was too young to remember really when Dad left—so she didn't remember how Mom fell apart. She's just really kinda pissed off all the time. I am the happy one. The smiler. The pleaser. But I feel like on the ocean, I don't have to be that way. Just do my work and that's all. I am scared a lot of the time. Not scared. Nervous I'll make a mistake, or I'm not doing something fast enough. That I'm a fake. Well, I am. But then, Magnus Sorensen has no formal scientific training—the scientist is his partner and girlfriend, Gretchen Handschuh. She interned with Sylvia Earle—I mean Sylvia Earle!! In English her last name means glove—hand shoe, get it? (I looked it up) I noticed that when she's on the boat—everyone, including—me—is in awe of her. She just knows so much, and not in a show-offy way. She is also quite beautiful—like a model. She really runs the place as far as I can tell. She and Magnus are really in love. They adore each other. I hope Anton and I will be like them. Anyhoo, yesterday Gretchen joined us on the zodiac, and we had a little chance to talk. I was surprised she knew my name, and quite a bit about me—I guess they really do read those letters of intent in the application! She asked about my being a Quaker, and I told her just a birthright Quaker—I don't really attend meetings. She was really interested, she said it seemed like the most gentle of religions—anti-slavery, pacifist, vegetarian, until you thought about Quaker history. My Quaker ancestors basically built the Nantucket whaling industry and slaughtered whales for centuries. They believed God himself had given them dominion over the fish of the sea, so they saw no contradiction between their source of income and their religion. Gretchen told me that Melville called them Quakers with a vengeance!! How did she know more than ME about my own history?? Maybe I am making up for the sins of my fathers out here on the ocean?? Ishmael, am I trying to find God in the eye of a whale? If so, I can't think of a better way to do it. I AM SO LUCKY!

Gretchen also told me that in the 1800s on Nantucket, (where her and Magnus have lived) the women kinda got to run the place, as their men were at sea most of the time. She told me the words to this song. (She knew them by heart—I wrote them down here to remember them). I think she said this was called the Nantucket Girl's Song:

Then I'll haste to wed a sailor,
and send him off to sea,
For a life of independence,
is the pleasant life for me.
But every now and then I shall

like to see his face,
For it always seems to me to beam
with manly grace….
But when he says, "Good-bye my
love, I'm off across the sea,"
First, I cry for his departure, then
laugh because I'm free.

Hahaha. I love it. Well, Ishmael, until tomorrow…sweet dreams.

Chapter 26

VICTORY

SUNDAY EVENING

Pierre Batmanian took his seat at the head of the imposingly long and thick oak dining room table and placed his cell phone in front of him. His brand-new third wife, who was not quite half his age, offered everyone at the table their choice of wine, beer, or house cocktail and then directed their maid to prepare them. On an elaborate side table were platters of finger foods that most of the guests were too shy or too preoccupied to dig in to. Except for one. Robert Renard helped himself to a generous plate of oysters on the half shell, vodka-cured gravlax, tuna carpaccio, and grilled beef ribs so perfectly cooked they fell from the bone like butter. There were also several kinds of exotic breads and colorful dips and a selection of cheeses, one of which Mayor Morin couldn't avoid inhaling from across the table. It smelled like her husband's sweaty socks.

Pierre checked the time on his phone as was his habit, letting everyone know that every minute with him was somehow more precious than anyone else. The maid placed a masculine-looking cocktail in front of him and all his guests except for two: Mayor Morin had a glass of prosecco, and her councilor Denise Duguay sipped primly on a Perrier. As Pierre cleared his throat, they all watched him anxiously. Mayor Morin felt sick to her stomach. She had heard the rumors and she was fairly certain he was about to confirm that they were true. Pierre leaned back in his tooled leather chair that looked like something out of *Dallas*. Robert tried to guess what this table and chairs alone cost. Twenty thousand? Thirty-thousand bucks? And the house was full of bespoke furniture like this, all twenty-two rooms. He'd snooped around as many of them as he could.

Robert looked around the table at the guests. The downwardly mobile Denise Duguay, once a provincial Member of Parliament, now a city councilor in a backwater town. Valerie Morin, who was well known to have been wild in her salad days, now a mother of four, and quite ambitious. She was still traumatized by the torching of her car and had kept at it like a dog with a bone. She insisted that something be done. Renard made a mental note to pay a visit to that shithead Cousineau. He'd shake a little information loose from him—the guy had been informing to Roméo for years. Across from the women were Jean-Louis Gingras, a local developer and owner of a fleet of snowplows and Luc Batmanian, Pierre's brother and fixer.

Pierre tapped his fork lightly against his glass.

"You've all heard the news, I think. Robert, could you fill everyone in?"

Robert quickly swallowed another oyster and took his seat at the table.

"Magnus Sorensen was found dead earlier today in Lac St. Simon His body was discovered next to the plane he was borrowing from an old friend, Mikael Rasmussen. The circumstances were deemed suspicious, but I can confirm from my sources that it was in fact a homicide."

A few people around the table gasped. Denise Duguay shook her head as though denying the news. Jean-Louis Gingras declared it was a terrible tragedy. Twice. Luc Batmanian furrowed his brow in thought.

"This is like—oh, what was her name? That movie star who died at Mont Tremblant? The wife of that guy—"

"What guy?"

"The movie star—English. I mean from England, I think."

The entire table tried to remember her name. They all agreed it was on the tip of their tongues.

"She died skiing at Mont Tremblant—she fell and hit her head. Don't you remember that?"

"It was terrible publicity for Mont Tremblant," Mayor Morin said, shaking her head. "This thing with…Sorensen may be very bad for us. Our investors' perception of our region. It could reflect very badly on our project. What are we going to do?"

Pierre waved a dismissive hand. "That story at Mont Tremblant was finished in a week. This one may last a bit longer. But, in the end, it has nothing to do with us."

"Good riddance, I say."

Denise Duguay was truly shocked. "Jean-Louis, that's an awful thing to say. My God, what's wrong with you?"

"I'm just being honest. Yes, it's sad when someone dies. But I say he got himself mixed up in something that's not his—business—good riddance to foreigners who tell us what to do. Now, I don't mean I don't like foreigners. I like *le Chinois* at the dépanneur—he learned how to adjust, he didn't come here and dictate to us our lives. I don't mind the Syrians who settled on rue Labelle. I don't like their hajib. Hibaj. The scarf on the head they have to wear. They keep to themselves, mostly. And they try to learn French. They're good people." He ended his speech with a satisfied nod and a swallow of his cocktail. Pierre Batmanian smiled and listened. If only they knew the half of it—who exactly had ponied up the money for this project. They'd be thrilled to have Magnus Sorensen back.

"I was at the protest earlier and one of them called me an *environmental racist*." He reported the insult in air quotes. "Whatever the fuck that is."

"I was called human garbage. *Garbage!*"

Suddenly, everyone at the table burst into a litany of complaints all at once.

Pierre got to his feet at the head of the table and appealed to them to calm down.

"I understand you. I do. We have tried to compromise with the other side. We have explained the forest's regeneration capacity. We have offered to plant trees after, to try and integrate parts of the preserve into the plan of the hotel. What a draw that would be! We have tried to alleviate the economic suffering of the area. But they will not compromise. It is zero-sum game for them, and that one *we* will win. Because my friends…," Pierre paused for effect. "We have met all the milestones the banks have asked of us. It looked rough for a while there, with all the press around Sorensen and the protests, but it is smooth sailing we hope from now on."

The relief around the table was palpable. Everyone in the room had money and their reputations invested in this. Robert felt like crying for joy.

"And, I want to announce that I have just received news

the injunction will be lifted at midnight tonight. Which means, ladies and gentlemen, our crews will be there tomorrow morning at the crack of dawn to start those chainsaws and begin the cut."

Just at the moment, the Batmanians' maid came out actually pushing a golden trolley containing a few bottles of Veuve Clicquot and a dozen glasses. She filled up their glasses as Pierre lifted his. "Leviathan, *mes chères amies*, is underway!"

Chapter 27

He had to pee. It was the curse of old men the world over. He gingerly got to his feet and hobbled over to a line of tall trees that marked the edge of the forest. Sometimes the urge was there but the body would not cooperate, and this was one of those moments. He waited as long as he could and then felt that glorious rush of relief. He noted that the sky behind the spires of balsams in front of him was turning a bruised mauve blue—weather was definitely coming.

By the time he returned she had fallen asleep, lying on her side, her cheek wrinkled into the blanket on the flattened grass. Her mouth was slightly open, breathing evenly and lightly. Louis slowly began his descent. He had to first get his hands down flat, pitching himself forward and hoping his arms would hold. Then his knees, one of which would often not bend at all. Then he had to swing his new hip around and plump down next to her. As he lowered himself beside her, Louis watched the breeze play with wisps of her white hair. There was just enough of it to cover her pink scalp. An ant was foraging amongst the crumbs left by their picnic, a bit too close to her face. He nudged it away from her face with his finger. She was so beautiful.

He wasn't surprised that Claire needed a little nap. The walk through the woods to his spot was a bit longer than he remembered, and the trail was more overgrown as well. A few times they'd had to stop and figure out where the path was. He hadn't anticipated how jungly these woods could get in the summer. In the end, they found their way to the little beach on Lac Sarrazin, on the side where there were no houses and no road. As Louis had hoped, Claire was delighted at the sun starting to set across the water, and she immediately slipped out of her shoes and waded into the lapping waves.

After, he had tenderly dried her feet, laid out their picnic blanket (the sheet he had borrowed from the linen closet), and helped Claire get comfortable before he took out each precious surprise from his knapsack and offered it to her. She ate like she hadn't in months, padding down the softened brie with her fingers onto torn chunks of baguette. She even had a glass of wine and toasted Louis. But the best part, the part that Louis knew they both loved, were the stories—especially the childhood ones they shared. They both had lost their mothers when they were very young. Louis was the middle child of nine, and he made Claire guffaw with glee at how he was the mama's boy—the *moumoune* of the family, even though he wasn't the baby, and his mother was dead.

"All my five brothers were real country boys, hunters and fishermen and loggers. But I hated hunting. I hated the noise. I hated cleaning the animals. I loved fishing, though." He described the many kinds of fish they used to catch in these lakes years ago, and how proud he was to bring some home to help feed the family. "There are no fish left in any of these lakes now," Louis explained. "You have to go way north of here to find them." Claire was about to tell him something when he continued.

"Did I tell you that I was supposed to be the priest of the family?"

Louis noticed the surprise on Claire's face. "Oui, Madame. I was the studious one. The one who went to mass and prayed the most fervently. Before my mother died, she always said I would be the one. The one who would go to seminary. But I was too scared *not* to pray. But my mother, she died anyway. And I didn't pray much ever again. Except when…," Louis faltered. "When Charles-Etienne died."

Claire took Louis's hand gently in hers.

"Did I tell you about *Matante* Albertine?"

Louis shook his head. "No. Tell me."

Claire looked out to the lake as though her image was unfolding there before her eyes.

"My aunt Albertine—we called her *Matante Titine*—was…she was not pretty. She had a face like a…like a…." Claire searched for the word. "Like a horse." Louis gave a sympathetic frown.

"And small eyes. And yellow teeth. Oh! And we always called those long hairs we get on our chins *titines*, after Matante, as she also had long ones that she forgot to…cut."

"Poor Albertine." Louis commented.

Claire leaned closer to Louis and continued.

"*Matante Titine* was a spinster. And she always lived with us—she was my father's older sister. But she was in love with our doctor—the one who took care of our whole family. I can't remember his name. Oh. What is his name? Oh. I can't—"

"It's okay. It doesn't matter," Louis reassured her.

"She would make any excuse to go and see him—she made up all kinds of, of woman problems. But the doctor was married to Madame. Madame *Daoust*! When Titine realized she couldn't have him, she had a plan. Every night before we went to bed, she would get me and my four sisters to pray with her. She went to mass seven mornings a week and was a very devout woman. We would get on our knees next to our beds, our hands like this," Claire pressed her hands tightly together, "and we would say, all together, Dear God in heaven. Please, please make Madame Daoust get sick and die so *Matante Titine* can marry Doctor Daoust."

Louis laughed so hard he sprayed the swallow of wine in his mouth onto his pants.

Claire wasn't sure she should laugh, but then she joined him. As he put his arm around her thin shoulder she wanted to melt with joy. And something else. Was that still possible? What if it was? What was she supposed to do? Louis leaned in and kissed her. On the mouth. Then he gently laid her back on the blanket and kissed her again. She felt wonderful. Like home.

The sky was darkening faster than he thought it would. To the south, he heard the rumble of thunder. Several times. It wasn't close yet, but it would be. Louis felt a stirring of panic. What was he thinking? They should've left a half hour ago.

"Claire?" He brushed her cheek gently. "Claire? Wake up. Claire?"

He wanted to kiss her again. But instead, he jostled her arm. Once, twice. She finally opened her eyes. They weren't focused. She startled into a sitting position and searched Louis's face for recognition.

"Who? Who are you? Why am I here?"

It was at that moment that Louis saw the lightning explode in the hills across the lake.

Chapter 28

MONDAY

8 AM

The drive back from Salmon River was endless. That morning at around five o'clock Roméo had woken Marie with a steaming cup of coffee. Once he had gotten her up and out of the cozy tent to sit by the morning fire and her head had cleared the night cobwebs away, he took her hands in his and told her the truth. Or at least what he knew so far. Marie listened, then looked him right in the eye and said, "What?"

Roméo repeated what news Nicole had messaged him. "When?"

"As far as we know, yesterday."

"When did you find out?"

Roméo hesitated. "Last night. Once it was getting dark, I thought it best to stay here—there was nothing we could do."

Marie just said, "Okay."

Then she stood up, dumped the rest of her coffee in the fire, and went back to the tent. Minutes later, the first of her packed dry bags went sailing through the tent flap, followed by her pillow, her folded sleeping bag, and a pair of sneakers. Roméo put out the fire, cleaned up the campsite so no trace of them was left behind, and started to load the canoe with all their stuff. Marie hadn't said more than a few words through the whole process, through the two-hour paddle back to the outfitter, and only responded in a few monosyllables to Roméo while they tied down the canoe to the top of their car and navigated their way out of the dense boreal forest that enclosed the lake.

As they left the potholed and rock-strewn gravel road and turned onto a larger highway, their phones started pinging and pinging, announcing the return of the human world to their lives. Marie's phone lit up with messages. As Roméo drove, she started to read them—from Ruby, Ben, Lucy, and a few other friends, many of whom had called or texted several times. Suddenly, Marie felt a wave of nausea, and had just enough time to yell at Roméo to pull over. He lurched onto the scrabbly shoulder and hadn't even fully stopped the car when Marie threw open her door and vomited up her breakfast.

They drove in silence for another twenty minutes or so, the tension between them growing with each passing mile. Roméo was furious with himself. He had clearly made the wrong choice not to tell her about Magnus last night.

"Marie?"

She shook her head. "I just need to not talk now. Is that okay?"

"I would like to call Nicole."

Marie nodded and said nothing. Roméo stuck his blue tooth plugs into each ear carefully and pressed Nicole LaFramboise's number. She picked up on the first ring.

"Are you awake?"

"Of course I'm awake. It's the middle of my day, for me." Roméo could hear Léo shrieking in the background. "How are you? How is Marie?"

Roméo glanced at Marie who was staring out the window at nothing. It didn't look like it, but he knew she was listening intently.

"She's…. She's shocked. And—"

"Please tell her I'm so, so sorry."

"I will."

"I know he was an old friend, and a big part of her life once, I think. I don't know what else to say."

Marie abruptly turned to Roméo. "Put her on speakerphone."

"Marie, I need to discuss a few details that will be disturbing—"

"Put her on speaker. I want to hear what she has to say."

Roméo shook his head and switched the call to the car's system.

"Nicole. You're on speaker. Marie is here."

"Mes sincères condoléances. I'm really sorry, Marie."

"Merci, Nicole." There was a long pause. Roméo went first. "What time did the…incident get called in?"

"At two-seventeen pm. Sorensen was found by a woman named…Emily Joly. His, um…colleague at *See Change*."

Roméo glanced at Marie. "Does that name ring a bell?" Marie shook her head.

"He was found in the water. At Lac St. Simon. By the floatplane he was planning on flying into the Leviathan protest." Nicole took a deep breath. "In my opinion, it is a suspicious death."

"You have secured the scene?"

"Yes, I put Joseph in charge. But it would be good if you were there. The locals are very…worked up, very excited about this, and I worry the scene will be compromised. Also, we have held the media at bay, but the news is leaking out and it's just a matter of time before the vultures descend on us."

"If it was reported at two-seventeen, Nicole, why wasn't I informed much earlier? I don't understand."

"That is a very good question, Boss. I checked in at the protest around one pm, and I was very...reachable. For some reason, the local police did not notify me until five-eleven pm. By then, I had to get to the scene, make sure the report was accurate. By the time I had the...confirmation, it was after seven pm. And I texted you. I didn't know—what exactly to do. I'm so sorry, Marie. I didn't want to interrupt you—"

"Where is this...Emily Joly now?"

"We had to take her to the hospital in Ste. Agathe. She was...in shock and she is, um...recovering there. She..." Nicole hesitated. "We'll get a chance to talk to her later today, I thi—"

Suddenly, Nicole's voice vanished. They were driving through a dead zone. When her voice came back, she was still talking. "...looked though those notes you gave me, the ones Sorensen received in the last few weeks? I mean, they seem like a warning—"

Roméo cut her off. "We can talk about those later. As soon as I'm back. Set up an interview for this afternoon with Emily Joly and me, as well as with the common-law wife, Gretchen—I don't know her last name."

"Okay, boss. Done."

Roméo suddenly heard the sound of something heavy crashing, and then a piercing scream.

"*Merde*! I have to go. I'm late to get Léo to the garderie. When do you think you'll be in?"

Léo let out another scream.

"I've got to get him out of the house now—"

Nicole hung up.

8∂

Almost two hours later, Roméo pulled into Marie's driveway and stopped the car by the house. He had been quiet the rest of the way home. Why hadn't he pressed Magnus about those strange notes he'd received? Why hadn't he taken them more seriously? It was not like him at all. The truth was he wanted to go on his honeymoon, and it was more convenient to accept Magnus's dismissal of them as just a part of his life. It was terrible policing. And now, he would have to explain to Marie what he'd done. Or hadn't done. He untied and unloaded the canoe in record time, and helped Marie toss all their bags of stuff onto her front porch. He raced through the house, grabbed his ID, and changed his shoes and shirt without even taking a shower. He felt a terrible, urgent guilt.

"Marie? I need to go. I'll let you know what's going on as soon as I can. Will you be okay?"

Marie was sitting at the kitchen table, the unpacked cooler of food beside her.

"I just can't believe it, you know? I just. Feel numb. I just need to process my friend being…dead. Okay?"

Roméo squatted beside her and took her hand.

"I am so sorry. I didn't tell you because, because there was no point in ruining your night. There was no point in telling you. There was nothing you or I could do."

Marie nodded and stood up. "I want to go pick up Dog and Barney at Manon's. Now. I'll put all this away later."

Roméo took Marie in his arms and inhaled her. She smelled of wood smoke and the last vestiges of her jasmine perfume. The honeymoon was over.

Marie wasn't sure what to do next. She felt empty. Not sad.

Not angry. Empty. She looked at all the gear piled up around her in the kitchen. Then she spotted it, tucked between the toaster and the coffee machine—the envelope that Magnus had left in her jacket pocket. Was that just two days ago? Was it possible? She had discovered it before she and Roméo left for Salmon River and decided to leave it behind. Marie hesitated. Then she retrieved the envelope and opened it carefully.

Dear Marie,
I can't tell you what good it has done me to see you
again and remember those years we had together. That
was when everything seemed possible and the world
was changeable—human nature, human behavior was
changeable, systems were changeable. I wonder now
what it all really added up to, if you can ever really
change people. I think it takes a collective epiphany, a
collective kind of moment where everybody realizes that
we have to do something. Our governments will not save
us now. Our wishful thinking will not save us.
But I fear with fewer and fewer people experiencing
and appreciating the non-human world—how could
they possibly value it? How could they possibly care what
happens to a butterfly, or a hummingbird, or a shark...
or the side of a mountain that contains such a diversity
it would take ten lifetimes to fully know? How could they
possibly understand how each and every one of those
lives is part of this giant ecosystem that still survives
despite our best efforts to destroy it?
I am looking at the stars now, and that delicious
feeling they give you—like you are everything and you
are nothing at the same time. To think I could navigate

*any boat by the stars, but of course only on a clear night.
If only I could have navigated us better, my dearest
Marie. What memories we made. Too many to describe
here, but one in particular came to me, and you might
be surprised that it is not one of our time on the ocean
but in Maine. On land, in Tor Hanye's backyard. Do you
remember?*

Of course she remembered.

*We had been up drinking Irish whiskey with Tor
and Virginia. We were still new together, still learning
each other. I think it was in late March, and we'd just
come up from our first season in Santo Domingo.
Everyone went off to bed a bit drunk, but you wanted
to go outside and look at the full moon. It had been a
mild day and all the snow had melted away. You dragged
me outside—I had no sweater, and I was cold—but the
moon was huge. We could clearly see the Sea of Rains
and the Sea of Tranquility. And then, you said, 'Look!'*

Marie smiled.

*Tor's entire backyard was moving. The earth
undulating in the moonlight. We thought we were seeing
things, remember? Hallucinating. But you looked it up
(of course) and determined that the earthworms were
coming to the surface in such numbers that the ground
was moving. You looked deep into my eyes and asked,
"Did the earth move?"*

Marie felt her eyes threaten to well up for the first time since Roméo told her.

I am sorry for what I did to you all those years ago. I don't know what came over me. Fear of losing a kind of control. I think I saw desire in your eyes for a different life, a more settled life than I could accept or thought I could live. A life with children and owning a home—quite ironic as I own a few homes now. And I think it scared me—maybe good old fashioned male fear of commitment. Peter Pan syndrome, refusal to settle down? And now? All these many years later? I watch you and your two wonderful children, your beautiful grandson and growing family, and I really do understand. Much more than you might know. I WISH YOU ALL THE BEST for this marriage with your man. I can see that he is a person of great depth and quality. And I still like him. See you in a minute!

Marie flattened out the letter and ran her fingers over the paper, feeling where the pen had pressed into it. Then she folded it up and slipped it back into the envelope. She felt exhausted. Flattened. Trying to figure out what to do next. A knock at the door startled her. Marie slowly made her way over to see who it was. Manon Latendresse was standing before her, with Barney curled up un the crook of one arm and Dog sitting anxiously at her heel, dying to go to Marie and lick every exposed part of her.

"I thought you might want your boys home."

It was then and just then that Marie started to cry.

Chapter 29

Olivier Ward was worried. Almost all of his regulars were at breakfast that morning, heads bent over their plates, their chins barely clearing the table, getting the food to their mouths as best they could. Others were engaged in boisterous conversation, heartily calling for more coffee or juice or tea, which Olivier cheerfully supplied. Madame Faustin, who was ninety-four years old and who'd had thirteen children, was absent. He heard she had an ulcer on her leg that had gone septic and had to go to hospital. Olivier cleared the last of the tables and scraped the remains into the compost bin. Monsieur Tardif never finished his breakfast, and he was as skinny as a pin. Madame Plante ate three plates of pancakes just that morning with enough maple syrup to drown a cat. But Madame Russell, his favorite of them all, was missing. Olivier loved Madame Russell.

Every morning she greeted him with a beautiful smile and told him how handsome he looked. She told him he was an excellent waiter because he never forgot to bring her extra cream for her coffee before she asked for it and extra cantaloupe when they had it. Olivier had never been told he was handsome before. And he had never been good at anything. Even though his teachers had tried to help him read properly since he was a child, he never could sort out the letters on the blackboard. The kids made fun of his cleft palate scar and mimicked the nasal way he talked. But when he started working at *Maison Soleil*, he felt like a real person. Like a man. He had even summoned up the courage to ask Karine, the front desk girl, out on a date although she had looked at him with such shock and pity that he had immediately retracted the offer and disappeared into the kitchen.

Olivier removed his apron and hung it carefully on the hook designated for his things. He would now normally change into his washing up clothes before getting the lunch tables set, but he decided to do something else first.

Karine was sitting at the front desk when she noticed him approaching, and he could sense her wariness. He had avoided her since their last disastrous encounter. She got very busy on her computer.

"Madame Russell wasn't at breakfast this morning."

"Oh no?" She returned to whatever extremely important thing was on her screen.

"Do you think she's in there?" he asked, nodding to her computer.

"I'm checking the morning report." Karine frowned. "Nothing unusual there."

Olivier persisted. "She never misses breakfast. Lunch, yes. Sometimes even supper. But never breakfast."

Karine rolled her eyes and sighed. "Okay, Olivier. We'll look into it." Her eyes returned to the screen.

"Now?"

She stopped tapping and sank into her chair. "Okay."

She swiveled her chair over to another part of the desk where her intercom was. Then she looked up who was on duty that morning and paged her over the system. Therese, a breathless woman in her mid-fifties, made her way to the desk.

"What?"

"Did you see Madame Russell this morning?"

She hesitated, scrolling through her overworked memory for an image of the woman.

"Yes. She was sleeping, so I let her have a lie in."

Karine shook her head and finally left her front desk chair. She grabbed the woman by the arm and pushed her ahead down the hall to the elevator.

It wasn't until Karine actually checked the lump in the bed that they all realized what had happened.

"Shit! Shit! *Shit!*"

Therese looked like she was about to cry. "I...I...thought she was asleep. And Carole called in sick today, so I had twice as many to check this morning and Madame Faustin soaked her bed. It was a big mess."

Karine turned on her heel and hastened back to the front desk. She immediately called the director of *Maison Soleil* and pushed the emergency button.

They looked everywhere. Olivier checked the yard, the garden, and beyond. Therese knocked on every door on Madame Russell's floor. Someone checked the pool and yoga room. Karine mobilized every staff member on break and called in reinforcements. Despite all their best efforts, they had to admit that Claire Russell was nowhere to be found. It was at that moment that the director's day got a lot worse.

Richard, the burly orderly who could lift an inert body like it was a kitten, jogged towards the group of anxious caregivers. They all looked to him with relief. He must have found her.

"Monsieur Lachance is gone. No one has seen him since suppertime yesterday."

The director ran her hand over her mouth as though to refuse to acknowledge what she had to do next. She returned to her office, sat down at her cluttered desk, and made the first of two awful phone calls.

Chapter 30

Roméo was driving way too fast, like he was trying to outrun the scorching heat which was already wilting the wildflowers and slumping the long grasses lining the road. The heat had eased up a bit after the thunderstorms of the night before, but still felt relentless. What would the rest of the day bring, if it was this hot and humid already? He flicked on the *Radio Canada* news to see if anything had reached them yet. So far, nothing. That wouldn't last. Instead, the news was all about a killer whale mother off the coast of British Columbia who had made headlines earlier that year for carrying her dead daughter seventeen days and 1600 kilometers in mourning her before she gave up the calf's body. She had broken hearts all over the world. The good news that morning was that she was now pregnant. It was the uplifting story to counterbalance the relentless tales of climate change horror that kept unfolding.

As much as Roméo tried, he couldn't shake the image of Magnus two days earlier. Pulling out the crumpled notes from his pocket almost sheepishly and giving them to Roméo.

Trusting him. Reaching out to him. He should have taken it more seriously. Roméo remembered watching a documentary about *See Change* battling Japanese ships that were still hunting whales in the Southern Atlantic and calling it "research." They were naming Magnus the natural heir to the man who first taught the world about the miracles of the ocean. Had Roméo allowed the next Jacques Cousteau to die on his watch?

Roméo suddenly skidded to a stop, the road beneath him kicking up gravel and stone. There was the gate with the two stags. Open. Roméo turned up the long driveway with a familiar and acute sense of dread. A flotilla of police vehicles was scattered around the semi-circular drive-in front of the house. Roméo had taken the precaution of ordering the crime scene investigators there right away, and the CID van had already arrived. Nicole's car was there, too. There were also too many Sûreté du Québec vehicles for the area to be kept uncontaminated. Roméo got out of his car and headed down the long, sloping lawn towards the lake.

The scene looked like an old sci-fi movie. Masked figures in white CID coveralls were starting to collect evidence. Hopefully, there would be trace materials—blood, body fluids, hair or other tissues that might provide DNA. There were no yellow numbered markers placed anywhere yet, so they must have just arrived. Or there was little evidence to record. The local cops were milling about, sipping from foam coffee cups, smoking, or both, trying to look cool and calm but talking excitedly amongst themselves. Whatever footprints might have assisted this investigation were long obliterated by now. Roméo raised a hand. They were all silent in a few seconds.

"I want everyone, and I mean *everyone* who is not on the CID team, is not Detective LaFramboise, Detective Tremblay,

Chief Denis or me to remove themselves at once. Go back to your precinct and do your job, and let the people here do their jobs. Thank you."

Of course, there was grumbling. This was way more exciting than hiding in your cruiser aiming your radar gun or giving someone a ticket for insufficiently securing their boat trailer. Sometimes they got to chase the Thibodeau twins, the local B and E experts who after a stint in jail were back in action. More and more often they were called to intimate partner violence cases, some involving members of their own force. But a high-profile homicide? It didn't get much better than this.

Detective Nicole LaFramboise spotted Roméo, gave him a little wave of greeting, and headed over to him, stepping carefully around a white-clad tech on his knees brushing for fingerprints. Despite wearing a T-shirt and loose cotton pants, Nicole looked like she'd just stepped out of a sauna. Marie didn't handle heat and humidity too well, either, he thought, but Nicole was practically soaked. A small bead of sweat was making its way down her forehead and threatening to drop off her nose before she wiped it away.

"Are you okay?"

Roméo nodded.

"How's Marie doing?"

Roméo didn't answer, just frowned and shook his head. Nicole continued.

"So, the body was taken to the morgue in Ste. Agathe. I just got the call from the ME. Preliminary? He died by drowning. But there was blunt force trauma to the back of the head, and as far as we could tell he fell face first into the water. It would appear that Sorensen did not hit his head accidentally.

This was a homicide." Roméo couldn't help but think of the notes Magnus had received. The first in the mailbox at his rental house with his partner. *The last big hurrah.* The second at the wedding. *I had lived enough.* And the third. *Today is the* day. Left in his shirt pocket at Roméo and Marie's house. Magnus had never left the wedding. Whoever wrote those notes had been there. If not a guest, was he or she working for the caterer? A wedding crasher? And were they written by his killer? He watched as one of the CID team dropped a yellow cone with a number 3 on it. They'd found something, at least. He wondered how they managed to survive in those suits in this heat. Maybe there were naked underneath.

"Make sure that they go over this place with a finer than fine-tooth comb. I want every inch covered. All latent print evidence meticulously logged. All footwear and tire track evidence as well. Despite the circus we have going on here, we cannot make any mistakes because the media will be all over this like flies on shit." He immediately regretted the simile. "Get Tremblay on all digital evidence—cell phone, email, etc.... And I want you to look into those notes that were left. But first, I need you to go and bring Gretchen, Sorensen's partner, to the morgue. She needs to identify the body."

Nicole raised one crooked eyebrow. "You don't want one of the baby cops here to do that?"

"No. I want you. And I want you to observe her carefully. Anything that seems odd, or inconsistent or out of...whack. Just make a note of it, okay?"

"Yes, boss."

She turned on her heel and started to move back towards the house. Then she stopped.

"Oh, I don't know if you heard. Ti-Coune Cousineau?

He's been arrested. They're holding him in Ste. Agathe."

"*Ciboire.* What did he do?"

"Assaulted a cop. Plus ca change—"

"What happened?"

"At the protest. It was that guy, you know that asshole from Lanthier who can't take his eyes off my boobs? He provoked him. It wasn't black and white—"

"Ouah, pauvre Ti-Coune. He was provoked by a cop, so he had to attack him."

"Ti-Coune got the worst of it, believe me."

"He usually does." Roméo hesitated. "Is he okay?"

"A black eye, a couple of bruised ribs, and maybe a bruised ego as well. Always thinks he's a tough guy, you know?"

Roméo looked off at the team working by the water and then back to Nicole. "I'll look in on him."

At that moment, a very large man in his mid-fifties with a greasy faux hawk and biceps so huge he couldn't swing his arms when he walked, approached Roméo. A nervous baby cop who seemed diminutive beside him cleared his throat and announced, "Detective Inspector Leduc? This is Karl…." He checked his notes. "Slo…bodjian." He pronounced the name like toboggan. "The caretaker."

Karl Slobodjian watched the police suspiciously, like they were going to steal something. He nodded at Roméo but said nothing. Roméo introduced himself.

"I understand you were not here yesterday at all."

"My day off. I get one. My replacement was sick. I told Mr. Mikael that we needed someone, but he thought it would be okay. I told him we needed a caretaker here twenty-four seven. He was wrong."

Roméo asked for the name of his replacement and wrote

it down. Karl watched the pen and notepaper intently as he did this, as though checking its accuracy.

"Has a police officer already retrieved the CCTV footage? From the front gate and by the house? If not, we'll need that now—"

"No cameras."

"I saw cameras. All over the place."

Karl shook his head and spat at his feet.

"Mr. Mikael didn't believe in them. They're all fake. They don't work. I told him to get proper cameras. Proper security. Despite all this," he gestured to the mansion behind them, "he's very...." He stopped himself before he said cheap. "Frugal."

Roméo wondered if Magnus's killer knew this.

"I told Mr. Mikael not to let any Tom, Dick, or Harry just come in here whenever they wanted to. But he doesn't listen to me."

Slobodjian punctuated that complaint with another stream of saliva. Was the man blaming his boss for one of his friends being murdered on his property? Of course, Mikael Rasmussen would have to be interviewed. He was currently in Svaalbard in the Norwegian Arctic.

"Well, thank you for your help, and we will probably be in touch. Please stay in the area."

"Where would I go?" the man asked Roméo balefully. But Roméo had already turned away and was headed to the water.

ଚଚ

Roméo walked down to the end of the dock and stood there as quiet and as focused as he could be. There were a few more little yellow flags placed around the cordoned off area. But no one had called him over to show him anything, any bit of compelling evidence. So, he did what was his habit. He tried to get a feel for what happened. Tried to tell himself a story about what went on here that had led to the violent death of his wife's former lover. In the murder mysteries that Marie liked to watch on TV, he himself might be the prime suspect, of course. If he didn't have a solid alibi.

He gestured to one of the younger detectives.

"Make sure the plane is dusted inside and out. Every inch. Got it? And everything photographed, everything."

"It's very hot. Those guys are going to broil in that plane—"

"A man lost his life here! Tell them to drink lots of water. Look the lake is right there."

Roméo turned away from the sullen detective and walked to the end of the dock. The body had been found here. He looked at the photographs that Nicole had sent on his phone. His assailant must have clocked him one. Hard, on the back of the head. Not enough to kill him, but enough to make him stagger and fall into the water. It looked like he hit his head just over his right eye again on one of the boulders by the dock, fell face down, and drowned. Hopefully he was already unconscious when he went in. The ME would most likely be able to determine that. Roméo stared into the water, mesmerized by the play of sunlight on its surface. He was not a swimmer, but today he would love to dive into that lake and come back when the sun went down. Suddenly, something flashed in the water. He thought it was just the sun, but then it flashed again. Roméo quickly removed his shoes and socks, rolled up his pants, and waded into the water. It felt glorious. Wonderful. Turning his head away from the water's surface, he reached down to the bottom of the lake to retrieve the object he had noticed. He thought his arm might just be long enough. And there it was. Roméo lifted it dripping out of the lake. A small pink stone set in a silver claw. He summoned one of the CID people and asked them to bag it for evidence. It could have been sitting there for months. Years. Dropped by the owner of this castle, or one of his hundreds of guests over the years. It also could belong to Magnus Sorensen. Or his killer.

Chapter 31

Paul Pellerin sat on the edge of his bed at the St. Moritz Motel which looked like anything but its namesake. There were no alpine vistas and no glamorous Euro jet set checking in. There was an outdoor pool that badly needed a paint job and a sign boasting Bain Tourbillon, but four of the neon letters were burnt out. The Vietnamese proprietor was so delighted to have a customer stay on past the weekend that his cheery mood stood in stark contrast to Paul's. He'd received the call the afternoon before. A young policewoman had gently spoken to him in English with such a thick, incomprehensible accent that he asked her to repeat the news in French, even though his French was very rusty.

Paul was the descendant of French Canadians who had poured out of Quebec to find work in freshly industrialized New England in what they called *la grande saignée* or "the great hemorrhage." Paul's people had moved to Massachusetts, but only his grandparents had spoken French. He admired the Quebecois for preserving their language and culture in the overwhelming sea of English North America. Paul had thanked her for making the difficult call and had assured her he would stay in the area until the investigating team said they no longer required his cooperation. They would be contacting him shortly to arrange an interview with the chief investigating officer. Paul stared blankly at the wall, at a very amateurish painting of the real St. Moritz in Switzerland, where he wished he was right now. Skiing down some powdery slope into oblivion. The enormity of Magnus's death had flattened him. Paralyzed him. What *the fuck* happened? What *the fuck* was he going to do now? This was not *not not not* how it was supposed to go. He had called Gretchen about a dozen times, but she didn't answer. Then he had texted her. Repeatedly and with increasing panic. She finally responded, telling him she was headed to the morgue with the police, and she would call him after. He had offered to go with her, but she had simply answered *No*.

So here he was, sitting on a grubby gray and purple bedspread, waiting for the rumors about the death of Magnus Sörensen to be confirmed to the world. When Paul allowed himself to actually think about it all he could barely breathe and had to put his head between his knees to stop himself from passing out. He wished Tor Hanyes could be here with him. Tor would know what to do. He always knew what to do. How to dodge crazy Russians firing on your zodiac in the middle of the Southern Ocean. How to bring a boat into harbor in the middle of the night with no lights and a foreign navy ready to blow you up. How to walk away from an organization you built with your own blood from the ground up when you thought it had lost its moral compass. How to leave a life you'd lived every minute with dignity and grace when cancer was devouring you whole. Paul knew he had to brace himself for the dizzying numbers of letters, emails, texts, and calls of condolence, shock, disbelief, and horror. He also knew he'd be hearing from his creditors over the next few days and weeks. He figured he had about a week's grace period before the jackals would be after him. But maybe, maybe, somehow, Magnus could still save him. He had to talk to Gretchen. How dare she blow him off like that? And what about Emily? He had to talk to her, too. Paul needed something to do, or he would go mad.

He pulled himself off the bed and went to his laptop. He had deleted everything he could think of. But he would go over them all again just to be sure. Didn't the cops have ways of checking the hard drive? Then he must give them no reason to do so. As he reached down to retrieve his glasses, he noticed the diary, one pink edge protruding from his bag. He pulled it out and ran his hand over the cloth cover, but he couldn't bear to look at it again. What would he do with it now? He wondered how many people kept a diary anymore. Although this one was only twelve years old, it was such a testament to another time and sensibility, one that was probably never coming back. Paul opened it to one dog-eared page. Then he hurriedly returned it to his bag. What had he done? He removed his glasses, dropped his head into his folded arms on the motel's scratched and greasy desk, and began to sob.

Chapter 32

Molly

Dear Ishmael,

Last night I had this nightmare AGAIN—the same one
I had when I was a kid.... It came from this picture in my
Children's Illustrated Bible. It's the one of Jonah and the whale
(of course!) Jonah is desperately trying to get away, his arms
reaching up to heaven, but the whale (which looked like a
freakish giant carp) had this gaping mouth and two very
human-looking eyes staring at him as it chases him—and
catches him and swallows him. The next picture was of Jonah
standing in the belly of "the beast." He spends three days and
three nights in there—in the pitch-black darkness all alone
until the whale opens its mouth to eat and a little light comes
in. But every time he almost drowns or gets sucked out to sea.
I used to wonder what Jonah did that was SO BAD that he
deserved to be swallowed by a whale? If I remember well, it's
because Jonah refused to go to Nineveh and warn everyone

there that God was about to smote—smite? them. For their terrible behavior which is never very clear or specified. (It WAS a kid's bible). Jonah was called (very dramatically) THE MAN WHO RAN AWAY FROM GOD! And I was so scared to run away from God myself—what if I was asked to warn an entire city about its bad behavior? And then there was the part where he is with the sailors on the boat (the way he escaped from God) and a terrible storm comes up, and the crew decide that he is the problem and toss him overboard. I used to DREAM THAT WAS ME. Trying to defend myself. After that trauma it's a miracle I'm out on a boat at all! After Jonah gets spat out by the whale and finally agrees to warn Ninivah, God decides not to destroy it after all—(weird and unexpected show of mercy!) and Jonah is pissed because God didn't destroy it. I think the takeaway was God was merciful and we are all worthy of forgiveness. I wonder if that is true, Ishmael. The God of Second Chances, my book called him. If only that was the case for all those others who got slaughtered in the Old T. Anton told me that in his class he learned that in Jung(ian)? analysis the belly of the whale is a symbol of death and rebirth. But enough about Jonah.... (The name means dove by the way.)

The Two Amazing Things That Happened Today:

It rained all day, teeming, BIBLICAL rain, so we couldn't do much but match fluke photos all day. I really like the work—I find it very meditative. It also gave me a chance to poke around the house, where I found this amazing old book—Photos that Changed the World—full of these pictures of these important moments in history in the last 100 years. The assassination of Franz Ferdinand (vaguely remember from high school history class) The opening of Tutankhamun's tomb. A little Jewish boy arrested in the Warsaw ghetto. The bombing of Hiroshima. The I Have a Dream speech. First Man on the Moon. There's so much I don't know!! But there was another picture, of a zodiac, just like the one we do our work in, being fired at by a water cannon as the people in the boat are dodging them to supply the oil rig they had occupied. And driving the boat? None other than the man I am working for this summer—none other than Magnus Sorensen!! He's like a real bona fide hero. And that's just ONE of many campaigns he has been a part of. He said he switched to defending whales because they're safer than people. That's if the Japanese whaling ships (pretending to be research vessels) aren't chasing you and trying to kill you.

At the end of the afternoon the sky cleared out and the rain finally let up, and someone proposed a little lookout ride. I said yes, of course. The sky was so beautiful. Anyway... Magnus decided to come along, and when we got a bit offshore, he let me drive the boat. He let ME drive the boat. He stood behind me and showed me how to steer it into the waves so as not to flip it. And I felt like this...electric connection between us. This heat. His breath on my neck. His scratchy face next to mine. It lasted a few seconds. I've never felt anything like that in my life.

Chapter 33

As Roméo pulled into the parking lot of the Ste. Agathe hospital two enormous tom turkeys stepped out in front of his car. He slammed on his brakes and pitched forward violently in his seat. There was an explosion of the turkey population in the Laurentians, most likely due to climate change. They were everywhere and growing bolder and bolder. Marie admired them, of course. They can fly fifty miles an hour. They are smart, playful, and according to Marie, sensitive. They hold funerals for deceased flock members. She also often pointed out to Roméo, when yet another one materialized at the side of the road, how beautiful they were, but he found their blue heads and garish red wattles quite off-putting. He half-expected some Elmer Fudd to appear with an oversized gun to go after them in cartoon pursuit. But they just wandered away across the parking lot, quite unfazed by their brush with death. The lot attendant shook his head and smiled ruefully at Roméo as he waved him through.

The hospital was unusually quiet. Winter was always busier because of the ski and snowmobile accidents and the ravages of flu season. But summer could bring its own share of broken bones from boating collisions to underequipped and ill-prepared neophytes trying all the adventure tourism the region offered. As Roméo made his way to the elevator, he saw only two people in emergency: a young woman nursing what looked like a broken nose, with a man sprawled on the plastic chair beside her scrolling through his phone. Roméo rode the elevator alone down to the basement and took a moment to steel himself for what was coming. Despite being a homicide investigator with years of experience under his belt, he still didn't feel cavalier or casual about an encounter with a dead body. He was startled as the elevator doors opened and there stood Nicole LaFramboise and Gretchen, who seemed just as surprised to see Roméo. He took Gretchen's arm very gently and guided her back into the corridor.

"Please allow me to offer you my deepest condolences."

Her strikingly sculpted features looked even sharper and thinner, and her tanned face was ashen. Those blue eyes had not lost their intensity, though, as they looked directly into Roméo's.

"Thank you."

There was an almost awkward pause, and then Gretchen moved past him to the elevator.

Roméo turned to Nicole.

"You'll take Ms. Handschuh back to her house, and make sure she is all right? I would like to interview her as soon as possible. Later today or tomorrow morning."

Nicole nodded, and without another word exchanged, the two women got into the elevator, turned around, and stared straight ahead of them into the closing doors.

୫

The body was lying on the metal examination table covered in a pale blue sheet. The medical examiner Roméo often worked with was not on duty this time. Instead, a man who seemed too young to be in university, let alone be a doctor, was tapping at a laptop at remarkable speed, his mask pulled down under his chin. He didn't look up when Roméo entered the room, so he cleared his throat and flashed his badge. The man raised one index finger and then continued entering data. Roméo decided to ignore him as well and went to examine the body. He paused for just a moment, then he pulled the sheet back away from the head and torso. It was a shock to see Magnus like this. The man was alive not forty-eight hours earlier. More than alive. Brimming with vitality and carrying the hopes of so many people on his surprisingly narrow shoulders. His gray-blond, thick hair was combed away from his face in long, stringy waves. His hairless chest was that of an older man; muscles that were once carved and full had gone soft and puckered. Like every corpse Roméo had seen, the wrinkles that life and age had lined the face with were gone. All worries, all earthly cares seem to have vanished as well. But to see that face, the color of plain candle wax, devoid of life, was always shocking. No matter what the cop shows say, Roméo thought. Or how they normalize death. Or make murder seem commonplace in quaint little towns. The soul—whatever that was—was gone. The big mystery no one will ever solve. As a young Roman Catholic Roméo was taught that the soul went to hell. Or heaven. Or limbo, until that got eliminated by one of the popes. Or purgatory, the place the boy Roméo was most terrified of. He'd rather burn in hell than be stuck in between the two possibilities forever. He had long since rejected the idea of a binary afterlife. He imagined it as circular, not vertical, more gray, not black and white, the way life really was.

"He is remarkably intact and untouched for a drowning."

Roméo startled to the voice beside him, a gravelly baritone that should have belonged to an older and larger man.

"There was no postmortem wandering because the body wasn't in the water long enough to start decomposing and become buoyant. The travel abrasions we usually associate with drowners are absent. Except for that."

The ME pointed to a deep gash over Magnus's right eye.

"I think he hit his head on a rock, or some sharp object falling into the water. However, there were petechiae that we associate with drowning—caused by pressure on the carotid artery. And in the photos taken at the site there was a foam column at the mouth and nose. So. I am fairly certain death was caused by drowning. But as I mentioned, he wasn't in the water long."

The doctor folded the sheet back completely, exposing Magnus's entire body. Roméo averted his eyes involuntarily from where they would naturally go. He returned his attention to the doctor who was now gently turning Magnus on his side. He pointed to a contusion on the back of his head.

"Could he have slipped and hit his head?" Roméo asked, peering closer at the injury.

The man tilted his own head to one side and frowned.

"He would have had to fall backward, hit his head hard enough for a traumatic injury, then somehow catapult forward and hit his eye, and *then* land in the water somehow. He may have done so. Staggered to his feet and thrown himself into the lake? But it is extremely unlikely."

"So, in your opinion, he was struck by something on the back of the head, then the force of that propelled him into the water, where he did in fact die by drowning?"

"I'm not absolutely committing to anything yet. But yes."

Roméo noticed the man had one green and one brown eye. Then he returned his attention to the wound and touched it gingerly with gloved hands.

"What do you think? A metal object? Wooden?"

The ME went back to his computer and tapped at a few keys.

"Not sharp. Blunt. But the lab work's not ready yet. I pulled a few traces of some material out of the wound. I'll know by tomorrow at the latest."

Roméo whistled.

"Any chance that could be later today?"

"DNA sampling has gone to the lab already. But we *are* in Ste. Agathe. In July. In the biggest heat wave since ever. This is more work than these guys have seen in months. Give them twenty-four hours."

Roméo felt his phone buzz. It was a call from Ti-Coune Cousineau.

"I have to take this."

He stepped out of the room, into the barren corridor by the elevator, and answered the call. The familiar, raspy voice caused by years of smoking and boozing said a curt, "C'est moi."

"Oui. Je sais. Ça va?"

"I have a pretty shitty headache, but no worse than my boozing days. Two broken ribs. That asshole will fucking pay for this, Roméo!"

"We'll be investigating. But, *sacrament,* Jean-Michel. What did you think you were doing? The guy's a cop—"

"Listen. Are you alone? Are you at the station?"

"No. The hospital. Why? Where are you?"

"I'm at Manon's place. Not going to my house. Those fuckers already trashed it, and who knows what they'll do next?"

Roméo could hear at Ti-Coune's end what sounded like a dozen dogs suddenly start barking hysterically.

"*Cristi.* I love those dogs, but…." Ti-Coune obviously closed a door to the noise, then lowered his voice. "Listen." He paused, then continued. "When I was sitting in the hole at the station, I had a lot of time to watch. And, er…observe. And listen."

Roméo wondered where this was going. At least it didn't sound like they'd beaten him up a second time.

"Anyway, I think they stopped noticing that I was even there. And I heard this one cop, not sure of his name…talk about that guy, Magnus? The one half the people around there hate even more than me? And then I heard one of those assholes bragging that one of their guys was going to take care of him. Of the Norwegian."

Roméo thought it was pretty ironic that Ti-Coune, an informant of many years to Roméo, had now turned the tables. He wondered where this was heading.

"And guess who this tough guy is?"

Roméo shook his head. "Tell me."

"I'm sorry to say it, Roméo. I heard them loud and clear. It's Renard. I know he's your old friend. But he's the biggest asshole of them all."

Roméo had another incoming call. Marie.

"Écoute, Jean-Michel. I don't know what you heard, but Robert's got nothing to do with this. I have to go."

Roméo hung up and answered Marie.

"Roméo? Roméo!"

"What? What is it? What's wrong?"

He could hear Marie trying to control herself, but her voice trembled with mounting panic. "My mother has gone missing."

Chapter 34

12:30 PM

Marie pulled up to *Maison Soleil* and took a few moments to hang on to her steering wheel with her head bowed. She had to compose herself. She could not completely lose it right now. Her mother needed her. As she got out of her car she had to stop to take in the scene before her. It looked like the entire Laurentian region Sûreté du Québec police force had arrived. There were half-a-dozen of their SUVs in the parking lot, their many red lights flashing incongruously on such a beautiful, hot summer day. Another twenty or so people from town had already gathered—the volunteer search team, Marie hoped. She recognized several faces in the small crowd and smiled wanly at them. Then she made her way to the front of the residence where the director and what looked like most of the staff waited for her, the women in matching baggy blue pants and floral tunic tops, the men the same except their tops were solid navy. They were all watching her with guarded sympathy. No one wanted this to turn out badly, but if it did, no one wanted to lose their job, or worse, see *Maison Soleil* shut down.

Lucie Lapointe, the director, took Marie's arm and led her into the lobby of the residence, away from the crowd. Marie felt like ripping her arm right off.

"I am so very sorry, Madame Russell. We are always so very careful with our residents. I...I just don't quite know yet what happened, but we will find out and deal with the person responsible—"

"It seems to me that you're the person responsible." Marie knew the woman would pass the buck as quickly as she could.

"Well, yes of course, but I was not here when the incident happened, and couldn't possibly know—"

"Listen, Madame Lapointe. I don't really care right now. I care that my mother is found as soon as possible."

"Of course. I will—"

But Marie had moved away from the woman and started down the wheelchair ramp towards Roméo, who was just getting out of his car. He stopped to confer with one of the SQ officers, then half-jogged to Marie. He took her in his arms and squeezed tightly.

"We'll find her."

He led Marie back to Lucie Lapointe and introduced himself, shaking her hand.

"Tell us what you know."

"We think they...left the premises this morning before ten am—"

Roméo raised a hand to stop her. "They?"

Lucie Lapointe took a breath before she continued.

"We think Mr. Louis Lachance may be with Madame Russell."

"What? Mr. Lachance, *mon homme a tout faire*? Monsieur Lachance, who used to work for me?"

"Yes, we think they're together. They're both…not here. And they have been spending a lot of time together. It's very sweet to see them—"

"Madame Lapointe, when were they last seen?" Roméo interrupted.

Marie could *feel* the woman deciding whether or not to give an honest answer.

"Last night. At supper."

Marie felt like she was going to pass out. "Fuck. Oh, fucking hell, Roméo."

Roméo put his hands on Marie's shoulders and looked her directly in the eye.

"They can't be far. I have a helicopter coming in any minute. We have eight hours of daylight left."

"There was that huge thunderstorm last night. What if they got caught in that? What if she's lost in the woods somewhere, hurt? Oh, I have to sit down."

Marie suddenly went very pale and started to droop. Roméo caught her and half-carried her over to the stairs and sat her down.

"I'm okay. I'm okay. It's just all of it. It's been a bit too much."

Roméo advised Marie to breathe and keep her head between her knees. Out of the corner of his eye he noticed Robert Renard get out of his car. He saw Roméo and headed right for him. He nodded at Marie.

"*Salut.* I heard the news. Looks like the two of them are on an adventure." He winked at Roméo. "My team are just arriving." He gestured over his shoulder at a group of about twenty people, wearing neon orange vests and carrying what looked like staffs. They all seemed to be chatting, excited and serious at the same time. "They had their training just two weeks ago, but they know how to conduct a ground search. I trained them."

Roméo nodded and pulled Renard aside.

"Merci, Robert. You and me, we have to have a talk a little later. When this is done."

Renard looked quizzically at his friend, then turned on his heel. "Ready to go when you are!"

Roméo watched Renard's people get into four long lines, ready to fan out and start the search. Marie's phone suddenly rang. It was Ben.

"Mom? Me and Ruby and Sophie are coming to you. Pénélope got a bunch of friends to come out and help, too. We'll find her. I promise you. Be there in about twenty-five minutes."

Ben hung up and Marie got unsteadily to her feet. She returned to Lucie Lapointe who was busy consulting with another SQ officer.

"Is Monsieur Lachance's family coming? His daughter? Do they know?"

The director of *Maison Soleil* shook her head. "Of course, we have informed Madame Poirier. Dominique. She is unable to come right now. She can't get away. We assured her we would call with news as soon as we know."

Marie felt her heart break a bit for Louis Lachance. She couldn't imagine not dropping everything if a family member was in trouble, but she only raised her eyebrows and said nothing. Maybe there were extenuating circumstances that made the behavior understandable. Roméo returned to Marie to explain what the next steps were, but his phone began to buzz. Nicole.

"Salut. Emily Joly is able to make a statement shortly. The hospital released her and she's at some motel...the...Radisson on the one-seventeen highway. Can you meet me there in one hour?"

Roméo explained to Nicole what was happening.

"*Tabernac*, Marie is having a time of it, *hein*? Do you need me?"

"No. But listen, Nicole. Go talk to Joly without me. Okay? We need that statement asap."

"Sure. I'll take Tremblay with me. Second pair of eyes and ears."

Roméo agreed and was signing off when Nicole interrupted. "Um, Boss, I've got some more news. The word is out. And the media are all over Ste. Agathe. Every news channel, Radio Canada, BBC, CNN, they're all here. All here for Sorensen. Wait until you see it. A three-ring circus."

Just what Roméo needed right now was a media feeding frenzy.

Chapter 35

MONDAY

2 PM

Detective Sargent Nicole LaFramboise was smiling, which was weird, given what was happening all around her. An international eco-celebrity had been murdered on her home turf. Her boss's girlfriend's, no *wife's*, elderly mother had gone missing. But she was smiling because she'd just read a text from Steve Pouliot. *Thank you for your hospitality this weekend.* Hospitality? He'd helped her get Léo home after a meltdown and slept on her sofa. *Could I pick you and Léo up this Saturday for a swim at Lac des Sables and an early supper at Café des Couleurs?* He sent no accompanying dick pic. No request for her to send one of her tits or pussy. The tone was perfect. Matter of fact, not corny, not too pushy. It was an afternoon date and *included her son*. The café he suggested was charming, quirky, and very kid friendly. She wanted to answer him right away, but she would give it a few hours at least. Nicole's track record of dating, since Normand walked out on her and Léo and she'd gotten back in the game, had been awful. One guy had asked to meet her in the Tim Hortons parking lot in St. Jerome, where he said they'd decide where to go out for supper. They ended up staying at Tim Hortons and eating a donut, which she paid for. Nicole had gotten dressed up for a fancy restaurant and felt humiliated and stupid. Another guy, a cop from Joliette, had invited her out to a big party after they'd gone on two pleasant lunch dates. He seemed fun, smart enough, and not entirely self-involved. They'd had a good time, until he started drinking too much and got very competitive at limbo. In the course of the limbo-off between him and another macho fool, her date had lost his shoes. They spent the rest of the evening looking for them, him trailing after her in his stocking feet. When she told him she had to leave and would find her own way home, he started to cry.

Nicole wondered what was wrong with Steve. He was too short, that was clear. He seemed very fastidious, especially about his personal appearance. Maybe he was like that guy she'd dated before Normand, who had to shower immediately before and after sex, and insisted she do the same. Maybe he had a very small penis. They keep saying size doesn't matter, but Nicole knew different. Of course, when Roméo was single her girlfriends were always bugging her to go out with him. They did have their one night together, and she was still so relieved that their relationship, both professional and personal, had survived it.

Nicole pulled into the parking lot of the Radisson Hotel and put the car in park. Time to shift mental gears as well. She had a statement to take that could make or break this case, and she would not screw this up. Just at that moment, DS Rejean Tremblay stuck his face into her window, his mouth and lips pressed up against it in a squishy grimace. Great. He had a clownish side to him that made her uncomfortable. He also had hit on her several times. And he was married. Very married, with three kids.

౸

Emily Joly was sitting in gray chair between the gray bed and a matching gray coffee table, her bare feet pulled up before her, her arms wrapped around her knees. She seemed to be wearing some kind of pajamas or sweatpants and a loose T-shirt that camouflaged her very large chest, but not entirely. Nicole knew that strategy well and had survived high school because of it. Emily had purple circles under her eyes and was very pale, her large brown eyes peering out at Nicole and DS Tremblay with trepidation. Her long brown hair was pulled up into a loose topknot. Even in the disheveled and traumatized state she was in, Nicole could see she was a beauty, the kind that probably had guys falling over themselves for her before she was even a teenager.

After Nicole introduced herself and DS Tremblay, she explained why they were there and asked Emily to tell them exactly what happened on Sunday. Emily recounted in painstaking detail everything she could think of until the moment she found Magnus.

"I'm going to stop you there, Ms. Joly, and just go over a few things again, okay with you?"

Emily eyed Nicole warily. "Okay."

Nicole flipped through her notepad. DS Tremblay was recording it as well of course, but Nicole preferred to keep her own notes.

"You said the entrance gate to the Rasmussen place was open when you arrived, correct?"

Emily hesitated just for a second. "Yes."

"Did you see anyone at the house or around the property at all?"

"No. It was strange. Like it was completely deserted. Unusual for a place that size. No...lawn guy, no gardener, no...I don't know—maid? Caretaker?"

"You are absolutely certain?"

Emily nodded.

"Was there anything or anyone else you noticed? Anything else that struck you as strange, like the deserted house, or anything happen that was odd?"

Emily chewed on a cuticle and thought about Nicole's question for a few long seconds. They her eyes widened and lit up.

"Oh! I'm not sure I did mention this. Just before I turned into the gate to Rasmussen's, a car went racing past me. Way too fast. I had to kind of swerve to get out of his way. He came over the top of a hill, so I couldn't see the car coming—"

"Did you see the car come out of the gate?" DS Tremblay interrupted.

Nicole shot him an irritated glance. "Let her finish, please."

"I would say he came out of nowhere, but it's just because I didn't see him come up over the rise in the road." She turned to DS Tremblay. "I don't know if he came from the Rasmussen place. I have no way to know that. But he was in a crazy hurry, that's for sure." She paused and continued. "Fucking idiot."

Tremblay leaned in. "Did you see the make of the car? The license plate number?"

Emily shook her head.

"Anything that could identify the car or driver?"

"He whipped by me. I looked in my rearview mirror, but there was so much dust I saw nothing. I mean—no. Really, nothing."

DS Tremblay sat back in his chair. Nicole pressed her. "Can you describe anything about the car you saw?"

"It was a car, not a truck or a van. And maybe dark blue. A small car. Not like a mini or anything, but like…a Honda. Or a Toyota?"

Nicole smiled encouragingly. "We can have you work with someone to help re-visualize the car. Maybe even the driver. This could be very important. You'd be surprised what you can remember with a little guidance."

Emily smiled wanly. She removed the elastic from her hair, let it fall in thick waves to her shoulders, then gathered it all and retied it on top of her head. She shifted in her chair.

"Are you comfortable? Would you like to take a little break?"

Emily shook her head. "I'm okay."

Nicole decided to explore something else. "So, before we review your original statement to the police about finding the…victim. I'd like to just verify why you were meeting him there at the Rasmussen place?"

Emily looked out the window before she answered. A family had just pulled up in their van and she watched as first one, then two, then three kids hopped out. The kids each wore a little backpack and looked very excited to be staying at a motel.

"Magnus called me the evening before and asked me to join him at the action for Mont Baleine. He didn't want to fly alone. And he had a stunt—what he calls a mind-bomb—to manage—"

"What was this stunt?"

"Do I have to tell you? They're heavily guarded secrets."

"Do you usually join him on an action? I looked at lots of past footage of *See Change* and their actions. It is often Gretchen, who I believe is his…partner who joins him. Or Paul Pellerin? His old comrade? As head of…," she checked her notes, "social media, would that normally be your role?"

"No. Not normally. But Gretchen wasn't…feeling well and he asked me to come along."

"At the last minute? Sort of?"

"Sort of."

"And you dropped everything and came?"

Emily unclasped her hands from her knees and raised them, palms open. "Of course. He's my boss."

Nicole reached into a plastic file case and pulled out several clear plastic baggies. In each one was a photocopy of each of the three notes Magnus received. The ones he had given to Roméo. She laid them out of the coffee table before Emily.

"Can you take a look at these?"

Emily leaned in and examined each one. Her face remained expressionless.

"What are they?"

"Notes that were recently sent to Magnus Sorensen. Please take a close look. Do these mean anything to you?"

Emily picked up each one and examined it. "No."

"You are absolutely sure?"

"Yes. What are they?"

Nicole sighed. DS Tremblay caught her eye. This was going nowhere. Nicole put the baggies aside and pulled out her tablet. She turned it for Emily to see. It was a photo of the talisman that Roméo had found in the water by the body.

"Do you know what this is?"

Emily peered closer. "Yes! It looks just like the one I have. Where did you get that?"

"Is it yours?"

Emily looked confused. "Um…no. Mine is here, I think."

Nicole watched her carefully. "Can you check?"

Emily unfolded herself from the gray chair and went to retrieve her bag. She looked like she was carrying the weight of the past few days heavily on her small shoulders. She rummaged through it.

"It's here. I know it."

"Who gave it to you?"

"Magnus. Magnus gave it to me. Oh my god, where did I put it?" She started to empty her purse, a large, sack-like, canvas shoulder bag with a whale's tale embroidered across it. The needlework was exquisite. Out tumbled keys. A wallet, hairbrush, a wayward mascara, hair elastics, and a pair of sensible underwear. A notebook. Pens. And finally, the little pink stone in a silver claw. Emily sank into the bed, all energy drained from her body.

"I always have it with me."

"Why? Is it very special?"

Nicole could see Emily preparing an answer. For the first time since the interview had begun, Nicole was sure Emily Joly was sleeping with Magnus Sorensen.

"Where did you get this photo? I don't understand."

"A…what do you call it? Talisman? Or charm? It was found in the water by the body."

"But how is that possible?"

Nicole exchanged glances with DS Tremblay, who seemed to be smirking.

"I suppose yours isn't the only one."

"Maybe not so special," DS Tremblay opined.

Emily suddenly raised her hand to her forehead. "I'm feeling quite dizzy. Can you give me a minute?" She cradled her head in her hands. They were shaking.

"We can stop for now, Ms. Joly. We can take a break."

Emily nodded but said nothing.

Nicole gathered her tablet and file. She and DS Tremblay got to their feet.

"Just one more question for now. Can you think of any reason someone would want to kill Magnus Sorensen?"

Emily answered quickly without looking up. "He's been shot at with guns, water cannons, tasers, pepper spray. You name it. He gets death threats all the time." She slowly got up from the bed and made her way back to the gray chair. "But that doesn't mean someone wants to *kill* him. You know what I mean?"

Nicole and her partner were ready to go. They hovered by the motel room door.

"We'll need to talk to you again."

"Do I have to stay here? Am I free to like, step out? Get a decent meal somewhere? I also have…work to do. *We* have work to do."

"Just stay close. In town. Just for a few days until we complete your statement and get all the assistance we can from you."

"Of course."

Nicole lifted her hand into a wave and stepped across the threshold.

"Oh! Congratulations, by the way."

"Thanks!" Emily's hand moved to her stomach involuntarily.

"When are you due?"

She blushed. A startling change in her pale, exhausted face. "Not for quite a while."

Nicole smiled and turned on her heel. DS Tremblay was right behind her. They clicked the door shut. Had Magnus gotten Emily Joly pregnant and then asked her to terminate it? Had he ended their affair? Had she grabbed something hard and heavy and bashed him on the head? She was small, but she looked strong enough. And why on earth was a little pink rock in a silver claw, exactly like her own, found in the lake?

DS Tremblay waved Nicole off and told her he'd meet her at the precinct. He returned to his car. He had an urgent call to make.

Chapter 36

It used to be that once a storm had passed through, the air would clear and shed its humid heaviness. But since climate change had hit the region, much more violent thunderstorms could happen at any time of day, and one after the other. Last night's storm should have cleared out the skies for a few days, but as Roméo glanced up at the horizon in the west, he could see a darkening anvil cloud building itself. It was so humid it felt like he was drinking the air. There would be another one this evening.

Roméo had just gotten off the phone with his colleague in St. Jerome who had organized a bunch of cops to come and help out with the search. On their day off. Between their group and the many volunteers from the village, it was likely Claire and Louis would be found. But so far, nothing.

One group of searchers were sprawled on the ground, red-faced, sweaty, and holding out their water bottles for refills. A few had removed their neon orange vests to cool off. A few of the men had kept the vests on but stripped their wet shirts off. The other volunteers continued their methodical search, moving in deliberate, slow steps across the area that Robert Renard and his team had divided into a series of grids. So far, nothing had been found. No piece of clothing. No clear tracks. No object that belonged to Claire or Louis. Only pieces of a few ancient takeout coffee cups, two used condoms, and the remains of a decomposed rabbit.

Ben and Ruby were out ahead of him to the west, maybe by half an hour, calling sporadically for their lost grandmother. Sophie, Pénélope, and several friends who had driven up from Montreal to help were in another group fanning out to the east.

Roméo was very touched that Sophie and Pénélope had dropped everything to help out. Marie had had a rocky time sorting out her relationship to her stepdaughter and learning to understand the dynamic between father and daughter. But by sheer force of will, Marie had pulled Sophie into their new family, and after some strong resistance, Sophie had finally surrendered.

Although Roméo had warned her to pace herself, Marie had called out for her mother and Louis so many times, she had no voice left. He walked beside his new wife and took her hand.

"I think you should sit down for a few minutes. Rehydrate. Reset. Okay?"

"What if we don't find them?" Marie croaked back to him.

"We will find them, my love. We will. Look at all these people out here. They're here for one thing only. To find your mother and Louis and get them home safely."

Marie stopped walking and whispered, "Why does this feel like my fault?" But just at that moment the SQ helicopter roared overhead. Roméo heard nothing. They both watched it fly up over the crest of a small mountain, then disappear behind it.

Marie took a long drink from Roméo's water bottle, and lifted her thick, curly hair off her neck.

"I feel like I'm in a perpetual hot flash." She managed a weak smile. Roméo was relieved she was still capable of humor. Marie's initial anger with *Maison Soleil* had turned to rage. Then disbelief. Then panic. He suspected guilt was looming. The truth was, Claire and Louis had been missing for close to twenty-two hours, if in fact they had made their escape the evening before. Maybe they were fine. Maybe they had found shelter. It was not cold, but there had been a storm that had caused local microburst tornadoes to land, wreak havoc, and spin off. Localized flooding had been reported. And two octogenarians in wet clothes, with possibly no food or water and at least one with significant cognitive impairment, were out in it.

Roméo's phone buzzed his shirt pocket. It was the CID guy he'd spoken to at the crime scene. He let go of Marie's hand and turned away to answer it.

"DCI Leduc?"

"Oui."

"You wanted to know about the floatplane?"

"Yes. You got something?"

"There were no prints anywhere. None. No fibers, no trace material, no nothing. If someone was in there, he wore a hazmat suit."

"Okay. Anything else?"

"I don't know much about planes, so I called my buddy Pat Lemieux from the little airfield in Rawdon. He runs that skydiving business, gives airplane tours of the Laurentians, flies rich Americans up to Mont Tremblant in his chopper."

Roméo glanced at Marie who looked about to set off again. Without him.

"Yes. And so?"

"Pat found some very interesting things. *Very* interesting."

Roméo breathed in, trying to keep patient. He had learned over many years of policing that lab technicians needed their moment to shine.

"He inspected the water rudder cable and strut pulleys. Without free movement, directional control on the water is seriously impaired. He thinks someone rigged them so that control would be lost."

Roméo's breath quickened. "Okay."

"He also noted that the floats were sitting low on the water—if Sorensen had pumped them out, which he should have to prepare for his flight, they shouldn't be. They should be high and empty. On further inspection, there were tiny little puncture holes in both floats." The man paused before his final triumphant conclusion. "Someone tampered with your victim's plane."

"Listen. Contact DS LaFramboise and tell her to make sure *no one* goes near the plane. No one. Including Rasmussen. Got it?"

"Yes. I'm on it. Now."

Roméo ended the call. His mind was racing with possibilities. Suddenly, he felt an arm around his shoulder, squeezing him into a hug. It was Joel. Joel loved to hug.

"Hey, man. We heard about Marie's mother. And Louis. We're here to help."

Shelly, his wife, had arrived with several thermoses of

iced tea and a huge Tupperware full of cupcakes and muffins. Several of the volunteers started gravitating towards the food and refreshment. The heat was suffocating, even at six o'clock in the evening.

Shelly made sure Marie got a drink and a bite to eat.

Roméo needed to check in with Nicole. He was very curious to learn what had happened in the interview with Emily Joly. He looked over to where Marie was chatting with Shelly and Joel. Well, *they* were chatting. Marie was nodding her head and gazing somewhere past them, probably hoping her mother would just step out of the thicket of trees, her arms outstretched. They had three hours before darkness. And Roméo had a murderer who by now could be on a plane across an ocean. Roméo felt a heavy hand come down hard on his shoulder. Ti-Coune Cousineau was smiling grimly at him, his missing front tooth and black eye a reminder of the life of the old, unreformed Ti-Coune.

"Hey, I heard about Marie's maman. *Cristi, les vieux, anh*? What were they thinking those two? Off for a little picnic? They just forgot they don't walk so well?"

Roméo didn't respond. He was trying to figure out what to do next.

"Roméo? A minute." Ti-Coune pulled Roméo aside and lowered his voice to a stage whisper.

"Did you look into uh, the people behind the Projet Leviathan?" Ti-Coune glanced around like a conspirator in a bad movie and continued. "I heard Renard has a lot invested in Leviathan. Like his whole life savings. And that he's talked *a lot* of other people into sinking their money in it, too. He's way past his *couilles* in this one. He's up to his eyeballs and over his head. If this fails, he drowns."

Roméo nodded but said nothing. There had been so much ill will and damage already from this project. Vandalism, threats, emotions running dangerously high.

Roméo watched as Marie and some of the other searchers got slowly to their feet and prepared to move out again. Was it possible that one of Renard's people had gotten carried away and killed Sorensen? Was it possible his old friend was involved?

Chapter 37

She was in some kind of nightmare. When she finally left her hotel room to go and get something to eat, the world was just the same. Everything looked normal. The man at the front desk waved at her and wished her a cheery "*bonne soiree!*" Maude Laflamme, the taxi driver who picked her up kept asking her questions about what fun activities she had planned for her holiday in the beautiful Laurentians. When she dropped her off outside a little café in the middle of Val David, people were behaving like nothing had happened. They were strolling through town window shopping. Restaurants lining the *rue principale* were full of eating, drinking, chatting, laughing people. A group of buskers played a popular Beau Dommage song, and a few passersby stopped to join in the chorus. She decided to go directly to the Provigo and pick up something to put in her mouth. But everyone at the store was the same. Choosing which of the many kinds of bread to buy, picking up cucumbers and apples and beer and stuffing it all in oversized shopping carts. Shopping like the world was normal. Safe. It was unbearable. Emily wanted to scream. *What is wrong with you? How can you pretend the world didn't just have its heart ripped out?* But she forced herself to put some food in a basket. Cheese. Carrots. Milk. Bananas. Something green for folic acid—a big plastic container of spinach. When she went to the cash to pay, she felt like waiting in line was impossible. A little girl propped in the shopping cart ahead of her stared at her, swinging her legs and licking the end of a candy bar that had mostly ended up on her face. Emily suddenly felt like she would faint and grabbed onto the magazine stand. She had to sit down. The little girl stopped eating and stared at her. Her mother turned and noticed how pale Emily was, then caught her just as she was starting to sink to the floor.

୫ଠ

Emily woke up a few minutes later to the store manager, the mother of the candy bar girl, and a doctor who happened to be in the store all on their knees before her, peering anxiously at her. Once they determined that she seemed ready to get to her feet, she did. They insisted that she go to the Ste. Agathe hospital to get checked out, but she convinced them she was feeling much better. Just a little attack of low blood sugar. The same taxi driver was called and returned for her and chatted just as amiably all the way back to her hotel. On the way there, she noticed at least a half dozen television camera trucks in the parking lot of the Tim Hortons. Of course they were here. How had they not found her yet? She stroked her belly, willing her baby to be okay. Could she feel what had happened? How had she survived the shock of finding Magnus? Of finding her father? Of losing her father. Did she know, somehow?

Emily made her way slowly back to her room. The hotel

206

was quiet. Everyone was still out, enjoying the long, northern days before the darkness descended in November. When she rummaged in her bag for her key, she discovered that her door wasn't locked. It was the old-fashioned kind that didn't automatically lock behind you. Hadn't she locked it when she left? She couldn't remember. She pushed the door open with a shaky "Is anyone here?" There was no answer, the room as still and silent as when she'd left. After a panicky check of her few bits of jewelry and her computer, she was certain nothing had been taken. Nothing seemed to have been touched or moved. The room looked exactly as she had left it. But it felt penetrated. Invaded. And she could not shake the feeling that someone was watching her. She had sensed it when she left the hotel, and again on her return. Just a presence, a sense of someone at the periphery of her vision. Emily locked herself in and flipped the extra security lock in place. What should she do now? What should she *do*? She perched on the edge of her gray bedspread and flicked on the TV. CNN popped up, and there he was. Not on the main news, but in the breaking news crawl at the bottom of the screen. *Magnus Sorensen, 62, environmental activist and entrepreneur found dead in Quebec. Local authorities calling it a suspicious death.*

Emily looked at the bag of groceries at the foot of the bed. She should put the milk and cheese in her mini fridge. She should force herself to eat something. She should answer the many texts she had from *See Change* staff, from her best friend. From Paul. But she couldn't. Instead, she picked up her phone, punched in the number that hadn't changed in her entire life and called. As soon as she heard her mother's voice, Emily tried to speak, but she couldn't. She finally allowed herself to sob her heart out.

Chapter 38

Louis woke up with a start. He had been dreaming about his wife, Michelle. She kept telling him they'd been married for sixty-four years, and he still didn't use his head. She was the sensible one. She told him he was a dreamer, who took himself for more than he was. *What did you do, Louis?* She kept asking. *What did you do?* She threw up her hands and turned her back on him. *Ca c'est, Louis!*

The sky was a navy blue, that time *entre chien et loup* that would soon deepen to pitch black. There was no moon. How long had he been asleep? Was it the next day? He tried to sit up, but his bad hip sent a shot of electric, shocking pain that stopped him dead. Slowly he started to wake his body up and try again. Finally, he was able to sit up, unclench his stiff fingers, and rub his grimy face awake. Then he remembered. He leaned over her, grimacing in pain, and listened for her breathing. She was still asleep, and still alive. Louis readjusted the sweater that he'd wrapped her in earlier that day and dropped the picnic sheet back over her feet that she had kicked off.

They had spent a terrible night. The storm came out of nowhere—Louis couldn't understand—he had checked the *meteo* channel again and again, and there had been no announcement of bad weather. He had had just had enough time to wake Claire up from her little nap at the beach, but she was disoriented and unable to focus. He had to half-carry her into the trees for shelter. They stood there for—minutes? Hours? Waiting for the thunder and lightning to abate, but as soon as it seemed the storm had passed another wave came, driven by frightening winds that made the rain come at them sideways. He figured they'd wait it out and try to make their way back to *Maison Soleil*, but it was by then so dark he could barely see his own hand, except for flashes of lightning brightening the sky—but not the lightning that you would expect in the summer. No, the jagged bolts like you saw in a movie, where for a few seconds it was like daylight, and then descend into impenetrable blackness again. Louis had no idea how to get back to the residence, as they'd wandered into the forest, and now he was completely turned around. Everything that in the daytime was so innocuous and beautiful seemed so menacing at night, even though Louis had grown up in the woods. He had never been scared, until now. He led Claire along what looked like a path, but the going was very, very slow. Just as Louis thought *that's it, we will have to spend the night exposed to the storm* he tripped over something that caught his foot and almost fell. When he felt for what was at his feet, he discovered it was a piece of plastic tubing. When he yanked it up from the ground and followed along it, he realized with a relief that made him want to cry that they had stumbled upon what was probably the tubing from an old sugar shack. Louis felt his way along until out of the darkness what seemed like an old stone wall appeared. He thanked the God in heaven he didn't pray to much anymore that there was some kind of shelter over them. The remains of the shack, he figured. He settled Claire next to it, and then sat beside her. He could hear the rain pelting against it. They would stay put here, for the night.

The sun rose early of course, and thankfully was already hot. Louis tried to wake Claire up, but she mumbled something, and he left her in the safe oblivion of sleep. As he had thought, they were sheltering in the remains of an abandoned sugar shack. There was a derelict roof over them, and two crumbling stone walls. Twists of blue plastic tubing stuck out of the ground like bizarre sculptures. There were several ancient metal basins in remarkably good shape and very little rust. Louis got carefully to his feet, his bones stiff with the damp and clothes sodden from the storm. He wandered off a way to relieve himself. Then he tried to get some sense of where they were.

He glanced over at Claire who hadn't moved one inch. He wanted to get his bearings, try to figure out where they were. But Louis was too afraid to leave Claire alone. What if she woke up and wandered off? They might never find her. He painfully sat back down beside her and took her hand. It was cold and brittle, despite the heat. He lifted it to his lips and breathed on it. Then he kissed it. Surely someone would find them today. Louis decided to sit quietly and focus on mapping his memories to get a sense of where they were. If this was the old Lafontaine sugar shack, then they couldn't be too far from the 6th range road. He looked at the stone walls on either side of him and remembered the delight of drinking the sap straight from the bucket, the maple water that nature had created with such perfection. His grandmaman always said it was the healthiest thing they could drink and kept bottles and bottles of it. She was way ahead of her time because now they sold it in some fancy stores for a fortune. He smiled as he thought of her, long dead now, at the old wood stove where she baked the most amazing *feves au lard*, rocking back and forth as she cooked. She also rocked when she had to speak to people and would sway impressively when the local curé stopped to speak to her after mass. Louis adored his *grandmaman* because she understood him in a way his own mother and father did not. Louis lifted his nose to the air and closed his eyes. Oh, but the best was the smell of boiling sap as it turned slowly, slowly into syrup. Boiling all day, for days on end. And the taste! He knew he could go to any five-star restaurant in the world and never taste a dessert as sweetly divine as that new maple syrup. Especially when it was poured onto snow piping hot.

Louis opened his eyes as he felt Claire stirring. She was mumbling something again, but still her eyes would not open. He touched her cheek. The day was already steaming hot, but Claire felt cold to the touch. He had taken off his own shirt and extra sweater and tried to shelter her. He put the picnic sheet as well, but they had gotten soaked from the storm and the temperature had dropped overnight. She had never really woken up. What had he *done*? Louis leaned back and tried to recall his grandmaman's voice. *Oh, mon beau Louis. Mon p'tit choux. Toi, t'es le plus bon p'tit gars.* Louis started humming to himself, trying to stay calm. They could not spend another night here. She wouldn't make it. Suddenly, he heard his father calling for him. *"Louis? Louis? Allo? Vous-êtes la!?"* He shook himself out of the memory. He had to stay sharp. He had to stay awake. The voice was closer. More than one. And it wasn't his father at all.

Chapter 39

AUGUST 5

Dear Ishmael,

I should have been asleep two hours ago, but I am so excited I just can't turn off my mind. The news is National Geographic magazine has been with us here at base camp for the last three days, waiting for the crappy weather to clear and the winds to drop so we can go out and shoot a feature on Magnus and the work he's been doing here for the last eight years. I can tell Magnus is really excited—I mean, he's normally a pretty cool guy—I think Norwegians are like that—but this is a game changer for his brand-new baby, See Change—his new organization. The cover of National Geographic? That should launch See Change into the stratosphere. And a huge article on him? Well, the rest of the team will be in it, too, but of course, he's the star—plus the whales we've been identifying and learning about all summer. What A THRILL it is to think we will be in a magazine—the one I've read since I was a little girl! (Well, I probably won't be IN it, but still…. I'm just a lowly intern so I don't rate an actual interview.) But maybe I'll make it into one the pictures! A picture of me! Magnus has been so careful and generous to make sure we are all introduced to the National Geographic crew. They've been super nice and interested. One guy kept following me around, telling me how photogenic I am, and kept asking me if I ever thought of being a model. He said he could introduce me to some people in New York. Anton would be so mad because the guy was really flirty, but also because he says I am so naïve and gullible all the time. I do take people at face value—but I'm not stupid. I know it was a come on.

National Geo are going to follow us for the entire day—a day in the life kind of thing and see what it is we do. Hopefully our beautiful whales will cooperate and put on a good show! We also got a message from one of the whale watch boats this evening that two RIGHT WHALES were spotted in the area yesterday. I've never seen a Right whale yet—we see more humpbacks and finbacks around her, but I am so excited. There are only 400 North Atlantic Right whales left. FOUR HUNDRED. My ancestors hunted them to near extinction because they were the "right" whales to hunt—that's how they got their name. Because they were heavy and slow-moving—made it so much easier to kill them and harvest all that blubber. Let them be there tomorrow so I can see these beautiful animals before they're gone. That is my prayer tonight. OMG it's already midnight! What I am I doing up still writing to you, Ishmael? I need to sleep because TODAY IS THE DAY!

Chapter 40

Roméo woke up completely foggy and disoriented. He had slept on and off in a small plastic chair all night, and his neck was so stiff he couldn't move his head at all for several seconds. It also took him a few more moments before his brain processed where he was and what he was doing there. His mouth tasted like stale coffee and ashtray, even though he hadn't smoked in almost three years. He unfolded his long body from the chair, let his arms and legs stretch out their stiffness, and very quietly pushed open the door to Claire's room. She was sleeping peacefully, an IV drip rehydrating her, a heart and blood pressure monitor flashing green, and her daughter curled up like a child in a chair beside her, her head tucked into her right shoulder, her hands crossed over her heart, and her mouth slightly open. He was relieved to see Marie had finally fallen into sleep. She had been beside her mother every minute since they were found and was so terrified Claire was going to die, she had been up most of the night watching her anxiously. Claire's vital signs were fine, and she had a few minor scratches and bruises, but she had never really fully woken up. Roméo wondered if she had chosen to withdraw into a dream world where she wouldn't have to face anyone, or if she really was in some kind of semi-comatose state. The doctor couldn't give them any straight answers. She kept saying it was a wait and see situation. Roméo's thoughts returned to the night before. When they had arrived with Claire, frantic with worry, the hospital had been eerily quiet, until a young tourist couple were brought in by ambulance. They had been canoeing on Lac des Sables when a motorboat full of drinking partyers smashed right into them. The impact had broken the canoe in half, and the man and woman were catapulted into the water. She had a broken pelvis and ruptured spleen. He had traumatic head injuries. Roméo hoped that those kids in the motorboat paid big for this one.

Roméo leaned down and kissed the top of Marie's head. She smelled of sweat and hospital disinfectant. He didn't mean to wake her, but she began to stir, opened her eyes and smiled up at him weakly.

"Thank you."

Roméo squatted next to her and held her hands. "For what?"

Marie took one of Roméo's hands and kissed it. "For finding my mother."

"What did I do? Renard's team found them."

"All those people came to help for you, my love. Because they all respect you. But please thank Robert for me. And that boy who discovered they were gone? Olivier, I think? He's a hero."

"I will."

"Were you here all night?"

Roméo nodded.

"The dogs! Who's with them?"

"Ben and Ruby stayed at the house last night. Don't worry. The dogs are fine." Roméo hesitated. "Écoute, Marie. I have to go now. I need to go to work. And, uh, I have to deal with the media at some point, I think."

Marie looked confused, like she had no idea what Roméo was talking about. Then she remembered.

"Of course." She scraped her chair closer to Claire who hadn't moved so much as an inch since she was brought in. "You'll come back later?"

Roméo kissed her again, this time on the cheek, and left the room. He would have liked to check on Louis Lachance, but he really needed to get to the station. He had heard that Louis was doing okay, that he was alert and already asking to leave the hospital. His daughter Dominique was apparently on her way.

The second Roméo stepped outside into the parking lot he called Nicole. He knew she'd be up this early. She called it Léo Time—two hours ahead of the rest of the world.

"Hi. It's me."

"Good morning, boss! I heard the great news. Wow. Is she okay, Marie's mom?"

"We're still waiting. She was in pretty rough shape, not coherent, a touch of hypothermia."

"In this heat? I didn't think that was possible."

"Louis did his best to protect her, but she's eighty-six years old and she got soaked to the skin in that storm."

"Unbelievable. Where were they going? Making the great escape? Like that movie?"

Roméo yawned. "We don't know what they were up to yet. It will be a story for the grandkids, and great-grandkids."

"You must be exhausted."

"I just want to get caught up. I know you sent your notes from the Emily Joly interview, but I haven't had a chance to read them yet or listen to the interview. Can you give me a quick rundown, please?"

Roméo saluted the parking lot attendant and got into his car. There were no marauding turkeys here today. Nicole went over her notes, giving Roméo the details about Emily's personal history that she had dug up on social media and her job at *See Change*.

"So, nothing too weird or surprising. Yet. But the stone in the claw thing found in the water? The talisman? I showed it to her, and there was no reaction. Except…she has one *exactly the same*. She carries it on her, in her purse. She showed it to me."

"So, the one in the lake is not hers, obviously."

"Nope. Maybe it belonged to Magnus, and he dropped it in the water. Or whoever attacked him dropped it."

"Or threw it."

"I had the stone identified. It is—or it looks like Thulite. I'm not sure how to pronounce that—it is the national stone of Norway." Roméo could hear Nicole checking her notes. "It's from the…oh, hang on now this is not an easy one to say. Bl…åfjella-Skjæ…kerfjella National Park, which is the largest reserve in Norway. It's famous for its marbled pink color, and it's named for *Thule*—the mythical northernmost region of the world—as believed by the ancient voyagers. And…it is supposed to stimulate the life force, whatever the hell that means. Hey, Thule is the name of those roof racks, right? For skis? Anyway. So, there's a link to Sorensen."

Roméo's mind was racing. Something was nagging at

him, just at the edges of his memory. Nicole continued.

"Oh, a few fun facts about Norway. They still hunt whales and eat them! Did you know that?"

Before Roméo could answer, she went on.

"And, they still hunt the four hundred wolves left in Norway, so I guess Sorensen didn't stop that either. But *maudit*, boss, it looks beautiful that country. A bit like here, except with the ocean everywhere. And really good-looking men."

Nicole tried to swallow those words. "Not that the men here are ugly, but…I mean…."

Roméo smiled. "What's her state of mind? They released her from the hospital. Is she okay?"

"I think she's still in shock. It's not every day you find a dead body. Of your boss, you know what I mean?"

"Did she seem frightened? Did she have any idea who might have done this?"

"She seemed a bit scared, maybe? Or nervous. He may be more than just her boss."

"Oh?"

"Emily Joly is pregnant. I'd say maybe four, maybe five months? And if I had to call it, Magnus Sorensen is the father."

"What?"

"Oui, Monsieur."

"Did you ask her if he was?"

"No. She's not ready to say it yet."

Roméo took a few seconds to process that information. Was Magnus going to be a father? Had he gotten this young woman—an employee—pregnant and asked her to terminate it? He couldn't imagine Magnus caught like that. It couldn't be good for *See Change*. Or his partner. Gretchen.

"Are you sure, Nicole?"

"No. It's a hunch. But a pretty solid one."

Roméo turned in the driveway to Marie's house. *His* house, too. He kept forgetting that.

"Okay. We need to talk to her again."

"I'll get on it."

"And we need to interview Gretchen Handschuh as soon as possible. I'm going to go clean up, and then I'll meet you at the station. Can you go pick her up? Nine o'clock. Sharp."

"Yes, boss. Oh. I would try to go in from the back door. The media are just camped out there. Wait till you see it. They are *really* hungry for this story. And we've given them almost nothing. They might want a little piece of you."

Nicole hung up and immediately made the call to arrange for Gretchen to be picked up for an interview. Then her phone buzzed again. It was Steve Pouliot. She glanced over at Léo, who was on the sofa watching Thomas the Tank Engine for the thousandth time. He was sucking on his thumb and staring at the screen in a stupor. She decided to take the call.

"Hi. You never answered my text."

"I'm sorry! It's been crazy here—"

"I can imagine. We're reading all about it here. How are you guys holding up?"

"*Je suis complètement dans le jus*, Steve. And Roméo's mother-in-law went missing, but she's back. Some honeymoon he's having."

"Listen. If it's too crazy for you right now we can do it another time. I just got a new case yesterday morning. They found another woman, well, girl really. At a construction site. Looks like an overdose, but we're checking."

After the homicide case in Montreal that brought Roméo

and Steve together, Steve was named as one of the leaders of a Montreal police team to liaise with the Indigenous community and investigate violent crime in that population. It was seen as a demotion at the time, but Steve loved the work. He hated how thick the police bureaucracy was though, and how slow politicians were to make meaningful reforms. Nicole really wanted to see Steve again, which was a surprise. But Nicole knew she'd be in no state to go on a date that Saturday.

"Could we, um…decide to do this a bit later? When you're, you know, less busy and we've got this case more in hand?"

There was a brief pause at the end of the line, then Steve answered, "Absolutely. I look forward to it." Then he hung up. Nicole had hoped he might be a bit less decisive. She'd hoped there'd be a few awkward, nervous pauses, then a promise to secure another date and time. She had no time to dwell on it, though, because it was 6:57 and she needed to get Léo to daycare.

After a frantic search for a missing shoe and an accident involving an epic setback in potty training, Nicole finally clipped Léo into his car seat and started the car. Her phone buzzed again. This time it was Emily Joly.

"Madame Joly? Hello?"

"Hi. Is this…Detective Sergeant Nicole LaFramboise?"

"Yes, Emily. It's me."

"I'm…I think someone's following me."

"What? Are you sure?"

"No. God, this sounds like one of those movies, but I can feel it. Him. Her. Them."

Léo started kicking the back of Nicole's seat and whimpered, "My stomach hurts, Maman."

"Sorry. Am I interrupting you?"

"Emily, there is a lot of media and press here to, you know. Is it one of them, maybe? Maybe they think they've got a story with you?"

"Look, I don't know. But I feel this presence. Like, all the time. And I came back to my room and my door was unlocked—"

"Did anyone take anything? Disturb anything?"

"No. Not that I could tell. But…."

Nicole waited. "But?"

"I think this could, I think maybe someone inside our organization…did this."

Nicole waited.

"A few days ago, Paul Pellerin came to see me at my hotel and…he's Magnus's right-hand man, and *best* friend."

"Yes?"

"He basically…threatened me. Well, it wasn't a *threat* exactly. Like a warning."

"A warning? Against what?"

"I can't—I don't want to talk about this on the phone."

Nicole was minutes away from the daycare. She could be at the Radisson in twenty minutes.

"We'll send an officer to your hotel right now. I'll be there as soon as I can."

Just at that moment, Léo threw up his breakfast and most of last night's supper all over himself and the backseat of Nicole's car.

Chapter 41

You would think after all these years Roméo would have gotten used to talking to the media. God knows he'd done enough of it. The head of the Sûreté du Québec loved putting Roméo out there in front of the cameras, especially when the case was controversial or hopeless or the police had behaved badly. Roméo was good-looking in a non-threatening way, had a strong baritone voice that suggested confidence without arrogance, and a gravitas that people appreciated. Roméo knew a free and critical press was essential to a functioning democracy. He just really disliked most of them. Intensely. But given the relentless assault on the free press going on in the world, and most alarmingly, in the United States over the past three years, Roméo had tried to control his distaste. But in the face of the phalanx of trucks, vans, cameras and mics that greeted him at the back entrance to the precinct he felt his repugnance return. These people fed off tragedy. They sold it for their viewers to consume in bite-sized, simplified bits and then moved on to the next calamity. They feasted on celebrity disaster, so this qualified. As soon as they spotted Roméo they descended on him, like pigeons on a pile of breadcrumbs, he thought. He was spending too much time listening to Marie's bird stories.

"DCI Leduc!! Who killed Magnus Sorensen?"

"Your wife, Marie Russell, is an old girlfriend of his. What does she know?"

"Is Gretchen Handschuh a person of interest? Have you made any arrests?"

"What about Sorensen's opposition to the Project Leviathan?! What was the big stunt he'd planned?"

"DCI Leduc! Over here! Was this personal or political?"

Roméo raised a hand and swept past them with a grunted "No comment."

He knew though, that he would have to go out there and face them at some point. Some point soon.

To Roméo's surprise, Robert Renard was in the precinct office, manspreading himself across a junior officer's desk, swallowing the dregs of a cup of coffee. She had moved her papers and files over to one corner and was trying to work while Robert regaled everyone with the story of the morning—the rescue of Claire and Louis in the middle of the storm of the summer, three kilometers from *Maison Soleil*. They were all trying to do their work, but Renard was a popular guy and most of them recognized that he really missed being a cop. He was also quite lonely, Roméo suspected.

"Bonjour, Robert! What're you doing here?"

The whole room went silent.

"Just having a visit."

Roméo glanced around at the office. Most of them had gone back to their screens. Roméo tipped his head to the adjoining room, the kitchenette.

"Can I talk to you?"

Roméo would have preferred his office, but that was in St. Jerome. Here, in Ste. Agathe he just used the empty desk of an officer on maternity leave.

Renard hopped off the desk and followed him. Roméo offered him another coffee but passed on one himself. Marie had bought him an espresso machine a few months earlier, and he was now too spoiled by good coffee to drink the mud that was prepared every morning at the precinct. Robert looked at him expectantly.

"*Quoi de bon?*"

"I want to thank you for your help with the search yesterday. Marie sends you her deepest thanks as well, Robert. I mean it."

Robert looked away, embarrassed by the show of gratitude.

"It was nothing. *Pis? Comment vont Louis et sa blonde?*"

Roméo smiled at Claire being referred to as Louis's "blonde" or girlfriend. But maybe that's exactly what she was. And he, her boyfriend. In Quebec, her "chum."

"Louis is fine. Probably going home from the hospital today. Claire is in rougher shape. We're waiting to see what happens."

Robert nodded, frowning. He held his eyes level with Roméo's, trying to read his face. They had worked together for years on a number of very challenging cases. They had each talked each other down off the ledge several times. Through both their divorces, as well.

"Okay. *Arrête de niaiser avec la puck.* What do you want to say?"

"Where were you on Sunday between nine am and

noon?"

"C't un joke, ca?"

"No, Robert. A car like yours was seen leaving from where they found Sorensen."

"*Anh*?? Like mine? You mean a blue car?"

"The color and model of your car. Where were you on Sunday between nine am and noon?"

"Are you crazy?"

"I hear you're deep in this Leviathan shit, Robert. And if I learn that somehow, you're involved in any of this business with Sorensen...*estie* Robert, you'll be answering to me."

Roméo could sense the entire station straining with every fiber of their bodies to listen to the conversation.

"I was home alone from nine am to about ten. Then I went to Costco for some toilet paper. Then I drove by the Leviathan site to see how that was going. Just to check that there'd be no trouble—with MY people. Then I left with Yvan...*DS Yvan Tremblay*, by the way. Maybe around eleven-thirty? We went back to his place, and I helped him put in his new dock."

"Until what time?"

"Until about three or three-thirty."

"And DS Tremblay will corroborate this?"

"*Oui.* And fuck you, DCI Leduc."

Robert Renard pushed past Roméo and out the kitchenette door, slamming it so hard behind him that it sprung open again. Roméo watched as he exited the building, got in his car, and roared off. That went well. He returned to the main area, where each cop had a little cubby and desk. On the central wall was the evidence board, with a photo of Magnus Sorensen at the center of the wheel spokes, so to speak. Roméo wondered who else would be added to the board in the next few days.

He dreaded that it might be his old friend. He looked around the office.

"Where's Nicole?"

There was a pause. Then the uniform who gave up her desk to Renard's butt answered, "Léo. He's sick." She didn't add "again," but she wanted to.

Roméo nodded. Nicole was a very good cop and would probably be a great one. But she had been a single parent since Léo was eight months old, and it took its toll. The daycare wouldn't take sick kids, and her parents lived in Joliette, seventy kilometers away. Roméo wondered how she'd manage that morning. They all thought he put up with too much from Nicole because of their close relationship. Even the women did. Maybe it was true.

But Roméo didn't believe someone should be punished for having a baby.

He looked over at the evidence wall again. Would he have to add Renard? Batmanian? The others on Leviathan? He needed to assign someone to dig up everything on that project. Where was the money coming from? What politicians supported it? Who were its silent investors? He would normally put DS Tremblay on it—he was one of the Laurentian SQ's best researchers. Or was he involved, too?

Chapter 42

She lay flat on her back, her arms and legs spread eagled. Her eyes were closed, her nose and lips exposed to the air, the rest of her submerged. She wished she could stay like that forever, the soft saltwater embracing her, holding her, all sounds of the world muted. It almost felt like home. *Home* home. In Hout Bay. Where she swam every single day of her life, even in winter. She was the only one of her gang of friends who would do that. *Kom binne, Gretchen*, she could hear her mother calling to her. *Genoeg! Kom binne.*

She slowly brought herself back to the surface and a few short breaststrokes brought to the edge of the pool. She should probably start to get ready, as they were picking her up at 8:40. She patted herself gingerly with a towel—her legs were covered in mosquito bites from sitting outside the night before. They were inflamed and terribly itchy. She had hoped the salt water in the pool would help, but if anything, they were worse. What a crazy country this is, she thought. Freezing cold all winter, and then a very hot and humid summer comes—with swarms of mosquitoes the size of cockroaches. She and

Magnus had talked about going back to South Africa. Back to the Cape Peninsula where'd they met. Gretchen was living in False Bay, where she worked for a research organization that studied great white sharks—but she also worked with cage-diving operators, as the shark industry brought in huge tourist dollars—right up there with the famous vineyards, game preserves and Table Mountain. She had recently heard that the great white shark population had almost disappeared from those waters. It was an unthinkable tragedy. Gretchen remembered the very moment she first spied Magnus. He was living in Hermanus, a lovely little town that looked out on the Southern Ocean and further beyond to Antarctica. Gretchen smiled at the memory. In those days, you could stand on the boardwalk in Hermanus and watch hundreds of whales from shore. There was even a town "whale" crier who would announce the sightings for that day. It was a touristy gimmick, but it got visitors excited about whales, and that's what mattered. Magnus was part of a research grant to study Southern Right whales for the season.

He was sitting at the bar of a very popular barbecue spot, chatting up the very pretty bartender. Gretchen sat on the stool next to him, and soon enough he started telling her all about his whales.

"And what do you do?" he had asked her. He was so gorgeous she could barely get her answer out.

"I study great whites and climb into a shark cage once a day. Guess what their favorite food is?"

"Stupid rich tourists?"

"Second favorite. Their absolute number one preferred meal is whale. A lovely high blubber content, energy-rich meal is what they're after." She remembered Magnus's laugh.

An unexpected goofy guffaw. And that was it. They slept together two days later, and then for the next thirty years.

Gretchen wrapped a towel under her armpits and padded back to the house. She stepped through the sliding patio doors and immediately sensed something was different. She hastened over to the bedroom and checked for her private papers and laptop. Everything was there. But the laptop, which she always left centered on the table, always closed, was open and angled differently. She ran to the front door of the house. It was unlocked. Gretchen never left the door unlocked. Never. Years of global travel had taught her the hard lesson; if a door had a lock, use it. She stood in the center of the living room, glancing around her, not sure what to do. Then she ran to the kitchen, pulled the biggest knife from the wooden block on the counter and began to check the house, following the point of the knife from room to room. Nothing. There was no one. Now. But she had been in the pool, twenty feet from the house, and not seen or heard anything. Gretchen sat in the center of the sofa, in the center of the living room. What should she do *now*? She tried to control her breathing. She realized she was hyperventilating and feeling very light-headed. The knife shook violently in her hand. And then the doorbell rang. With her heart in her throat Gretchen went to the door and threw it open. A diminutive woman stood there. The detective. Nicole. Gretchen let the knife fall to her side.

"I'm a bit early. Sorry. Is everything all right?" Nicole inquired, checking the knife in the woman's hand. Gretchen stepped back.

"I thought…there was someone in the house. My computer was moved. The door…it was left open."

Nicole thought of Emily Joly and her suspicions of an

intruder. What was going on here? Gretchen turned away from the door, returned to the kitchen and slid the knife back in its slot.

"I need to get dressed. Obviously."

"Would you like me to have a look around?"

Gretchen hesitated for just a moment. "Yes, please. I would appreciate that."

Then she removed the soggy towel, draped it over the back of a chair and disappeared into the bedroom. The woman was magnificent, Nicole thought. Even though she was sixty-one years old, (Nicole had checked) she looked like those Wonder Women you see in magazines. Like it takes no effort to look like that. The luck of the gene pool. No cellulite anywhere. No rubbing, jiggly thighs or saddle bags or floppy overhang belly, like Nicole had from her Caesarian. All she noticed was a little puckering on her thin but muscular arms, and of course the giveaway—her hands. They were the hands of a capable woman, but a capable woman who was definitely in her sixties. Nicole grabbed a pair of gloves from her pocket and walked in and out of each of the rooms. She would send someone here to dust for some prints. Was someone after Gretchen Handschuh? Was she somehow the next on the list? The house had that staged feel of a rental, the only real lived life in it suggested by Gretchen's clothes draped across the sofa, and a pile of used tissues on the floor beside it. There were a few medications in the bathroom—for hyperthyroidism, for high cholesterol, and a little plastic vial of Ativan. Nicole called out to Gretchen in the bedroom. "I'm just going to look around outside." Gretchen didn't answer. Nicole checked the front door for any sign of force. Nothing. She walked around and looked at the ground floor windows, then she checked the patio doors. Nothing. No footprints, no broken shrubbery, no evidence at all that someone had entered the house in any unusual way. Did the intruder have a key? Or was there an actual intruder? Nicole leaned against her car and decided to use the few minutes she had while waiting for Gretchen to make a call. It rang four times before a slightly out of breath woman answered.

"Hi! How is he?"

"Oh, Nicole! He's um…fine. Very low-grade fever, but no puking. He's actually curled up on the sofa with Kutya. Louis Lachance's old dog? They seem to really like each other."

"That's great. What a relief! Thanks so much."

Nicole ended the call. She felt fortunate to have Manon Latendresse so nearby, who sometimes took in kids as well as dogs. When she had dropped Léo off at Manon's that morning, Ti-Coune Cousineau had answered the door, holding a trembling chihuahua in his arms. Nicole had marveled at what a weird, unpredictable world it was when she was leaving her kid in the care of the girlfriend of a known felon who'd just attacked a cop.

∞

Roméo and Nicole sat at a narrow plastic table across from Gretchen Handschuh in what was referred to as the interview room. It was really just an extra office with a door that locked. Roméo had considered bringing Gretchen down to the central precinct in St. Jerome for questioning, but that would just attract more unwanted attention from the jackals outside, and no one needed that. Nicole moved the box of tissues to the side of the table and started the recording.

ANN LAMBERT

"First of all, Ms. Handschuh—"

"Gretchen. Please."

"Gretchen. I would like to offer you again my deepest condolences on the loss of your...Magnus."

Gretchen nodded and again thanked Roméo for his sympathies. He looked briefly through his notes, and then asked her directly. "Who do you think would want to kill Magnus Sorensen?"

Gretchen looked at Roméo evenly. "Who wouldn't?"

"Can you elaborate on that, please?"

Gretchen nodded. "Of course." Gretchen lifted the glass of water to her mouth with trembling hands, the only indication of how devastated she was.

"Magnus is revered by many, many people around the world. He is an icon, the living symbol of the fight against global warming and *for* climate justice. He has led campaigns all over the world. And all over the world are people who support him and *See Change*, some of whom would have died in his place." Gretchen paused. She was clearly trying to control a wave of emotions threatening to overwhelm her. She swallowed hard, twice.

"There are also some people, not many, but they are out there...who hate him. Those on the right think he is a self-righteous, self-aggrandizing eco-terrorist, even though he has never advocated any kind of violent resistance. And on the left? Magnus is not radical enough. He has a platform that could change the world, but he is a sellout. Some think that his work—and the fortune he makes—as a celebrity speaker and motivational leader has pulled him further and further away from his roots as an animal rights and environmental activist. They think he sold his soul, Detective Inspector Leduc."

"Enough to kill him for it?"

"Maybe."

"Are there any of these people you could identify?"

"Yes, I suppose. I could send you a list of some people we might identify as 'enemies'—although that is a strong word. Most are former colleagues with whom Magnus fell out."

Gretchen took another sip of water. Her hand was steady.

Roméo leaned forward in his chair and opened his file.

"I'd like to move on to Sunday morning, the day of the… incident."

Gretchen glanced at Nicole and gave her a feeble smile. "Okay."

"As you may or may not know, I drove Magnus to Mikael Rasmussen's place that morning, as Magnus had stayed over at, um…our house after the wedding that night."

Gretchen said nothing.

"On the way there, he told me he had received these notes." Roméo put the three notes Magnus had given him before Gretchen. "Please look at them very carefully. Do they mean anything to you? Do you know who sent them?"

Gretchen picked up and examined each baggie with the note in it in turn. She shook her head.

"No. Nothing. Magnus has received many death threats, but mostly by email or text. These are quite…cryptic, aren't they?"

"These notes were left on or very near him. At the wedding. In his shirt pocket. By someone who got very close. And someone no one would notice, presumably."

Gretchen looked them over again. "I'm sorry. They don't ring any kind of bell."

It was so brief, so fleeting Roméo might have missed it

were he not on complete, acute alert. Did he see just a flicker of recognition? Of memory?

"We have his computer, of course. But it would be very helpful if you could flag some of those threats for us—the more egregious and recent?"

Gretchen nodded. "I could, yes."

"Or perhaps one of the staff could help you?" Nicole pretended to look at her notes. "Ms. Joly, maybe? She is head of social media, isn't she? And of course, she found um… Magnus."

Gretchen took a third sip of water. The room was so quiet they all heard the sound of her swallowing it.

"It has come to our attention that you were supposed to be on that action with Magnus that morning."

"Yes, I was."

"Magnus had a big stunt planned, and you were supposed to be a part of it. Why didn't you go?"

"I assume you are looking into the people who saw Magnus's presence as a real threat to that project? He draws the international media's attention and could have potentially blown up the whole development project."

"Yes, we are aware of that. Why didn't you go?"

"I got a call the night before that my best friend back in Boston—her daughter went into labor, and I promised to be there. She's my goddaughter."

Nicole wrote down the woman's name and contacts. Gretchen watched her.

Roméo smiled at her reassuringly. "Just a few more questions, if you don't mind."

"Ask all the questions you need to. I will do anything to find who did this. We all will. Everyone at *See Change*. All his friends." Gretchen's voice broke. Roméo waited while she composed herself.

"Where were you between nine am and one pm on Sunday?"

"At the rental house, where Detective LaFramboise picked me up. Where Magnus and I were staying."

"The entire time?"

"Yes."

"Was anyone there with you?"

"No."

"Can anyone confirm you were there all morning?"

"No."

"What were you doing all morning?"

"I was packing. My flight to Boston was at four pm, so as I think you know I was on my way to the airport on the shuttle when…when Paul called."

"Paul Pellerin. Magnus's best friend and—"

"*Oldest* friend. And closest colleague."

"If you were in a hurry to get back to Boston, why didn't you catch an earlier flight?"

"I wanted a direct flight. Even after all these years and too many flights to count, I don't really like flying. So, no stops. I could leave at eight thirty-five am or four pm. I chose the latter. My goddaughter had just gone into labor, so I had time."

Nicole took notes by hand. Roméo listened.

"Is there anything else you can tell us, Ms.…Gretchen?"

Gretchen suddenly looked like she was about to burst into tears. But she swallowed hard again.

"His…Magnus. It's a terrible, irreplaceable loss to the world. You have no idea what this means."

"And to you?"

She didn't answer the question directly.

"My life has been with, by, and...*of* Magnus for thirty years."

"And his with a few other women over those years, we understand."

Gretchen muttered, *"Nie belangrik."*

Nicole leaned forward. "I'm sorry. I didn't understand that."

"It's not important."

"How did that make you feel, Gretchen?" Nicole asked. "Magnus's other women? Girls, really."

There was a long pause. Then, she finally responded.

"How do you think? Do you think we were...*normal* people? Do you think that I got *jealous* of some *girl* and plotted revenge? Is that what you think?"

"Did Emily Joly have a relationship with Magnus Sorensen?"

"I don't know. Did she? If she did, she wasn't the first, as you so kindly pointed out."

"But she is the last."

"Touché, Detective."

Roméo's phone buzzed. He checked the caller, and then apologized for the interruption.

"Gretchen, I think that's all we need from you for today. I am sorry we had to put you through this, but everyone must be questioned."

Nicole stood up and gestured to Gretchen that she could as well.

"There was an intruder in my house. Are your people looking into that?"

"Yes. Of course. We will put an officer on the property there if you would like that."

"I would. What if whoever…did this intends the same for me?"

Nicole nodded. "We'll have an officer drive you home and stay with you."

Gretchen scraped back her chair, which made an awful noise on the floor. She extended her hand first to Nicole and then to Roméo. "Thank you."

"Oh, hang on, Gretchen. Just one more thing."

Roméo went back to the file case and pulled out the baggie with the pink stone in the silver claw.

"Is this yours?"

Gretchen looked at the object lying flat in Roméo hand. "No."

"Have you ever seen this before?"

Gretchen peered closer. "No."

Roméo closed his hand over it and returned it to the table.

"I am really very sorry for your loss, and that we had to do this. We have to interview every person who could shed some light on this case. I hope you understand."

But Gretchen had already turned away and was heading out the door.

Chapter 43

Even though the ceremony was supposed to begin at 4 o'clock, they started to gather long before that. Some rode their bikes from as far away as Montreal, while others just had to pedal a few kilometers down a country road. Some arrived by car, families pouring out of minivans, some with their pet dogs in tow. Some hiked to the summit of Mont Baleine, to take in the magnitude of the mountains unfolding in green-blue waves before them, and to watch the crowd below growing next to the sparkling diamond of a lake, where just two days earlier they had all waited excitedly for Magnus Sorensen to come and lend his support for their cause.

Down on the ground, the local *Sauvons Mont Baleine!* group had erected a platform and next to it an enormous screen. There were a few chairs placed for the speakers, and several microphones. On either side of the wooden platform, folding plastic tables were opened again, and on them were scattered their brochures and the petition against Projet Leviathan for anyone to sign who hadn't already. Downstage of the raised platform, was a beautiful spray of flowers encircling a poster-sized head shot of Magnus. Roméo and Marie had just arrived and stopped to watch as a long line of mourners shuffled by the platform one by one to pay their respects and place their own tribute at his portrait. There was almost complete silence, despite the presence of at least fifty people raising their protest signs. A little girl stood next to her father struggling to hold up a sign saying *You'll Die of Old Age-We'll Die of Climate Change!* Joel and Shelly lifted a photo of a burning earth with *People OVER Profit-There IS NO PLANet B!* scrawled across it. Roméo noticed Tracy Jacobs with a few of her Mohawk Council members. One was holding *STOP Environmental Racism-Climate Justice NOW!*

Roméo had read about environmental racism, the choices and policies that result in the disproportionate impact of environmental hazards on people of color. The worst polluters—toxic waste dumps, polluting industrial sites, chemical plants, animal production and other environmentally hazardous projects were often built near racialized and disadvantaged communities the world over. In Canada, many Indigenous people still did not have equal access to clean water—in a country with twenty percent of the world's supply of fresh water. He remembered the case of the Grassy Narrows First Nation being poisoned by mercury dumped into their water source. The government did nothing about it, even though they knew about it for years. *Years.*

Although Roméo had witnessed it for much of his life, he still could not accept that as a species, we had collectively decided that entire groups of people were expendable based on the color of their skin. Suddenly the huge screen on the raised platform came to life. On it was a scene of another group of people gathered to honor the memory of Magnus in Oslo, where even though it was nearing nine o'clock in the evening, the sun was still quite bright. Someone turned the sound on, and the image shifted to a little girl and boy solemnly placing flowers on a memorial in Magnus's home city. Roméo recognized the background music playing, the very dramatic "Death of Ase" from Grieg's *Peer Gynt*. He was a character in Norwegian folklore, a rogue who will be destroyed unless he is saved by the love of a woman. Roméo wondered if anyone questioned the choice of that iconic music.

Marie took Roméo's hand and squeezed.

"Can we sit down?"

She led him to a row of stackable plastic chairs that had been set up near the platform. Marie sank into one of them. The hot and muggy day was getting to her, and she had slept very little in the last few days. She had so much to process she couldn't seem to turn her brain off long enough to fall into the restorative oblivion she needed.

"I'll go get you something to drink."

Roméo headed off to one of the tables that had pitchers of water and what looked like iced tea on it. But first, he wanted to have a look around and see who had decided to attend the memorial for Magnus. Just at that moment a car with Massachusetts plates pulled up. A moment later, Gretchen Handschuh stepped out of the cool of her car into the hot sun. She was wearing a very large-brimmed straw hat, a pair of oversized sunglasses, and a simple print dress that made her look twenty years younger. She didn't see Roméo, and for a brief few moments, seemed entirely lost and out of place. Then she collected herself and made her way to the throng of people by the platform. There she stopped to talk with a very sweaty tech guy with plumber butt who was uncoiling a cable. No more than two minutes later, Roméo noticed Maude Laflamme's taxi arrive. He could see Maude chatting with her passenger, and then out of the back seat Emily Joly emerged. She looked pale and exhausted, and like Gretchen, at first seemed unsure of what she was doing there. Then a young woman with a *See Change* T-shirt on pulled her into a long hug. They made their way to a couple of chairs not too far from Marie. Roméo watched as the media vans and reporters vied for their spots near the makeshift fence that had been put up to keep them away from the area where people were honoring Magnus. By the time Roméo made his way back to Marie with a paper cup of iced tea, all the ice had melted. Ruby, Sophie, and Pénélope had found seats nearby, and a few people were starting to climb the stairs to take their places on the platform. Gretchen sat at the center of the stage, flanked by Manon Latendresse and Tracy Jacobs. They were joined by an older man with a grizzled beard and a mop of dank gray hair. He wore a Hawaiian shirt and a pair of wrinkled chinos. Roméo was certain that was Paul Pellerin, the man he had yet to interview. The sound of the memorial in Oslo on the big screen went mute. Paul nodded to Gretchen and the others on the platform and went to the microphone.

He cleared his throat several times before he began to speak, but he could still barely get above a whisper at first.

"As the world sinks further and further into eco-suicide—" the microphone screamed feedback. Paul stopped and waited for the shrieking to end. He started again. This time with a bit more volume.

"As the world sinks further and further into eco-suicide, Magnus Sorensen was like a beam of light. Showing us the way out. The path away—" his voice broke. Then he forced the words out. "—away from the edge of the precipice." Paul gestured to the screen. On it were powerful still images of his environmental activism over the years.

"Not that Magnus ever was afraid to tell people, to tell the world, the horrifying facts that no one wants to hear. How our addiction to fossil fuels is killing us. Our need to consume meat. Our treating our ONE ocean, because there is only ONE ocean, as our personal garbage dump. He knew this information could overwhelm us, could cause a kind of paralysis. But he knew that we had to get people to ingest and digest this information without losing faith. Without losing hope. How does one even understand the state of our ocean and keep going? Well, there's good old-fashioned denial. But Magnus forced us out of it. He showed us the world as it is, and what it could be." Paul paused to compose himself again, but when he continued, he spoke with even greater power. "Magnus always used to say, people want what they want. If it's fresh bluefin tuna although we hunt them till extinction, or fresh blueberries in the middle of January—will we ever go back to a sustainable world? Magnus made it seem like there was still a way. He wasn't a proselytizer—he didn't speak down to people. He didn't make people feel judged or immoral. We have seen in this polarized world where that gets us."

"It may feel like we're on a train to the end of our world as we know it and we can't get off. But we can. It will take enormous sacrifice, and…well, I'm afraid no one wants to go first. Will I go first? Will you? What will you sacrifice? Magnus sacrificed his life."

Paul had to stop. He stared down at his feet until he found his voice again. Then he looked out to the crowd of 200 or so people.

"I think we saw the measure of the man when he dropped out of his very busy schedule and came up here to support the fight against losing this beautiful and important piece of your world, of our world. I hope we can turn this...horrible tragedy into something that can inspire hope and change. So. I would like to invite Gretchen Handschuh, Magnus's partner in everything that mattered to him, to speak to you, and make an important announcement."

Gretchen stood up slowly, removed her hat, and left it on her seat. She then removed her sunglasses. As she made her way to the microphone, the image on the big screen changed to a shot of Matteo DiAngelo and Magnus, posing with their arms around each other's shoulders, standing on the pontoons of a float plane.

"On Sunday, Magnus Sorensen had planned to fly in here in his floatplane and drop hundreds of flyers announcing what you are about to hear right now. There was no big stunt, no wild eco-action. Just the result of him working hard to make a difference. To offer an alternative to the stalemate that you have here. And asking a favor of a dear friend who is equally committed to saving this planet, one day, one step, one acre at a time."

Gretchen nodded to the tech guy and all eyes turned to the screen, which shifted from the still shot of Magnus and Matteo DiAngelo to the movie star himself talking.

"Greetings, good people of Ste. Lucie des Laurentides of Quebec!" he said with such a thick American accent that the words were incomprehensible, but most people there figured out he was addressing them.

"My good friend Magnus has explained to me what's going on up there, and because I have committed to *See*

Change to do what I can to stop development of very fragile eco-systems that must be protected, I have an offer to make."

DiAngelo, ever the actor, paused for dramatic effect.

"I am offering to buy back from the developers of Project Leviathan their investment at a fair and equitable price. And ensure that the nature preserve at Mont Baleine forever remains just that. Not a tree will be cut. Or a lynx, or bear, or wolf driven from its habitat."

DiAngelo continued talking, but there was such a buzz amongst the people who'd come to honor Magnus that Roméo could barely hear the rest of the video. He was stunned. How would such a deal work? Why would the investors accept such an offer? Or given all the controversy, why wouldn't they? The image on the screen changed again. This time, it was one of Magnus on the bow of his beloved research vessel, *The Tempest*. The accompanying music wasn't Greig this time. It was a beautiful ballad by Beau Dommage, one of Quebec's most beloved bands. The crowd began to sing along.

As the music continued, Roméo watched as Gretchen, Paul, and the others left the stage, stepping carefully down the makeshift stairs. The media were going crazy, cameras and mics bobbing and thrusting trying to get to someone to talk to them about the bombshell announcement. And of course, to shed some light on who killed Magnus Sorensen. But Gretchen headed straight to her car and without any hesitation, got in and drove away, navigating past the gathered media banging on her car windows. Marie and Ruby headed over to speak to Paul Pellerin, whom Marie knew from many, many years before. Paul was being bombarded by people with questions, and people shaking his hand, people hugging him. Marie and Ruby decided to catch up with him later. As they headed back to their seats, which volunteers were already stacking and putting away, Marie noticed a man with his head bowed before the memorial to Magnus. He looked very emotional. Distraught. Magnus had meant so much to so many. Suddenly, Joel her neighbor grabbed her and squeezed her into a bear hug.

"I never got a chance to tell you how sorry we were. It must have been just *awful* for you this week. First your mother and your old…friend. But this is…this is unbelievable news!"

Roméo looked over at a stream of cars and bikes that were now making their way down the narrow gravel road out of the area. People were in a chatty, festive mood now, torn between the solemnity of the occasion and the good news they'd just been given. Roméo had told Nicole LaFramboise to position herself by the parking lot, where she could get a good look at everyone leaving the site. Magnus's killer could be close. He left Marie with Joel and Ruby and headed towards Nicole. She was in what looked like an intense conversation with Emily Joly by her car.

"Emily Joly. This is Detective Chief Inspector Roméo Leduc."

Roméo shook her hand. She looked him directly in the eye.

"You're in charge of the investigation."

"I am. I am sorry we haven't met yet. Please accept my condolences."

"Someone is still following me."

Nicole and Roméo exchanged glances.

"We put an officer at your hotel and advised you to stay there. Of course, we understand today was necessary. Do you sense you're being followed here?" Roméo asked.

"How would I know?" Emily looked up at Roméo with red-rimmed, but very large and deep brown eyes. "One of them did it. I know it."

"One of whom?"

She gestured to the now empty platform.

"His best…friend." She spat out the last word. "Or his partner. One of them did it, I'm telling you."

Nicole leaned in. "What evidence do you have? Did you think of something since we took your statement?"

"I was involved with Magnus. For almost a year. They want me gone."

"With all due respect, Madame Joly," Roméo interjected. "I think you are one of several women Magnus had a…liaison with over the years. No one ever killed him for it."

"I'm pregnant. Five months. Magnus is the father. We were planning to start our life together. They would do anything to stop that."

Nicole gestured towards her car.

"Let me drive you back to the hotel, and I'll take another—"

Emily waved her hand away.

"I've already called the taxi. There's nothing more to say. Just…it's the money. I'm sure of it. Magnus changed his will. He changed…it for me. And her." She put a hand on her belly. As if on cue, Maude Laflamme's taxi arrived and gave a quick honk. She leaned out her window and waved cheerily at the young woman flanked by the two police officers.

Emily turned and made her way to the taxi. Then they made a wide U-turn and disappeared down the road.

"You've got someone good on the finances, right? And the will?"

"Of course." Nicole looked a bit put out that he would even ask.

"He's looking into *See Change* and Paul Pellerin as well? Magnus was a very wealthy man."

"I'll ask him to look even closer. No stone unturned, no paper un…read. Sorensen's lawyers have turned up, so the whole process is MUCH slower."

Roméo looked up at Mont Baleine. A massive cumulonimbus cloud had started heaping itself over the summit. Another of those ominous thunderclouds they'd be seeing all summer. They appeared out of a perfect blue sky and suddenly the heavens opened and poured down on all those below what felt like every last drop of water the world had left.

It was time for him to go talk to Paul Pellerin.

Chapter 44

Paul

Paul Pellerin hated police stations. This was not surprising because he had spent a fair amount of time in them. Since he was a kid, he had been hauled into a cop shop for a wide range of offences. The first time, he was twelve years old. A bunch of his friends and him used to hang out by the railroad tracks in Lowell. There wasn't much else to do when you had no money and the ocean which was tantalizingly close was still impossible to get to by bus. They liked to throw rocks at the passing train cars. One afternoon, they were up to their preferred pastime, except the railway authorities called the police. All Paul's friends made a getaway, except him. The arresting officer gave him a hard smack on the head as soon as he got him alone in a holding cell. When Paul, sobbing, was finally allowed to call his mother she told the police to hang on to him for a while. She was in no hurry to rescue him.

Ten years later, he joined the PlowShares Movement that the Jesuit priest, poet, anti-war activist and Paul's hero,

Daniel Berrigan started. They engaged in many famous acts of civil disobedience directed against weapons of war, including breaking into a nuclear weapons manufacturing plant and pouring their own blood on blueprints. Paul wasn't part of that action, but he was arrested for chaining himself to the fence of a nuclear facility, demanding the disabling of the war machine. In the end, despite his love for the movement, it involved too much obsession with guilt and suffering for him. And Paul was offered a scholarship to study political science in London, where he dropped out after three terms. But he did get a first-hand look at Thatcher's England. He was arrested again during the coal miners' strike for a protest he went to—and in retrospect, an issue about which he had much to learn. When he followed a beautiful girl to Newcastle and found himself outside the town hall holding a cup that said "Dig Deep for Miners" he realized this wasn't his story. Besides, she had dumped him less than two weeks later. After he joined PlanetGreen UK he'd been arrested dozens of times. Paul had been pulled in by vicious cops, kind cops, stupid cops, and smart cops the world over. He had a deep and abiding suspicion of all people who chose to police others for a living. The attraction to that kind of fascism. He remembered reading somewhere there is a thin line between the policeman and the criminal, and the best cops are the ones who are able to think like criminals. But for a quirk of fate, they might have been criminals.

Paul was wondering how much longer he had to wait. A short, pretty detective had ushered him into this room, and then disappeared. The air conditioning was either non-existent or so lousy that it was uncomfortably hot. Paul could feel the sweat trickling down his back, and down the runnel of his chest. He'd like a glass of water. Or coffee. Or something. He scraped back his chair and headed to the door, but before he could open it, it opened. A very tall, dark-haired man stood in its frame, holding two cups of coffee.

"Paul Pellerin. I am Roméo Leduc. Detective Chief Inspector of homicide for St. Jerome and Laurentian district. Thank you for your patience."

Paul was immediately impressed by the smooth baritone of the man's voice. He returned to his chair and thanked Roméo for the coffee, although after his first sip he regretted doing so. A moment later, the short detective came back in the room and took a seat.

"This is Detective Sargent Nicole LaFramboise. We are running the investigation into the death of Magnus Sorensen. We are very sorry for your loss."

Paul nodded. "Thank you. How is the investigation going?" he asked in a voice more confident than he felt. Roméo ignored the question and asked another without looking up from his papers.

"Tell us about your relationship with Magnus Sorensen."

Paul rubbed his damp palms together. "Okay, then. We're jumping right into it."

Paul tried another sip of the vile coffee. "Personal or professional?"

"Let's start with the former. Personal."

"Okay. Well. Magnus and I met in nineteen ninety-two in London, and he joined the environmental organization I was coordinating at that time. Despite having little experience and no scientific background, Magnus became a leader in the movement."

"Unh huh." Nicole was taking notes, even though the

interview was recorded. "And how would you characterize your relationship?"

"Magnus is." Paul stopped to clear his throat. "Magnus was my best friend."

"And your boss." Roméo observed. "How did that work for you? Was it difficult?"

"No." Paul hoped he was sounding sincere. Of course, it was difficult. It could be awful. Managing his moods, his women, his manic elation went things went well, his despair when they didn't. Paul was like the steadying hand on the rudder. He never got to fall apart. Was never *allowed* to—the way Magnus could and sometimes did. Without Paul and Gretchen holding him up, he would have toppled over many years before and never gotten to his feet again. And yet, they stayed hidden in the shadows, the peons quietly toiling towards the continued creation of the great man. The visionary. But it could also be wonderful. Magnus offered him a life he couldn't have imagined in his wildest dreams. Paul knew that Magnus was, really, the love of his life.

"I am Magnus's right-hand man. And left-hand man. It's a joke. I'm left-handed."

Neither Roméo nor Nicole laughed.

"And *See Change*? I make it run. Without me, it would have been a second-rate NGO duking it out with the other wannabees. Because I knew that Magnus and I were an unbeatable combination. I stuck by him through the great rift years earlier when he and Gretchen split from Tor Hanyes and PlanetGreenUK. Magnus basically became his *own* brand and broke away from all the old eco-hippies whom he saw as less and less effective. Despite all the work he's done, he is perceived by some of his former activist friends of selling out and betraying the movement. They see his celebrity as just another…commodity for people to consume. They think he destroys the integrity of the movement. But Magnus is the *embodiment* of it. They said the same thing about Berrigan, the co-opting of this moral voice by celebrity. Do you know what he answered?"

Roméo and Nicole shook their heads but said nothing.

"One can't simply renounce one's voice or one's talent for helping people interpret the truth or turn a corner." Paul waited for their reaction. They remained silent.

"I mean, do you know how many campaigns Magnus has run in the almost thirty years I have known him? And now, he's fighting the clear-cutting and burning of the fucking Pantanal, which he believes will destroy the world either through unstoppable global warming or through the next zoonotic disease. When you disturb a forest, it upsets the balance between pathogens and people, so there's a strong correlation between deforestation and disease outbreaks because the disease jumps from animals to humans. Did you know that six out of every ten diseases in humans are zoonotic? So, we're just waiting for the Big One. Or the next Big One."

Paul emptied the cup of undrinkable coffee. Then he looked from Roméo to Nicole. They were checking their notes. He fiddled with the empty cup. Roméo noticed he had small, fine hands for such a burly man. Not the hands you'd expect on someone who had done plenty of work on boats.

"It would seem like your relationship with Magnus Sorensen, though, was more than the creation of *See Change* and changing the world. We've looked into your background. Magnus invested a significant amount of money in this company, *More Than Meat*, that you're building."

"Yes."

"Does he routinely invest large amounts of money in your business ventures?"

"No."

"We've also discovered that Magnus had loaned you quite a bit of money over the years. Significant amounts here that we're seeing."

Roméo pushed copies of the transaction papers closer to Paul.

"Borrowing huge amounts of money from your…best friend often ends very badly. Often destroys the friendship. Would you agree?"

Before Paul could answer, Roméo continued.

"It seems to me than Magnus is a very special friend. It seemed to me that Magnus is someone who has propped you up over the years."

"Propped *me* up?"

Paul stopped to take a breath and control his reaction. There was no amount of money—*no amount of money*—Magnus could have paid that would ever be enough for what they'd done for him.

"As you know, Magnus comes from a very wealthy family. Immensely wealthy. Oil money. Which he, by the way, turned his back on when his father cut him off. But his mother left him a significant amount of money when she died. So, yes. Magnus is very generous that way."

"What does his death mean for his investment in *More Than Meat*?"

"I don't know. I don't know what his death means. All I know is…it's the worst thing that has ever happened in my life."

Paul's hands stopped fiddling with the coffee cup. He had torn the foam into little pieces. Then he tidied them up into a little pile on the table. Nicole swept them aside and removed her notes from the file. She pretended to look them over again.

"Let's talk about Emily Joly."

"Okay."

"She's here. In Quebec. Is that usual for one of your employees to be traveling like this with you and Magnus?"

"Magnus wanted me here to be part of this important, amazing announcement that was made yesterday. And, um. Emily, as you know is our branding expert—she has rebranded Magnus and our entire organization. She's been a really important part of *See Change* for about, I guess, the last two years."

Nicole smiled, leaned in and addressed Paul less formally.

"She is more than just a branding expert though, right?"

"I don't know what you mean."

"She's been having a relationship with Magnus now for some time."

"Oh."

"You *did* know about that."

"Yes."

"We've talked to Emily, and she claims you came to her hotel room to warn her. In fact, she said it was kind of a threat. You *threatened* her."

"You *met* Emily Joly. She is not the easiest woman to *threaten*," Paul scoffed.

"But you did. Threaten her?"

"No. I didn't threaten Emily. Don't be ridiculous."

"Then what did you talk about?"

"I *reminded* her that what was important. What *mattered*

was *See Change*. And Magnus. And not…other concerns that she might have. That given the zeitgeist—I mean the #MeToo Movement—it maybe wasn't the time to um…publicize their…relationship. Magnus's age. And her age. And his, um…history with younger women."

"Did you know that she is pregnant?" Nicole watched carefully for Paul's reaction.

"No."

"Does Gretchen know she is pregnant?"

"I have no idea what Gretchen knows."

There was a long pause while the question Nicole had just asked hovered in the air. Roméo continued, "Could you please look at these notes? These were left for Magnus by someone who got very close to him in the days before he was murdered. We see them as a kind of threat."

Roméo placed the same three baggies with the notes before Paul. "Do they mean anything to you? Anything at all?"

"They mean nothing to me. Except, you know, that they're little…sayings you might see on someone's refrigerator, on a fridge magnet."

"Thank you, Mr. Pellerin. I think that's all for now. Of course, we would ask that you remain in the area for several more days until our inquiry is complete."

Roméo stood up and extended his hand. Paul did as well. Nicole did not. She remained seated and scribbled some notes. Just as Paul was almost out of his chair, Roméo stopped him.

"Oh, yes. Just one more thing. Do you know what this is?" Roméo watched Paul very carefully as he pulled out the baggie with the Thulite stone in the silver clasp and put it on the table. Paul didn't pull it closer to him or examine it or show it any reaction at all.

"No."

"Does it belong to you?"

He hesitated as long as a heartbeat, Roméo noted.

"No."

"Do you know if this belongs to anyone you know?"

Paul shook his head emphatically. "No."

"Well, then, Mr. Pellerin, that is all for today. Given the fact that one of the members of your organization was targeted, I would keep an eye out. Please be careful. Let us know if anything or anyone is of concern to you."

"What do you mean? Am I in some kind of danger?"

Roméo and Nicole exchanged glances. "We don't think so. But it's always a good idea to be prudent."

Roméo watched Paul through the precinct window as he hastened to his car. He stopped to grab what looked like a dirty towel from the backseat and wipe down his sweaty neck and damp hair before he got in. It was not the make and color of the car seen leaving the scene at breakneck speed. But he could have used another car. Roméo thought about the interview. He was certainly someone who kept his cards close to his chest. He gave away very little, but clearly there was a deep love for the murdered man. And maybe an equally deep resentment, the kind of hero worship that can so easily turn the other way. Was it enough for Paul Pellerin to kill him?

Chapter 45

Marie sat in the ancient armchair that had migrated through the decades and all the way from their family home on Woodgrove to take its oversized place in Claire Russell's little room. It was pushed up right against the side of the bed. Marie stroked her mother's right hand, feeling the bumps of arthritis and gnarled, swollen veins that old age brings. Although Claire was doing much better, well enough to be released from the hospital and returned to *Maison Soleil*, she had not yet come back to herself. She was sleeping much more than usual, and when she was awake, she seemed unsure of where she was and who she was. The doctor had said that given the shock of her night in the wilderness, it might take some time for her to recover. But Marie was worried. She was also very angry and resisted returning her mother to the residence. Roméo, Ruby, and Ben sat down with her and persuaded her that this was still the best, safest place for Claire. Marie was not convinced, but after reaming out the director and her assistant for their negligence, she felt that now Claire would be *very* well cared for.

Her mother was sleeping again. Marie brushed away a strand of white hair that had fallen over her eye. Claire stirred a little, and then settled again. It was hard to remember her as the dynamic and vivacious woman she once was. The woman who tried so valiantly to save first her husband, then her eldest daughter from alcoholism. The woman who watched them come and repossess her pride and joy—her blue Datsun sports car—that *she* had paid for out of her hard-earned savings. The money she had managed to protect from her husband Edward, and that in the end had gone to pay off his debts. The mother who, despite everything, told her three daughters every single day that they were beautiful, that they were smart, that they could do anything. The truth was, Claire was really describing herself, Marie thought.

Marie turned as she heard the door open. It took Roméo about two strides to cross the room and reach Marie. This was nothing like the last residence Marie had placed her mother in, *Le Warwick*, in Montreal. That was like a five-star hotel, replete with a luxurious living room with a grand piano, a state-of-the-art movie room, and an enormous swimming pool. Claire's living quarters had easily been twice the size of her tiny one and a half rooms at *Maison Soleil*. But Marie had made the horrifying discovery that *Le Warwick* used to drug their residents suffering from dementia with antipsychotics to keep them compliant and to make it more "convenient" for their staff. She got Claire out of that hell as soon as she could and moved her up north closer to where Marie and Roméo now lived. She had made sure that kind of thing did not happen at *Maison Soleil*. And now this.

"How is she?"

"Very sleepy. I'm scared she won't come out of it."

Roméo rubbed Marie's shoulder. "She's had an adventure. Her body and mind have a lot of processing to do. How is Louis?"

"Did you know he is almost *eighty-nine* years old? The guy is a wonder. All he has is a sore hip, and he's a bit tired."

Roméo smiled. "May we be so lucky."

"Oh, his daughter Dominique *finally* came to see him. A bit late, I'd say. I overheard her just *lose* it on him. She sounded like she wanted to kill him."

Marie let go of her mother's hand and sank back into the chair.

"What do you make of my mother and Louis Lachance? Do you think they're in some kind of *relationship*?"

"I certainly hope so. She did run away with him, after all. And they're *not* married." Roméo shook his head in mock concern. "What a scandal. I hope we can live it down."

Marie gave his hand a dismissive tap.

Roméo leaned closer to her and whispered, "Maybe they're in love."

"My mother and Louis?"

"Yes. Why not?"

"Well, as my mother used to say, nothing but *nothing* would surprise me anymore."

"When I spoke to…Olivier, was it? He said they were very fond of each other. *Very* fond."

Almost as though he'd been summoned, Olivier Ward suddenly appeared at Claire's open door. He stood at the threshold, his hands fidgeting with his apron.

"I'm sorry. I don't want to bother you. I'll just…." He turned and disappeared. Roméo hastened after him. They reappeared a few moments later. Olivier stood at the foot of

Claire's bed. He looked like a kid who thought he was in some kind of trouble.

"I just want to thank you so much, Olivier. For my mother's life. Without you...paying attention, being so...on the ball and sounding the alarm? She would probably have died." Marie took the boy in her arms and hugged him tightly. "You are my hero."

Roméo hugged the boy as well. Olivier received the hugs with his arms at his side, like he didn't know what to do.

"*Merci,* Olivier. I hope they know what a great person they have working here. We have written a letter already to your boss. Please continue to take such good care of the people here. It's a very important job."

"Not as important as being a policeman," Olivier offered.

"They are both important jobs. But taking care of our elderly the way you do? The ones who raised us, who loved us, who made us? It's the most important."

Olivier beamed at Roméo.

"Oh! I have to get back to work now."

Before either of them could say anything else, he was gone.

"A man of few words," Roméo observed. Then he turned to Marie.

"I'd like to take you home now and fix you something to eat. I bet you're starving."

Marie looked back to her mother who was still sleeping peacefully.

"*Maman*? I'm going to go home now. I'll be back soon."

Marie kissed her mother's forehead and pulled her duvet up a bit on her, even though the room was very warm.

"We need to...*I need* to spend more time with her. Get

her out more. Go on little excursions. I don't know why I do less of that. I guess because it's hard, you know? She's not the mother I used to know, and sometimes I find it too sad. I get frustrated and short-tempered with her."

"I think that most of the time, you're quite patient with her."

"Maybe we could take her and Louis out some time."

"Maybe *drive* them to that beach they escaped to. Have a picnic?"

Marie nodded. "That is a *great* idea." She gathered her phone and purse and adjusted her mother's duvet one more time. They walked up to Karine at the front desk and informed her they were leaving for a while. She assured them that someone would be looking in on Madame Russell regularly. For a moment, Marie thought that Karine might apologize, but it passed. She waved them off with a cheerful *Bonne soiree* and was already staring into her computer screen before they reached the front door.

∞

Marie and Roméo were sitting in their porch, the thin metal mesh of the screens the only line of defense against being eaten alive by mosquitoes. At that time of day in late July in the Laurentians they were still voracious. The heat and humidity of the last few days made them even worse. Marie watched the mosquitoes clinging to the screens and pointed out to Roméo that a change of shift was going on. The day mosquitoes found their prey by sight. They were quitting work for the day. The night mosquitoes hunted by smelling carbon dioxide. They were just starting.

"They're all females, though," Marie said. "They need our blood to reproduce."

"The most dangerous animal on the planet," Roméo offered.

"Except for humans." They both said at exactly the same time. And then laughed. *We already know each other's punchlines*, Marie thought. And they'd only been married for four days.

Marie had inhaled the bean salad with fresh arugula and garlic from their garden that Roméo had prepared. Now she was working on the hamburger he'd grilled for her, slathered in Dijon mustard, piled with onions and mushrooms and topped with a thick slice of cheddar. Roméo, of course, was eating his Beyond Meat burger, which to Marie tasted like wood shavings. She'd also had two glasses of a bottle of rosé Roméo had opened and counting. She wasn't. He was.

They stopped to watch a male hummingbird that flew in like a torpedo to the sugar water Marie had hung in a feeder under the eave of the porch. Then the female bombarded the feeder and they squabbled and squeaked viciously for a second or two. Then they both zipped away to their respective perches before resuming battle. Marie moved on to glass of wine number three. They sat and looked out at the sun starting to settle itself on the horizon of their little lake, hidden just beyond a thick stand of trees. The few clouds that had appeared were tinged salmon pink. Marie listened to a couple of jays chatting. They were probably on the hunt for the newly fledged songbirds, very vulnerable to predation. Their sometimes-nasty behavior and reputation were in such contrast to their beauty, Marie thought. She loved listening to their dozen or so calls. Sometimes they sounded like a mewing cat, sometimes a rusty clothesline—each call with a specific purpose. Warning. Gossip. Affection. Marie had actually heard one imitate the screech of a hawk so as to frighten the smaller birds away from the feeder.

Roméo wiped his mouth, crossed his fork and knife on his plate, and took Marie's hand.

"Do you feel up to talking about Magnus?"

Marie stopped in mid-sip. "Now?"

Roméo nodded. "I have a few questions you might be able to help me with. Can you do that?"

Marie hesitated for a few seconds. She freed her hand from Roméo's. "Why didn't you tell me right away that night—that…he had died? I just can't get my head around it."

Roméo shook his head. "There was nothing we could do. It was too late to go home. And, and I didn't want to ruin the first night of our honeymoon. But it was already ruined. And it was…selfish. I should have told you."

Marie looked directly into Roméo's green eyes. He didn't look away.

"How did he die?"

"He was hit in the back of the head and fell or was pushed into the lake where he drowned. It looks like a heavy blunt metal object, like a pipe, or a crowbar, but heavier. Never mind. The blow must have stunned him or knocked him out." Roméo paused. "There is Gretchen Handschuh's DNA on him. Not surprising, obviously. But there was also Emily Joly's DNA—"

"Who?"

"The woman who found him. Who was…replacing Gretchen on the flight into Mont Baleine? She is the social media and branding expert at *See Change*."

"Well, that would make sense, too."

"Who is now five months pregnant. And Magnus is the father, apparently."

"What?"

"They've been in a relationship for almost eighteen months."

"Oh, good God." Marie let that information sink in. "Wait. Does Gretchen know?"

"We're not sure. It is one of the questions I intend to ask her when I interview her again."

Marie covered her mouth with her hands like she was praying and let out a long exhale. "Wow."

"But the plane Magnus was supposed to fly into the Mont Baleine protest, we believe it was also tampered with. The floats had small puncture holes. The struts were compromised."

"The plane?" Marie repeated.

Roméo nodded. Marie poured herself another glass of wine.

"So, they wanted to kill Magnus *and* Gretchen?"

"Or Mikael Rasmussen."

"You can't tell how recently it was—what's the word? Sabotaged?"

"No, but we found a note on the dashboard of the plane to Magnus that indicated that Rasmussen had the plane checked out and everything was good to go. So, presumably the person tampered with the plane after Rasmussen left. Or, whoever inspected his plane tampered with it. Or the inspector was a total incompetent."

"But...who would do that? It's so...you know... diabolical."

Roméo frowned. "I haven't heard that word in a while.

Maye we should ask your neighbor—the one who specializes in the devil? What's her name?"

"Laura. And she's the sweetest, most harmless person in the world." Marie stared out at the lake as thought the answer might be there.

"Could it be one of the pro Leviathan guys? Would they *do* something like that?"

Roméo threw up his hands. "Anything is possible. Sabotaging the 'stunt' might have been very satisfying to one of them. There's a lot of anger towards Magnus—"

"Enough to *kill* him?"

"Maybe."

Marie cradled her head in the heel of her hand and sighed.

"I can't believe we're talking about this. This whole week has been…wonderful. And awful. Surreal."

"Can I talk to you about Magnus?"

"I haven't even had time to process this. Or think about it, really. Or help. What do you want to know?"

"Just talk to me about him. Whatever comes to mind— that you feel comfortable sharing. Then I'll ask some more directed questions, okay?"

"Okay. Um…I met Magnus in…nineteen eighty-eight? Or…was it 'eighty-nine? We were working together on a research project funded by the New England Aquarium, at Stellwagen Banks near Boston. It was a *coup de foudre*—love at first sight. For him—so he always claimed. It took me maybe three encounters before I knew. That I wanted to spend my life with him. Long story short? He met Gretchen in South Africa, Hermanus, I think. I was supposed to be joining him there, and then we were heading to Mauritius for a project we'd gotten some money to run on Sperm whales. After two years together, I got *the* call." Marie took a deep breath. "It was gutting. Devastating. It took me years to get over it—well, you already know some of this. The life that he had with Gretchen? That was going to be *my* life, was *supposed* to be my life. *Our* life." Marie smiled wanly at Roméo. "Well, you know what that feels like. Elyse dumped you for your best friend."

"Maybe I didn't love her the way she needed to be. The way you loved Magnus."

"The way I love you."

Roméo took Marie's hand. "Do you have regrets?"

"Me? How could I? *I* didn't make the decision. It was Magnus's choice to end…us."

"Was it?"

"Absolutely—"

"Because Gretchen said—oh, nothing."

"Gretchen said what?"

"It was nothing. I misheard."

"Roméo, I have Ruby, and Ben and Maya, and Noah—my heart. And you. I can't have regrets about that. And I wonder how long it would have lasted with Magnus. With that *presence*. With that ego. He is all-consuming, as you might have noticed."

"Do you have any idea about who might have killed him?"

Marie shook her head. Roméo pulled his tablet over and showed Marie the photographs of the notes left for Magnus and explained their sinister provenance.

"Do these mean anything to you?"

Marie looked them over carefully. "Nope."

"I didn't take them seriously enough." Roméo's voice

caught. "That's not true. I thought they were a legitimate threat. But I wanted to get away with you and passed them to Nicole to deal with. But it was already too late. I am very, very sorry about that."

He waited for Marie's response. She pursed her lips and said nothing.

"What else would you like to know?"

Roméo felt such relief that he'd told Marie about the notes he felt like someone had taken a terrific weight off his shoulders. And stomach. And heart.

"Can you tell me a bit more about *See Change*?"

Marie told Roméo what she remembered and had read about the organization. Most of what she said matched what Paul Pellerin had told him and Nicole in his interview. She reiterated that she thought Gretchen, the scientist with the hard skills, was the driving force.

"Magnus was the germinator of ideas. She was the terminator; she executed them. She is kind of like…Yoko Ono to his John Lennon. Although, for the record (pardon the pun) I think all his music once he met her went to shit."

Roméo typed a few notes into his tablet.

"I wanted to ask you about this…accident I read about— just as *See Change* was really starting to grow. It was in…two thousand and seven, I think. Do you know anything about it? Can you tell me anything I might not have read about it?"

Marie leaned back in her chair and stared up into the rafters of the porch.

"It was way after my time with Magnus, obviously. I probably don't know any more than you do. There was a terrible accident with one of the interns. What was her name?"

"Molly Meader. Twenty-five years old."

"Oh, right. From what I remember, she was in the bow of the boat and was crushed to death. Getting too close to a right whale, I think, to disentangle it from fishing lines."

"But she shouldn't have been doing that in the first place, right?"

"Absolutely not. That's a job for very experienced people. From what I remember, she was in the wrong place at the wrong time. But just so you know—there have *literally* been no recorded deaths caused by a human and whale encounter *ever*. I mean, not counting old time whalers who hunted them in rowboats and hand-held harpoons, like in *Moby Dick*."

"So, this was a freak accident, then. It never happens. Except to her." Roméo referred back to the screen on his tablet. "There was an inquest. A thorough investigation was conducted. She died immediately. On contact. There was nothing to be done."

Marie nodded. "I remember the inquest. I wrote to Magnus and the team after. They were completely eviscerated."

"Gretchen Handschuh and Paul Pellerin were in the boat as well. So was Magnus. Everyone testified that it was an accident. Terrible and tragic. But an accident."

Marie stacked their dinner plates and rose from her chair.

"You know that kind of thing would have destroyed so many organizations. I was surprised and impressed that *See Change* came back from that."

Marie disappeared into the kitchen. Roméo heard her emptying the scraps into the compost bin and rinsing the plates. She returned with another bottle of rosé. He was still looking over the coverage of the accident. Marie peered over his shoulder.

"Let me see that?"

She pulled the tablet closer and examined the screen. Then she pointed to a man who was talking to reporters after the inquest had concluded. Marie pointed her finger at the screen several times before the words came out.

"I saw him at Magnus's memorial! He stopped at the portrait they'd put on the stage. You know, for a brief flash, I *thought* he seemed familiar."

"Anton Volkov. Molly Meader's fiancé?"

"Yes. I think that's who I saw!" Marie sat down beside Roméo. "Why on earth would he be at Magnus's memorial?"

Roméo quickly tapped in his name. He had almost no footprint on social media. He had no Facebook account. No Instagram. No Twitter. But an article describing the couple in the local news identified him as a mechanic. Roméo typed in another search.

"Anton Volkov is a mechanic. An airplane mechanic. Employed at Pratt and Whitney in Connecticut."

"What the hell? Do you think this guy sabotaged the plane?"

"I don't know." Roméo stood up and pulled his phone from his pocket.

"But I think we better give Gretchen Handschuh a call."

Chapter 46

She sat on the edge of the king-size bed that she had made that morning with the same precision she had made her bed every day since she was a little girl. The way her mother had taught her. Fold each corner of the sheet in neat right-angles and tuck in securely. Then fold the duvet back six inches; the edges of the two pillows meeting the fold perfectly. Pillowcases with openings facing out, every wrinkle pressed and flattened. On the bed, however, a well-traveled black leather satchel lay open, its contents still undisturbed—except for one thing. A blue and green Hawaiian shirt with humpback whales chasing each other around it in playful spirals. They had bought it together in Na' Pali at least twenty years earlier, both enchanted by the expert illustrations of the whales, and bemused that they were swimming in and out of palm trees. He had worn it so often and washed it so many times that the neon bright colors had faded to pastels, and the fabric was as soft as a baby's cheek. Gretchen held it to her face and inhaled, hoping to breathe him in, keep his essence in her lungs forever. But the shirt had been washed just before they'd left home, and all she could smell was the laundry soap and fabric softener their housecleaner favored. Gretchen refolded the shirt carefully and tucked it neatly back into his bag. She stared at the wall in front of her. On it was a large, conventionally composed photograph of spires of balsam trees silhouetted against a winter sky. Exactly the current view out of the living room if you removed the mounds of snow. She briefly wondered why someone would decorate a wall with the same image they could get just looking out their window. She gathered her blue dragon robe around her and tightened the belt. The two Ativan she'd swallowed just after her evening swim had barely taken the edge off, and at this rate, she would never make it through the night. What she needed was a glass of something strong to settle it with and headed toward the kitchen.

She felt the breeze flutter the bottom of her robe before she realized that the patio door was open. She had closed and locked it.

"Nice to see you again, Gretchen."

She felt her heart constrict. Then her entire body began to tingle, goose bumps exploding on her arms, neck, and legs. She drew her robe tighter around her and considered making a run for it, but in two steps he'd made it to the patio doors and locked them—with the actual key that she never used. She glanced at the coffee table where she'd left her phone, but it had disappeared.

"What are you doing here?"

"Oh, come on now. You were always the smartest one. I think you know."

"I have absolutely no idea." She continued on toward the kitchen as though he was a guest she was entertaining. "But while I give it some thought, I'd like to fix myself a drink."

The man moved shockingly fast for someone his size and weight, blocking her way. He grabbed her wrist in his gloved hands and half-threw her into the armchair, as easily as he would a small child.

"Sit down and shut the fuck up."

Gretchen rubbed her wrist which was starting to throb. She took in the man standing over her. In any other circumstance, his was a forgettable face. Even, undistinguished features except for a wide mouth with full lips. Skin slightly pocked from old acne scars along the cheek line and down his neck. His hair, which had been plentiful and hung down to his shoulders, was tucked tightly into a black knit cap. He had put on at least fifty pounds—but most of it seemed to be muscle.

Although she seemed as calm as someone could be in the situation, Gretchen was frantically considering her options. She could jump out of the chair and run for the front door, but he'd beat her to it, that she knew. She could try to arm herself somehow—there was the fireplace poker, but she had moved it next to her bed for protection two nights before. She saw no weapon on him, but she knew in her bones that he could overpower her and hurt her very badly if he wanted to. She pulled her robe even tighter. She wasn't wearing underwear and felt horribly vulnerable. *What did he want?*

He sat on the edge of the L-shaped sofa across from her and steepled his gloved hands under his chin as if in prayer.

"How does it feel now that he's dead?"

His accent had faded but was still slightly detectable. Gretchen said nothing.

"I asked you a question."

"What is it you want?"

The man withdrew his hands from his face and let them fall between his thickly muscled thighs. He exhaled with an exaggerated sigh.

"What. Do. I. *Want?*" He emphasized the *want* and punctuated it with air quotes. "Well, that is the million-dollar question, isn't it?"

They both briefly glanced out the window to the pool which was so peacefully illuminated in the evening dark as though the answer lay there.

"I want you to tell me the truth."

Gretchen closed her eyes and cradled her head in the arm that wasn't injured. So, this is what he was after. Again. Maybe there was a way out.

"Can you ask me a specific question?"

The man ran his hand over his cap and pulled it lower.

"Sure. I can be specific. Why was your *forty-eight-year-old* boyfriend fucking my *twenty-four-year-old* fiancée?"

"He wasn't."

"And why did your *boyfriend* play with her heart like it was worth *nothing*?"

"I don't know what you're talking about. Why are you here? Why are you talking about this *now*?"

Gretchen cringed as the man reached into his jacket pocket. Did he have a fucking *gun*?

He pulled out a sheaf of folded papers. He opened them carefully, and pulled out one of several that had been marked with a tiny colored tab. He began to read.

"At the end of the afternoon the sky cleared out and the rain finally let up, and Magnus proposed a little lookout ride. I said yes, of course. The sky was so beautiful. When we got a little way out, he let me drive the boat. He let ME drive the boat. He stood behind me and showed me how to steer it into the waves so as not to flip it. And I felt like this…electric connection between us. This heat. His breath on my neck. His scratchy face next to mine. It lasted a few seconds. I've never felt anything like that in my life. *I had lived enough, that is all!* It's from a poem but I can't remember the rest—"

"What is that?"

"Shut your mouth." He looked at her with such hatred that he could have incinerated her on the spot. He continued reading.

"When we got back to the house, Magnus took me aside, and told me to close my eyes. I hoped he was going to kiss me. Then he told me to keep them closed and to open my hand. He placed something in it, and gently closed my fist over it. You can open your eyes now, he said. It was a little pink rock, inside a silver claw. Now you're a whale warrior, he said. One of us. And then he went to join the others. I wonder if he knows the effect he has on people? On me? He makes me feel like I can do *anything*. Like the world is my oyster—I don't know what that really means. I will always carry my special charm that Magnus gave me. I am protected by it. I am invincible. I am Molly Meader, WHALE WARRIOR!" The man's voice broke on the last few words. Then he reached into his breast pocket and removed a small pink stone inside a silver claw. He held it on his open palm as though he was offering it to Gretchen, then just as suddenly tucked it to back into his pocket.

"Where did you get that?"

"No, Gretchen. The question is—*how* did I get this?" He lifted the wad of papers above his head like a preacher brandishing a bible. "How did Molly's diary *finally* find its way to me? How is it possible no one included this—THIS—in her personal…things that were given to me and her parents? I just got it. A few weeks ago. Anonymously, in the mail. Photocopies, though. Not the original. Why didn't you tell me you had it all those years?"

"I didn't—"

"Don't *lie* to me!"

But suddenly Gretchen knew. She knew who'd sent him the diary. Who also knew something else that was very, very important?

The man pulled a roll of duct tape from his pocket, grabbed her wrists, and taped them together, twisting her injured hand so badly she thought she might pass out. Then he grabbed her ankles with one big hand and taped them together. As he began to tape her body to the chair, her robe slipped slightly. He grabbed the lapel and pulled it roughly across her.

"I don't fucking want to see that."

Gretchen felt the panic rise in her like vomit. She tried to steady her breathing.

"What do you want, Anton?" she asked as gently and evenly as she could, making direct eye contact. He actually had rather beautiful eyes, with long lashes like a woman's. He unrolled more tape and wound it over her forehead and around the back of her head to the chair, so her head was completely immobilized, like an accident victim. Then he ripped a short piece off and slapped it roughly over her mouth. He went back to his spot on the sofa and began to speak.

"You know, all those years ago—after the inquest. I *wanted* to believe you. I really did. That fairy tale you all told? I *knew* it was a lie. I *knew* she died because someone didn't look out for her. Someone convinced her that she had to sacrifice herself. She would never have run to the front of the boat—she wasn't *stupid*—if that boyfriend of yours hadn't told her to—"

Gretchen began vehemently shaking her head.

"What? What's that, Gretchen?"

He ripped the tape from her mouth. It felt like he'd torn the skin right off her lips.

"No one told her to, Anton."

"'You have to be willing to put your *body* on the line. To sacrifice yourself.' She wrote it right here!" He smacked the folder of papers over his heart. "The cameras were there. It was your boyfriend's big moment. And he wasn't going to miss it, was he? She died, because of him. Because of his arrogance. His ego. She wanted to please *him*. To impress *him*. She was his little *whale warrior!*"

Gretchen licked her swollen lips and tasted blood.

"Anton? Do you know what it's like to see an entangled whale? It's horrifying. The whales are in terrible pain, they're scared, and often try to escape from rescue efforts. When we...came upon the whale that morning, fishing lines were wrapped around his body and flippers, and through his mouth—many times. We were the first to see him, but we *did* radio for help, for the disentanglement team. The truth is, we didn't prepare her for what she saw that morning. She spent the summer playing in the zodiac, matching fluke photos, doing a bit of basic research. Nothing prepared her for what she saw. And Molly reacted—"

"Do *not* say her name. Don't you speak her name."

Gretchen tried again. "She reacted like most deeply caring, brave people might—she ran to the front of the boat to get closer, to try and *do* something. But the whale was not... exhausted enough, and he was still terrified." Gretchen's voice softened. "And for some reason, probably to get away from us—he lifted his flukes, and they came down on the boat. She didn't suffer. She did not—"

"You shouldn't have been there. You got too close. Everyone said so—"

"We were trying to see what we could do until the Marine Mammal Rescue boat arrived."

"I want you to tell the truth about what happened that day. Not the fairy tale you and your buddies made up at the inquest. The truth. *Now.*"

"It was a freak accident, Anton. Thousands of whales are disentangled over the years. Only one person has *ever* been killed in all these years. One person. Besides—her. It was terrible luck. I am so sorry."

"You shouldn't have been there. You knew it was dangerous and you sacrificed her for the fucking *National Geographic*. You refused to admit it to protect that prick."

He was right. They had all closed ranks. To protect Magnus. To protect *See Change*. To *save See Change*. And themselves. Gretchen had nothing more to say. Anton closed his eyes.

"For a long, long time, I thought I'd never get over her, you know? Then one day, I woke up and I realized that I could breathe again, that rage, that anger that had its hands around my throat? It was gone. And I was really okay for a while. Then, I got this package in the mail. No identified sender. It was like living the whole thing over again—but so much worse. Because everything was a lie. And a beautiful young woman who'd dreamed of whales and dolphins since she was a little girl gave her life for a photo op. Because she loved *him*."

He abruptly stood up and pulled a long, thin rag from his pocket. Gretchen realized what it was for. She tried to pull her mouth away from him.

"Everyone will know it's you—Paul will know. He sent you her diary, didn't he?"

"Don't you worry about Paul."

He forced Gretchen's mouth open and pushed it in like a horse's bit, gagging her completely. Anton quickly slid open the patio door. Then he started to un-tape Gretchen from her chair and ripped the tape from her ankles.

"I hear you like to swim."

He wrenched Gretchen from the chair and frog marched her out the door and to the pool, which looked very inviting, the embedded pool lights turning the water to a lovely turquoise reminiscent of the Caribbean.

"Two down and one to go. Get in!"

Gretchen raised her taped hands. Anton took out a knife and slit the tape from her wrists. Then he slapped Gretchen hard. Right into the pool. As she felt her body slip into the water, she felt for just one moment, that she would let herself go. Just let herself sink to the bottom and stay there. But of course, no one drowns like that. Drowning is a horrible struggle. Gretchen kicked her way to the edge of the pool, but Anton was there before her, and pushed her head under water. She tried to pull him off her, she grabbed, she scratched, she clawed his arms. But he held her fast. She was going to die. Like this. Like an animal nobody wanted.

⅋

Roméo was concerned. He had called Gretchen Handschuh several times, and each time it had gone to her voice mail. It seemed odd to him that she would not answer the phone from the senior detective on her partner's murder case. He also wondered what on earth Anton Volker was doing at Magnus's memorial.

"Are you sure it was this man, Anton Volker you saw at the service for Magnus?"

Marie shook her head. "I'm not *positive*. He looked a lot fatter—bigger—and had way less hair. But don't we all?"

Roméo rubbed his face and checked his watch. "I'm going over there to take a look."

"What? Really? Are you worried?"

Roméo was already looking for his keys. He hesitated, then decided to grab his gun and shoulder holster.

"I'm coming with you."

"No, Marie. You're staying here."

But she was already on the phone to *Maison Soleil.* They assured her that they'd just checked on Madame Russell, and she was sleeping comfortably. Roméo was already out the door and in his car by the time she caught up to him and hopped into the passenger seat. They sped off down her little dirt road.

⅋

By the time they found the turn off to Gretchen Handschuh's rental, it was well past dark. There was no moon, and the sky must have been overcast as no stars were visible. As they first saw the lights of the house, Roméo spotted a car—a compact sedan parked off to the side, hidden in a copse of trees. Ontario plates. Not Gretchen's car. Roméo decided to park away from the house and cut the engine. He eased himself out of the driver's seat.

"You stay here. Give me a couple of minutes to see what's going on, okay? Sit tight."

Roméo closed his door shut without making a sound and walked very lightly on the gravel driveway towards the house. Marie watched as he peered inside the front windows. Then he disappeared around the side of the house into the backyard. He could hear splashing water, like someone was diving repeatedly into the pool. Was Gretchen taking an evening dip? Is that why she didn't answer her phone? Roméo left the shadow of the house, bolted towards the sound and practically ran into the man who was watching a woman, floating face down in the pool. He stood stock still. Roméo drew his handgun.

"Put your hands up. Hands up where I can see them! On your head"

The man slowly raised his hands.

"Turn around."

The man turned around. He looked directly at Roméo. A huge grin broke out on his face. Marie suddenly came at a full run around the corner of the house and was shocked into stopping at what she saw before her. She jumped awkwardly into the pool and waded over to the body. Gasping with the effort, she managed to pull and drag the body to the top of the concrete stairs in the shallow end. Although Marie hadn't had to do CPR in years, and couldn't exactly remember what to do, instinct kicked in. The man suddenly turned and bolted for the thicket of trees that opened up to hundreds of acres of unspoiled wilderness. Roméo saw Marie was trying to revive Gretchen, tucked his gun in his pocket, and ran too, following his suspect blindly into the woods. The man was big and could probably easily take Roméo in a fight, but his weight slowed him down. Roméo aimed for his knees. It felt like throwing himself at a running bull, but Anton Volker went down. To Roméo's surprise, he didn't fight at all. Roméo struggled to his feet and pulled his gun from one pocket, his flashlight from the other. Anton lay face down in the dirt, his arms stiffly by his side, like a fallen tree. His eyes were closed. Roméo prodded him with his foot. No response. He took a few steps back, never taking his eyes off the unconscious man and called an ambulance. A few moments later, Gretchen Handschuh found herself gazing into the terrified eyes of Marie Russell.

Chapter 47

Ti-Coune Cousineau and Manon Latendresse waited impatiently at the door. They could hear Dog barking frantically inside, but no one seemed to be home. Ti-Coune had a case of twenty-four under his arm, even though he didn't drink beer anymore. Watching other people drink a few Molsons was his way of celebrating now. Manon deeply respected his self-control, but she knew it was a fragile truce with the demons that chased him straight to the bottle. She had made sure to bring soda as well and carried a jumbo bottle under her arm. They were both practically dancing with excitement and the anticipation of sharing their news. Manon knocked again. Finally, they heard a voice shushing the dog, and then Marie Russell opened the door.

"Are we disturbing you?"

Manon knew the answer as soon as she had asked it. Of course, they were disturbing her. She looked like she hadn't slept in days, with blue half-circles like bruises under her eyes and her summer-tanned face drained of color. Marie was exhausted, but she saw the case of beer and the excitement on the faces of her neighbors and invited them in. They followed Marie to her screened-in porch, Dog nuzzling Manon for more attention and hopefully the treat he knew was in her pocket. Barney was sound asleep on the sofa, all four legs in the air, oblivious to the intruders. Roméo was sitting in the porch, hunched over a laptop. A sweet breeze was blowing though the screens, softly rustling the papers Roméo was also consulting. Ti-Coune pulled up a rattan chair to the table and popped open the soda bottle with a loud hiss. He poured himself a glass. Manon and Marie opened a beer each, and in unison took a long swallow from the bottle. Roméo passed on a drink and looked up inquiringly at Ti-Coune and Manon who were clearly poised for a toast.

"The Sauvons Mont Baleine committee has just gotten word from your wonderful daughter and the legal team that the injunction has been reinstated!"

Marie and Roméo looked puzzled.

"Projet Leviathan is on hold. They can't proceed!"

Ti-Coune and Manon scanned their hosts faces for a reaction, and Manon continued.

"You should've seen it. Hundreds of guys were there for the last two days, happily mowing down trees, destroying as much as possible. It was awful to see. And we could do nothing about it—"

"But what about the Matt DiAngelo's offer? Didn't they even consider it?" Marie asked.

"Well, that's the best part. Apparently, they're all duking it out with each other. Some want to take his money and run, the ones who were always in it just for the money—"

"That would be *all* of them!" Ti-Coune interjected.

"And the others want to continue with the Leviathan

project anyway. Unbelievable! They're the ones who still see this as a necessary development for the region."

"I don't understand. Why was the injunction reimposed?"

"Hello? Hello!"

Joel's head popped up at the bottom of the exterior stairs to the porch. Closely followed by Shelly's.

"Did you hear the *fantastic* news?"

Marie's dearest and nearest neighbors pulled up two more chairs to the table. Joel gave everyone an impressive hug. Shelly opened a large plastic container full of homemade chocolate banana muffins that were irresistible even to people who didn't like chocolate or bananas. The woman was a diabolical baker. As they washed down the muffins with beer, soda, and the prosecco that Joel had brought, they continued to discuss the amazing revelations that had come to light in the past few days.

"So, as we suspected, they found evidence of illegal influence, *and* a city councilor has come forward and told the police that death threats were made against her—the Sûreté du Québec had to post a squad car at city hall and at her home. There were also death threats made against at least one other councilor who opposed Leviathan." Shelly announced all this with great satisfaction. Joel nodded in approval at everything she said.

"And this is just the tip of the iceberg. The anti-corruption squad is launching an investigation into the silent partners in Leviathan. Turns out they're not such upstanding citizens."

"And whatever investors are still in, well, they're sure to run for the hills now."

Ti-Coune looked at Roméo. "I think Renard is fucked."

Manon gave him an admonishing tap on the leg. "On parle pas de ca, Jean-Michel. Don't say that."

Shelly poured herself another glass of prosecco.

"And they think they found the little prick who trashed Ti-Coune's house and painted *swastikas* on ours."

Joel shook his head. "You won't believe it." He paused for effect. "Jean-Louis Gingras's kid—Marco."

"Our snowplow man?" Marie confirmed.

"With a few of his buddies. One of them was bragging about it at some party, and one of the kids told his parents."

"They found the spray cans, and a bunch of white supremacist paraphernalia. I mean, you can't make this stuff *up*!"

Ti-Coune said nothing. He knew what could happen to a bunch of bored and aimless young men who felt like they had no future. Boys who wanted to feel like men. They looked for purpose and meaning in places that readily accepted kids like them. Those often happened to be the real, nasty fringes of society. He planned to have a chat with the little shit who had trashed his house.

Manon swallowed the last of her beer.

"Did they find out who torched Mayor Morin's car? Was it one of them? Or one of us?"

'No idea. It remains a mystery."

"I wonder if it was that guy—the one who never talks? He was really pissed at the protest—"

"Who?"

"The mailman. The mushroom expert—"

"*Lucien*? Lucien Picard?" Shelly and Joel asked, laughing. "He doesn't have a violent bone in his body."

"Maybe we all do when we are pushed hard enough,"

Ti-Coune offered.

Joel watched Ti-Coune carefully.

"And your assault case?"

"Going to court. I have witnesses."

"So does he." Roméo shook his head. Manon put her arm around Ti-Coune.

"My boyfriend punched a cop defending my honor. And what if I was the town slut? It's my business." She sighed and rolled her eyes. "Men. Always ready to defend our honor, when it's really all about them."

Everyone sat silently for a few moments, perhaps realizing that in their excitement they'd all forgotten about the murder of Magnus Sorensen.

"We hear you made an arrest, Roméo?"

Roméo nodded. We have someone in custody now."

"The media is going crazy in town. I saw them camped outside the hospital. Is the…um…suspect there?" Shelly asked, probably already preparing who she'd share the news with.

Roméo smiled enigmatically. "I really can't discuss this right now."

"Of *course*." Shelly said. She was *dying* to know who it was but took Marie's hand and squeezed it. "How are you holding up?"

Before Marie could answer, Roméo's phone rang, as if on cue. He grabbed his papers and retreated inside the house, closing the sliding door behind him and muffling the animated conversation that continued without him.

"Hey, *patron*. How are you feeling?"

Roméo instinctively massaged the back of his neck.

"My shoulder's really sore, and I think I gave my neck a

good twist. Other than that, I'm okay for an old guy."

"Okay. Good. So, I have lots to report. Where are you? You want me to come over?"

"No, Nicole. I've got a house full here, and I have to get to the hospital early tomorrow."

Nicole cleared her throat. "The car seen leaving Rasmussen's by Emily Joly was NOT Volker's. Not Gretchen Handschuh's, either. The car seen leaving the scene could have been Robert Renard's. You know he might be in trouble with this project? Well, he seems to have disappeared. We've got an alert out on his car, and we'll bring him in for an interview if. If that's okay."

"Of course, it's okay."

"Anton Volker is still semi-conscious. As in not talking. We found no weapon on him. But we did find this kind of photocopied diary he had on him and guess what else?"

What?"

"*Another* of those pink stone talismans—"

"What?"

"He's got one, too. I mean, how many did Sorensen buy?"

"We need to interview Anton tomorrow. Can you talk to the hospital tonight and set that up for the morning? We'll get a statement from Gretchen Handschuh as well. I assume they've kept them as far apart from each other as possible?"

"Not a problem. She just got released from the hospital."

"What?"

"She left about two hours ago."

"That seems very quick for the injuries she sustained. What are they thinking at that hospital?"

"Just letting you know, boss. Do you want me to check up on her? You want to take her statement tonight? I'm off to pick up Léo, but I could see if Manon is available—"

"Manon is here."

"Oh, okay."

"Tomorrow morning is fine. I'll meet you at her house at nine am."

Nicole hung up. Roméo stared at his phone as though it was about to tell him something important. It didn't. He had been certain the talisman he'd found in the lake was Anton Volker's. And where the *hell* was Robert?

Suddenly, the porch door slid open, and Marie announced that their visitors were leaving. By the time Roméo stepped out to say goodbye, they were all getting into their cars, cheerfully wishing Marie and Roméo a good night's sleep. Ti-Coune had taken the rest of the beer and soda with him, of course. But to Marie's delight, Shelly had left all the muffins.

Chapter 48

FRIDAY MORNING

He had been driving all night. The first stop he made was at a Tim Hortons just before he hit the border. Ironically, he had acquired a real affection for their Boston Cream donuts while he was in Quebec. He considered making his second stop in Lowell, but that would involve too long a detour off the highway. And there was no one he really knew there anymore—only his cousin who was in his late fifties and still dealing dope to teenagers and an old girlfriend who was a grandmother several times over now. He decided just to pull over for a piss stop at one of those tourist information places that were closed at this time of night. Still, they were safer than the side of the highway, where he'd risk being hit by one of the giant transport trucks that rattled his entire car as they lumbered by.

Paul's mind was racing over all that had happened in the last few days. He just had to get away, so he got in his car and headed south. When he saw the US customs sign, he realized where he was going. As he zipped up his pants and got back in his car, the light briefly illuminated the bright pink cover on the passenger seat. He picked it up and opened it to the first page again. *So, dear...whatever you are...I shall call thee Ishmael.* She was from Fall River, an absolute armpit of a place, but that's not where he was taking her. She was heading out to sea. As Paul pulled back onto the highway, he could just make out the first streaks of the sunrise to his left. His timing would be perfect. And once this was done, he would continue to their office in Cape Cod. Things were going crazy down there. Since Magnus had died, *See Change* had received almost a *million* dollars in donations. It was insane. They'd had to hire someone just to manage the traffic on their website. What would he be without Magnus? How was he *possible* without Magnus? But Paul knew that now, his company would make it. And for that, he felt an immense relief.

He glanced down at the diary again. He tried to decide if he felt guilty for what he had set in motion. When he sent Anton the copy of the diary, he had no idea what Anton would do. The idea was to threaten Magnus so he would need Paul more than ever. So, he would need Paul to back him up if Anton was going to make things difficult again. But the attack on Gretchen? He could not have seen that coming.

As he drove through the town, it was just waking up to the new day. A few drunks were wandering home, and a couple of fishermen were heading to the pier. Paul knew the way to Good Harbor beach with his eyes closed. The parking lot was closed, but he knew a special spot even closer to the water. He picked up the diary and ran his fingers over the embossed letters on the cover. The memory of that day was still so very vivid. Horrific. They had no business going near that whale. The Marine Mammal Rescue boat hadn't arrived yet, and they had little experience with disentanglement. The whale wasn't tired out enough. But the National Geographic team was there, and it was show time. The driver of their boat got too close to the whale and somehow got on top of her. She panicked, flipped her flukes up, and they came down on Molly. Paul closed his eyes. He told the investigators that he was driving the boat. The truth was, Magnus was driving the boat and knew they were too close. Recklessly, dangerously close to a fifty-ton animal. He had said it was an unavoidable accident. So had Gretchen. They had both lied. For Magnus.

Paul got out of the car and headed down the boardwalk that cut a straight line to the water through the dunes and sea grass, tinged the sweetest pink by the rising sun. When he got to the beach, he pulled his shoes off, and curled his toes into the sand. It felt delicious. The ball of sun was well above the horizon now. The wind had picked up, and the waves were hurling themselves against the shore. That ancient rhythm, that old story, told again and again. Straight out there was Stellwagen Bank Marine Sanctuary. Where Molly had really fallen in love. Paul walked well out into the ocean, the water so cold it took his breath and shrunk his testicles. He threw the diary as hard as he could into the waves. Then he stumbled back to the beach and sat down hard on the sand. There was one more thing he had to do. Paul pulled out his phone, copied the number from the card in his pocket, and texted his message to the detective. He waited for the whoosh that said the text had been delivered. Paul bowed his head over his knees and began to sob.

Chapter 49

She had to tell someone. This could *not* be happening. There was a room full of people enjoying a sumptuous meal upstairs, including her friend, Lucy, Lucy's husband Graham, and her two grown sons. When she went down to the basement to use the bathroom, she could hear a *baby*. It wasn't crying, just sort of moaning. She followed the sound, and discovered a baby girl, maybe two years old, in a crib way too small for her. She couldn't talk, she had a rash all over her body, and her nails were so long they'd grown back into her skin. She looked so damaged and delicate, Marie was too afraid to pick her up, so she ran back upstairs and demanded to know what was going on. The dozen or so people at the table lifted their wine glasses to her and laughed. She kept screaming *What is wrong with you? What is wrong with you??* until suddenly her eyes were open, she was in her bed and there was no baby. *What the hell was that?*

She glanced over at her ancient clock radio and saw that it was 7:38.

"Good morning, sleepy head."

Roméo was fully dressed in his work suit and sat on the

edge of the bed. He ran his fingers through her unruly curls.

"You feel okay?"

Marie sat up and described the nightmare she'd just had.

"It's odd that it would be Lucy, of all your friends. Arguably, the most maternal. And kind."

Marie shook her head. "It was just like this story I read once—when I was in high school, I think? About this city where everyone is happy and healthy, and life is good. There's no war, no hunger, no disease—a kind of utopia. Except underneath the city, a young child has been locked away and forced to live in chains—in misery. He's never allowed to leave and is fed just enough to keep him alive. The city's happiness depends on the terrible suffering of this one child. But sooner or later, everyone knows about him."

"What happens?"

"Nothing, really. Some people walk away, and never go back. Others just accept it and rationalize it and stay."

Roméo kissed Marie on the cheek and got up from the bed. "I did not see that story coming at me this morning. Wow."

Marie was still trying to clear her head. She had slept a full two hours past her summer wake up time. By now, she would normally have had her morning swim, two cups of espresso, and breakfast. She watched Roméo expertly add a tie to his ensemble.

"Where are you going?" she asked, stifling a yawn.

"To the hospital. I actually had a chance to chat with the attending doctor this morning. Volker's coming out of it."

"I hope that fucker is good and awake for you. I just can't believe...after all these years. He held that grudge, that... hatred for so long."

Roméo stuck his wallet, ID, and keys in his jacket pocket. "I'm stopping in at Gretchen's first."

"Aren't you were meeting Nicole there at nine?"

"I thought I'd go a bit early."

Roméo disappeared into the kitchen. Marie could hear him pouring a coffee and adding his oat milk, the familiar sounds of Roméo's morning ritual that had become dear to her.

"Marie?"

He stood just inside their bedroom door, his tall frame almost filling it.

"Do you want to come with me?"

"To Gretchen's? Why?"

"Because you saved her life. Maybe we should see how she is together."

જી

The day was already much cooler than the last week. It was about as perfect a summer day as one could hope for. A cloudless sky. The softest of breezes, and the humidity dissipated to another part of the world. Although Gretchen looked like she hadn't eaten anything fattening in forty years, Marie brought Shelly's muffins anyway. Of course, she'd already inhaled one and a half on the way there. She tried not to think about the last half she wanted to eat. They were quiet for much of the drive. Roméo had to answer several calls, but no information of any real significance came his way, except that they still hadn't found his friend, Robert Renard. Roméo had also called him three times and discovered his voice mail was full.

As they pulled into the long driveway of Gretchen's

rented house, they saw that her car with the Massachusetts plates had the trunk wide open.

"Do you think she's going somewhere?"

Roméo shook his head. "I doubt it. She had mild hypoxia and a broken hand. She should not be driving at all."

As they waited on the front doorstep, Marie could make out a Canada warbler twittering to the trees. Before long, that tiny, pretty bird would be making its 3000 mile migration to South America. Roméo knocked again. Just as he was headed around the back of the house to see if she was outside, the door finally opened. Gretchen looked shaken. There were pink marks on her neck. A nasty bruise on her cheek. Her right hand was in a splint. Still, her intensely blue eyes matched that morning sky, and she managed to look like someone hadn't tried to drown her.

"Good morning, Gretchen. We thought we'd stop in a bit early to see how you are. Your trunk is open. You want me to close it?"

"Thank you, yes. I just unloading a few groceries and forgot to close it." She hesitated. "I wasn't expecting you till nine, but come in."

Gretchen beckoned them into the house, which was immaculate. Marie was always amazed by people whose houses looked like no one lived in them. When she and Daniel used to rent a beach house in Maine for a week with the kids, within minutes it looked like a family of twelve had lived there for years. Gretchen turned and took Marie's hand in her uninjured one.

"Marie. I tried to call you yesterday—but I didn't have my cell phone, and they weren't letting me do anything." She pulled Marie into a gentle hug. "The whole thing was like a movie. Like I was watching some awful movie. What can I say? *Thank you.*"

"I brought you some muffins."

Gretchen smiled and took the box from Marie. She padded into the kitchen and put the four remaining muffins on a plate. She returned it to the coffee table with a few paper napkins. Then she cut one into quarters and nibbled on it. When she was a kid, she was probably the kind who waited for everyone else to wolf down their candy, and then ate hers last, Marie thought. Her sister Louise did that. It was torture.

Gretchen put the muffin morsel down and moved back into the kitchen.

"I have some fresh coffee made. Would you like some?"

Roméo said yes and thanks. Marie passed. One more coffee and she'd be ricocheting off the walls.

"I wanted to know if you could tell us anything more about what happened with Anton Volker. We have your initial statement, but we always like to double-check a few things. Do you feel up to it?"

Gretchen folded her long and pretty feet under her. Marie noticed her toenails looked freshly painted. "I'm not sure what more I can add, but I feel fine."

"Oh! Do you have any milk for the coffee?"

Gretchen went to get up, but Roméo stopped her. "Please. I'll get it myself."

The fridge was empty except for a bit of milk, an apple, and a few eggs. He poured a little cow's milk in his cup, barely enough to change its color.

Gretchen recounted in detail what had happened when Anton Volker broke into her house two nights earlier.

Gretchen took another tiny nibble of her muffin, and

delicately wiped away a trace of chocolate with her pinky.

"I'm curious. Why did you and Marie show up like that? I don't understand—"

"Marie had remembered the...accident all those years earlier. And that she had seen Volker at the memorial for Magnus—"

"What?"

Marie nodded. "I didn't recognize him at first, but when we looked up Molly Meader later, I realized it was him, her fiancé. Then we found out he was an airplane mechanic at Pratt and Whitney, I think."

"The fact that the plane Magnus was going to fly in with—with you—was sabotaged. It wasn't a huge deductive leap to figure Volker might be involved."

"It was just horrifying to think he still held us responsible after all those years. To think he hated us still."

"He must have loved that young woman very much."

Gretchen looked out the patio door to the pool and back to Roméo again.

"Well, yes. But at a certain point, love becomes obsession. It doesn't create. It destroys."

Roméo looked evenly at Gretchen.

"The thing is, we had a chance to question Volker yesterday—"

"Oh? My understanding was he had a head injury and wasn't conscious."

"It's not as severe as they thought. He was able to communicate with us for a few minutes."

Marie opened her mouth to say something and closed it again.

"He claims he had nothing to do with Magnus's death.

Nothing."

"Well, he would, wouldn't he?"

Roméo smiled and nodded. "The thing is, we're fairly certain he sabotaged the plane."

"Yes, you mentioned that. He wanted to get both of us. Two birds with one stone."

"I guess we're wondering why...why he would go to all the trouble, I suppose you could say, of tampering with the plane, and then just assaulting Magnus like that—taking the risk, if you will. Risking DNA tracing, the possibility of some-one seeing him. Why would he just...kill Magnus?" Gretchen took a sip of her coffee.

"I don't know. Maybe...maybe Magnus surprised him?"

"We also found—in Volker's pocket—this object." Roméo showed Gretchen a photo on his phone. "I guess we're won-dering why Emily Joly has one, and Molly Meader had one that obviously Volker received in her...effects when she died."

Gretchen shrugged her shoulders.

"Detective LaFramboise took a look at the diary Volker had on him—it was Molly Meader's of course, and the pink stone talisman was given to her by Magnus. She wrote that it made her feel...what was the word? Invincible."

Gretchen said nothing.

"As you know, we found an identical one in the lake where Magnus's body was found. We assumed Volker had tossed it. A kind of parting gesture. Closure, maybe."

Marie leaned forward and covered her mouth with both hands.

"But it obviously wasn't hers. Or his."

"So?"

"Did Magnus also give *you* a talisman like this, Gretchen?

It seemed he gave one to quite a few of the important women in his life."

"No, he didn't." She turned to Marie and raised her eyebrows in question.

"Did he give *you* one, Marie?"

Marie shook her head.

"Not *every* important woman, apparently."

Gretchen went to take the last sip of her coffee, but her cup was empty.

"Do you think I didn't know who Magnus was? He *loved* the kind of vacant beauty whose ideals hadn't been... tainted yet, who didn't know the disappointment of compromise. Who still believed the world was always, always going to be better. Please.... They were girls who loved going for boat rides who thought they were saving the world. Do you know how many of those Magnus went through? If you think I would sacrifice all the work we've done for *that*? You don't know *me* at all, Detective."

Roméo scrolled through his phone again.

"This morning, very early, I got a message. From your friend, Paul Pellerin."

Gretchen showed no reaction.

"Here. You can read it yourself." Roméo held the phone out to Gretchen. *Gretchen has a talisman.*

"Can you show it to me, Gretchen. Do you have it?"

Gretchen ran her hand through her thick, silvery blonde hair.

"This is getting ridiculous."

"Was it because he'd gotten this last one pregnant? It must have happened before, no? So why *her*? Why was *Emily Joly* so special?"

Marie looked directly at Gretchen over her clasped hands.

"Gretchen. You didn't do this."

Gretchen gazed out the patio door for a few moments. Then she turned back to Roméo with her startling blue eyes.

"Have you ever heard of a whale fall, Detective Inspector Leduc?"

She glanced at Marie. "I know you know what it is. I'm curious if he can guess."

"I'd like you to tell me."

Gretchen suddenly stood up and headed to the kitchen. She emptied what was left in the coffee pot into her cup and returned to her place on the sofa.

"I'd offer you both some, but I'd have to make another pot. Would you like me to?"

Roméo and Marie both shook their heads. Roméo said, "No, thank you."

"When whales die and sink to the bottom of the ocean, the whale carcass provides a sudden, concentrated food source and a bonanza for all sorts of organisms in the deep sea. This is called a whale fall. The whale becomes an energy-rich habitat—it even become a kind of eco-system unto itself. At deep sea levels they form a new food web and add to the ocean's food chain. So, while the death of the whale is sad, it is a wonderful opportunity for other ecosystems to feed off it and to flourish. It is critically important to the overall health of the world's ocean."

Roméo crossed one long leg over the other at the knee.

"Well. That's not what I would've guessed at all, but it's fascinating."

She turned to Marie with a bemused smile.

"What would *you* do when the man you basically had *made* accepted all the accolades and praise when you were the real *visionary* behind it all? Society almost always thinks it's the men, but it is more often the women who are the real creative thinkers. Don't you agree?"

Gretchen didn't wait for an answer.

"What would you do if you had been humiliated repeatedly over the years? Oh wait. You were, of course, Marie." She paused then went on. "But you weren't ready for the life that Magnus offered anyway. You wanted a…smaller life. The life you got."

Marie opened her mouth to protest, then decided against it.

"He killed me just as he killed that intern—only over years and years…of erosion of…my very soul. And I realized he was worth more dead than alive to me. But I didn't…I didn't *plan* anything. I just went there that morning to talk to him. Magnus was surprised. He wasn't expecting me, of course. He was expecting her. I told him I knew about Emily. About her being pregnant. I asked him how he could be so *stupid*. At his age. A pregnancy? With a twenty-nine- year-old? Had he not read a newspaper in the last four years? Men bigger and much more powerful than him were taken down for much less? Is THAT what he wanted for us? For *See Change*? How could you be so STUPID?"

Gretchen looked out the window to the pool, which was half in shade, half-illuminated and sparkling in the morning sun.

"For the first time in thirty years, for the first time ever, he looked at me with *pity*. It was *unacceptable*. It was *unforgivable*. Because, you see, he said—and he took my hand in his first. Gently. He said, 'I wanted the baby.' *I wanted it.* He was *thrilled* about it. And he *informed* me that he would be running off to playhouse in Norway with her. Well, that's not how he phrased it, exactly. He told me he loved me and would always…and would always take care of me. Blahblahblah, who cares?"

Marie suddenly exhaled. "Oh, Gretchen."

Gretchen wagged a finger and tsked at Marie.

"You're thinking, poor Gretchen! She went crazy because she wanted a baby and to be a mother, so she could be a *complete* woman. A *real* woman. Women don't have to reproduce to *matter*. That's patriarchal, insulting crap. I did it because I was being left behind like, like I never mattered *at all*."

Gretchen paused and let out a huge sigh.

"I just couldn't breathe. I couldn't even feel my body. It was like I was out of my body, above it, looking at it. And then, amazingly, my hands and arms still worked. And he turned his back to me. He was getting the *plane* ready. So, I picked up a shovel. Or a spade. Or an oar. I can't remember. And I whacked him on the back. He *flew* right into the water. I didn't expect that."

"Where did you put the shovel?"

"Oh, I don't know. Somewhere. Good luck finding it."

Gretchen undid her thick hair from its topknot and tied it up again. It was perfect.

"I could have saved him. I could have lifted his head out of the water. I didn't."

Marie couldn't listen anymore. "Oh my God, Gretchen. Oh my God."

"And you threw your talisman into the water, the one Magnus bought you?" Roméo asked.

"What?" Gretchen regarded him with those relentless blue eyes. "Oh that. Maybe."

They were all startled by the sudden ringing of the doorbell. Gretchen started to get up to answer it, and Roméo ordered her to sit back down. It was Nicole LaFramboise. It was nine o'clock. Nicole looked a bit confused when she spotted Marie, and then waved a quick hello. Roméo took Nicole aside and quickly went over what had just happened. He handed her his cell phone, with which he'd recorded the entire exchange from his pocket. Nicole pulled her handcuffs from her jacket and approached Gretchen. She explained that Gretchen was being arrested on suspicion of the murder of Magnus Sorensen, that she had the right to keep silent, and that whatever she did say could be used in evidence against her in court. Gretchen listened patiently with a slight smile. She turned first to Marie, then to Roméo.

"I just made all that up. Now go try and prove I did it."

Chapter 50

ONE WEEK LATER

She rode along highway 20 due west, until the sign for Pierre Elliott Trudeau International Airport loomed to her right, and her taxi driver shifted to the exit lane. She read his plasticized ID photo and name. Ethiopian, if she had to guess. Normally, she would engage her driver in a conversation, ask where he was from, what brought him here to Canada, how many kids did he have. But Emily Joly just didn't have the emotional resources to do even that. The last two weeks had been so shocking and surreal, she felt like it had all happened to someone else. Waking up was the worst. Every morning she opened her eyes and for a moment or two she still lived in her old life. Magnus was alive. They were in love and going to have a baby together. They had a whole life waiting to be lived. And then she remembered. Some terribly damaged and crazy man had tried to avenge his fiancée's accidental death, but he failed. Gretchen Handschuh's took up the quest where he left off and succeeded. Every time Emily thought of those last moments of Magnus's life, she thought she would throw up. She had had to work very hard to put it all aside for the time being so she could focus on the health of their baby.

"Madame?"

"Yes?"

"Which airline, please?"

"Oh. KLM, please."

He glanced at Emily in his rear-view mirror.

"You are going to Amsterdam?"

Emily shook her head. "No. Well, yes. Amsterdam first, and then to Oslo. In Norway?"

"I know Oslo! My brother lives in Oslo. He says it's very beautiful."

"I hope so."

She was actually spending a few months in Oslo. The entire team of *See Change* Norway consisted of two older veteran activists who could barely manage social media. Their organization was in a shambles, but money was pouring in. Emily had asked if she could work with them, do a little restructuring and rebranding. She wanted to make it a going concern. Then, if her plan worked, she would move into the little wooden house in Balestrand, the one that had belonged to Magnus's grandfather, and where Magnus had spent many idyllic summers away from his parents. Their baby would be born there. Emily had asked her mother to join her there in three months' time, and she had agreed immediately. She had never been to Europe and was beside herself with excitement. She tried hard not to be as gleeful as she felt, given the circumstances that made her participation possible.

The taxi pulled over at the KLM exit. Emily paid the driver and got out of the backseat while he pulled out her large suitcase from the trunk and placed it on the sidewalk. Just as she went to say thank you, she suddenly felt something she never had before. Like a butterfly fluttering deep inside her. The baby books called it "the quickening." She stopped and put her hand on her belly. She felt it again and gasped.

"Are you all right, Madame?"

This was really happening.

"I'm fine. Thank you!"

"Good luck to you, Madame. Safe flying."

Emily had already headed off, wheeling what few things from her old life she wanted to take along behind her.

"To you, too, Monsieur. To you, too."

Chapter 51

Marie watched as Maya waded out of the lake and back to the sturdier chair they had brought along just for her. At almost thirty-eight weeks pregnant, getting in and out of a folding camp chair was no joke. The baby had dropped, and she was walking like she had a bowling ball between her legs. That was still better than feeling like you were giving birth to one, Marie thought. Maya wasn't due for another three weeks, but Marie was certain she wouldn't go that long. Despite her many pleas to Maya and Ben to reveal the gender of Mystery Baby, they wouldn't. Another boy, a brother to Noah would be wonderful. But a girl? A granddaughter? Marie didn't even dare to hope for that. She watched Ben, who was now floating on his back, spit a fountain of water into the air like a blowing whale. How had her sweet baby boy, who used to sing at the top of his lungs in his stroller to anyone who'd listen, who used to climb into bed with her almost every morning and ask her to read the same book again as he curled his tiny fingers into her hair, how was it possible he was about to have his *second* baby? She felt especially lucky, as she knew so many young people today were opting to be *child free*—choosing not to have kids. Because of the ravages of climate change, many believed this was no world to bring a child into. Others because of the impact yet another human being would have on the planet. Ruby had discussed it with her, and informed Marie she would most likely not be having children. Marie believed that every generation had had these doubts before but understood that the profound existential crisis facing them all had created a tectonic shift in thinking.

Ruby was standing up to her waist in the lake, holding Mohammed afloat as he practiced his dog paddle. She had been teaching him to swim every chance they got. He had quietly explained over dinner one night that at the refugee camp in Jordan where he spent five years of his childhood, they didn't offer swimming lessons. Suddenly, Mohammed said something to Ruby that Marie couldn't hear. Ruby exploded in laughter, her head thrown back, that gorgeous red hair glinting copper in the afternoon sun. Marie couldn't help but feel sad at the thought of her choosing not to have kids.

Roméo nudged Marie gently and filled her glass with the cheap rosé that she loved. Then he gestured with a nod at the two people they had all gathered to celebrate. Louis and Claire sat facing the lake on two camp chairs pushed together. The same spot on the same lake they had gone to on their epic journey together a few weeks earlier. They were slathered in sun block from the tip of their noses to the tips of their toes. Claire wore a hot pink, wide-brimmed straw hat, and someone had stuck a *Sauvons Mont Baleine* baseball cap on Louis's almost bald head. They were holding hands. Roméo wondered if he and Marie would be like that? He was ten years younger than her. Would he get the chance to take care of her the way Louis did of Claire? Or would she end up wiping the drool from his chin and reminding him who his grandchildren were again? Marie had invited Dominique, Louis's daughter, and her family to the picnic, but she was away on a golf vacation in Prince Edward Island. Roméo couldn't imagine such a thing. But then, how could he possibly have pictured the life he had somehow been given now?

He smiled at the sight of Sophie and Pénélope playing a vicious game of badminton, Sophie laughing like he hadn't heard in years. Sophie had been a really difficult teenager who couldn't seem to make one good choice for herself. Ever. She was diagnosed with ODD—oppositional defiant disorder in grade seven. When the teacher explained it to Roméo he thought she was kidding—he assumed all teenagers had it. But he was assured it was a condition and that she should be treated for it. Sophie had watched her parents' marriage fall apart spectacularly. She had reason enough to rage at the world. But after all that, and several boyfriends who ranged in quality from useless to abusive, she had fallen for this young woman, who seemed to ground her—to make her feel like being just herself was enough. She seemed fully alive and engaged in this life. What more could you ask for your child, really? What a wonderful generation of young people, he thought. They were changing the world is so many fantastic ways. They didn't put up with the crap his and Marie's generation had. Roméo looked at the empty beer in his hand. Was that his third or fourth?

His tipsy musings were interrupted by shrieking laughter. Léo and Noah had for once been playing quietly, each devoted to digging up the gravelly gray sand and dumping it on Steve Pouliot's prone body. As soon as they got him buried, he'd kick his way out of it. Their reaction to that could end up in tears, but today both little boys found it hysterically funny, one feeding off the laughter of the other. Steve, Roméo knew, had put up with repeated homophobic attacks, and criticism for calling out the racism in the Montreal police force. The man was small but had more courage than almost anyone he knew. Not the least of which was dating Nicole LaFramboise and taking on her beautiful but very *challenging* boy. Nicole was keeping a quiet eye on her son and her new boyfriend while she scrolled though her phone. They still had a lot of work to get done on the Sorensen case. And the SQ anti-corruption squad was discovering more and more evidence of bribery and interference in the Projet Leviathan case. Roméo had been relieved to learn that his old friend and colleague, Robert, did not seem to be involved in anything overtly illegal. Yet. And they had never sorted out whose car had left the Rasmussen estate at breakneck speed. If it was Robert, he was not admitting to it. Matteo DiAngelo's offer was still the talk of the town. Pierre Batmanian immediately offered to withdraw his interest in the project for the actor's cash, but many of the local investors wanted the project to go forward—they believed in it. Roméo didn't think this fight was over yet.

He looked over at Marie. She was standing at the edge of the water, shading her eyes against the sun which dazzled the surface. She had not really spoken about Magnus since his murder. He wondered if she ever would. And Gretchen's name had never been uttered again. *The most unkindest cut of all.* Roméo remembered that from *Julius Caesar* in high school. The knife held by the person you trusted the most. The thin line when great love turns to profound hatred. The crazy, unpredictable journey both love and hate take us on.

Marie made her way to the picnic tables and started to clean up the epic remains of their feast. Was it that time already? Soon, they would have to take Claire and Louis back to *Maison Soleil*. But Roméo and Marie had promised each other that they would do better by her mother and her mother's *gentleman caller*, as Ruby referred to him. They would take them out of the residence once a week at least. Until Claire really wasn't able to anymore. Roméo hoped that day was still a long way off.

As he got to his feet and went over to give Marie a hand, he took one last memory snapshot of the people who had become his family. He and Marie never did get to have their romantic honeymoon. But maybe, this was even better.

ABOUT THE AUTHOR

ANN LAMBERT has been writing and directing for the stage for thirty-five years. Several of her plays, including *The Wall*, *Parallel Lines*, *Very Heaven*, *The Mary Project*, and *Two Short Women* have been performed in theatres in Canada, the United States, Europe, and Australia. She has been a teacher of English literature at Dawson College for almost twenty-eight years in Montreal, Quebec, where she makes her home.